WHISPERS OF LOVE

POSSUM RUN DUET

DARLENE TALLMAN

WHISPERS

POSSUM RUN DUET *of Love*

INTERNATIONAL BESTSELLING AUTHOR
DARLENE TALLMAN

CONTENTS

WHAT I LIKE
about Sunday

INTERNATIONAL BESTSELLING AUTHOR
DARLENE TALLMAN

COPYRIGHT

This is a work of fiction. Names, characters, places, and incidents are either the product of the author's imagination or used fictitiously, and any resemblance to actual persons, living or dead, business establishments, events or locales is entirely coincidental.

EDITORS: MARY KERN, MELANIE GRAY, NICOLE MCVEY, JENNIFER CORBIN, STEPHANIE ELLIS, BETH DILORETO, SYLVIE HOWICK
PROOFERS: NICOLE MCVEY, NICOLE LLOYD, CHERYL HULLETT
FORMATTER: LIBERTY PARKER
COVER BY TRACIE DOUGLAS OF DARK WATER COVERS

ACKNOWLEDGMENTS

Back in December, my PA, Nicole Lloyd, gave me a task. To go through the manuscripts I had "out there" that weren't done yet and pick one to work on that was outside any of my series I was working on, or any of my cowrites, then pick one of the many premade covers I have in yet another folder. I went through several, sent her the blurb and she said, "That one!"

However, no book is ever a solo project and when I got sick a few days before I was going to need to upload the book, I had several folks jump in to help get it polished for me so I wouldn't blow my deadline and disappoint the readers. Nicole McVey and Cheryl Hullett threw their two cents in, as did Liberty Parker, even though she was faced with her own deadlines. They made sure the story made sense and even tossed in some ideas to expand it in some places and this book wouldn't be complete without acknowledging that fact!

XOXOXO

Dar

DEDICATION

This one is dedicated to my favorite oldest granddaughter, Maddison. She turns 17 the day "What I Like About Sunday" releases, and while I haven't seen or spoken to her in almost eight years now, not a day goes by that I don't miss her.

MaddiBelle, if you ever see this, just know you're loved and prayed for every single day, and I'll always love you to the moon and back.

Love,

Grandma

BLURB

Growing up in the same small town where everyone knows one another, Sunday Cross has watched Jett Blake's life from afar. Not because he's several years older and ahead of her in school; no, it's because of his girlfriend, who makes the mean girls in the movies look like choir girls. She's focused on her own goals and dreams, determined to use her GI bill to become a nurse like her mother, and grandmother. Instead, she returns to town shattered and scarred, her military service over and any dreams she had for a future with her fiancé ground into dust. Now, her days are filled with surgeries and physical therapy instead of patients and missions.

Jett Blake was the golden boy of the town. Star quarterback. Exemplary student. All-around nice guy, despite the fact his girlfriend wasn't well-liked. His life reads like a blueprint for success; college athlete, drafted into the pros. He never expects to find himself home again, now, a single dad to a four-year old little boy, divorced, and broken.

Can two broken souls, who were aware of each other years ago, find their way to happiness?

PROLOGUE

"Where's your cross, Sunday?" the group of girls chanted, using my last name as a pun.

Shaking my head at their obvious lack of originality, I ignored them as I headed to my locker. Why, oh why, was I blessed with a surname that begged people to make fun of me? Sighing, I switched out books, closed my locker before turning around, and crashing straight into a hard, muscular male chest.

Looking up, I saw the senior that every girl in the school was panting over.

Jett Blake.

Star quarterback. Star of the cross-country team. He had so many athletic skills and commendations that he

1

was being offered free rides to all of the major, top tier colleges. As if that wasn't enough, he was smart as well, holding down a near-perfect grade point average despite all of his extracurricular activities. The only downside, as far as I was concerned, was his girlfriend. She was horrid, what my friends and I would classify as a 'mean girl', yet she had him snowed somehow, believing she was a caring, empathetic girl, which was a shame because she was anything but that.

His deep blue eyes looked down at me, and I said, "I'm so sorry, I wasn't watching where I was going."

"Don't let them bother you, Sunday. They're just jealous because they have nothing unique about them." I knew my mouth was hanging open at his words. How in the hell did he even know who I was, for heaven's sake?

"I try not to," I softly replied.

He smiled at me, and was about to say something in response when his girlfriend, Stacey, came up next to him. "What are you doing, Jett? We're going to be late!"

"We're fine, Stace. I accidentally ran into Sunday, and wanted to make sure she was okay."

I looked at him and couldn't believe he was pretty much lying to his girlfriend, since it was me who ran into him, not the other way around. Then again, Stacey was a bit of a bitch, and if he had said what truly happened, she would have made my life a living hell. Where she was concerned, I preferred to stay way under the radar. Which has me confused, because we've all been convinced that he bought into her fake smiles and personality. Maybe he's not as clueless as we thought? Maybe he saw her flaws but turned a blind eye to her rude behaviors.

"Well, I'm sure she's fine since she's still standing. I don't see any bumps or bruises on her. Let's go," Stacey said, pulling on his arm.

"Sorry again, Sunday. See you around," he said.

I watched them go, my mind still replaying his words as I wondered... what did he mean that I was unique?

TEN YEARS AGO

Graduation over, I prepared for basic training, getting all my ducks in a proverbial row. Thankfully, I was involved in several different extracurricular activities, so as far as the physical fitness aspect was concerned, I wasn't too worried. I had chosen to do a delayed enlistment in the Navy, and received a significant scholarship for college that I planned to utilize, once I had honored my military commitment.

"Honey, are you sure this is what you want to do?" Mom asked, coming into my bedroom with a basket of my washed laundry in her arms.

"Mom, I want to be a nurse and going into the Navy, I can get a lot of experience as a medic that will eventually help me. I'll be fine. Plus, I was going to get my clothes in a

few minutes, you didn't need to bring them to me, but thank you."

"You know your dad and I will worry, honey. We're not exactly at peace these days."

"I should still be just fine, Mom." I'd roll my eyes but knowing her, even though her back is turned, she'd still see me and it's not worth the smack, that's for sure. As a teenager, I learned the value of making sure to not to express what I was thinking, at least not where Mom could see me. We've got a good relationship, but we definitely butted heads when I was younger. The bottom line, though, is she loves me.

"Did you hear about Jett Blake?" she questioned as she started folding my clothes.

I closed my eyes and breathed in deeply. Being in a small town, I knew the gossip and tried to ignore it, but hell, everyone had known that he got Stacey pregnant right before they graduated. They ended up having a miscarriage shortly after they got married, according to the gossiping townspeople. I just remembered how kind he was any time I saw him at school, even though he was an upperclassman, and I was a lowly freshman. If memory served, they recently had a little boy, Dusty, but I wasn't sure how old he was right now.

"What about him?" I finally asked.

"Well, apparently Stacey left town," Mom replied,

folding a pair of my socks, and putting them in a growing pile for me to add to my suitcase.

"Oh no, what about Dusty?"

"Honey, she left the baby too."

"Are you kidding me? I always knew she was a bit of a witch, but how can a mother leave their child behind?" I questioned. There's no way on earth I would ever leave my child.

"No clue, but he has moved back home with his folks, and is going to school to become a paramedic, I think. Although, the high school has approached him about becoming their head football coach, and with his experience, he'd be a fool not to take that offer instead."

"That's nice." Why on earth was she sharing this shit with me? It's not like I ever had any in-depth conversations with him. Most of our interactions were rather banal; the only thing is, I held each one, as well as every time he glanced at me, close to that secret place in my heart.

The admonishing one that said a guy like him wouldn't ever want someone as average as me. I would never be able to compete with the likes of Stacey, so I never bothered to try.

"So, what time do we leave in the morning?" Mom asked, thankfully changing the subject.

"I have to be at the airport by seven for my nine o'clock flight."

"Then we'll leave around five, okay? Let's get this

wrapped up, so your dad and I can take you out to eat, since we have to be up so early."

"That's fine, Mom."

Part of me was excited about my upcoming adventure, even though I knew it would be challenging, and probably harder than I was anticipating. Regardless, I felt like I was finally stepping into the adult world. I'd be making my own money, dealing with the consequences of my actions without parental involvement, and learning how to be a productive member of society.

FOUR YEARS AGO

"I love you, Sunday, will you marry me?" Jonas asked.

Looking at him, I smiled before answering, "Yes."

"I know you still have this last tour, but maybe when it's done, we can get married?" he questioned, the hopeful expression on his face nearly wearing me down.

"Jonas, are you saying you don't want to travel around the world?" I replied. One of the best parts of my Navy experience so far, was that I had been stationed in several different countries, places I would've never likely been able to travel to on my own. The experiences I'd had, the people I'd met; all added perspective to my life, in some way or another.

"Well, no, not really, but if that's what we need to do until you are out, then I'll manage."

I sighed before replying, "I had planned to possibly make the Navy my career, Jonas." Which I had considered, since nurses were in high demand, so I could pretty much write my own path according to my commanding, and reenlisting officer. It hadn't been easy juggling getting my nursing degree with my military commitment, but I'd done it, with a lot of my field experiences counting toward the clinical knowledge I had to have. I was proud of the fact I was an actual registered nurse, something I could carry into the civilian world when I was discharged.

"Yeah, but that was before you met me, right?" he inquired.

Damn, what an ego! It was definitely a detractor from his overall personality, and one I was coming to realize I might have a problem handling in the future if he kept pushing the issue. While I loved him, I had re-enlisted, so I had another four years to serve my country before I could even remotely think about whether or not I'd stay in, or resign my commission.

"I figure it's something we can work out, and discuss," I replied.

"You're right. How about we celebrate our engagement?"

TWO YEARS AGO

I looked around the base we were currently stationed

at, and cringed. Going into the medical tent, I was glad to see that at least it was well-stocked. Doing a quick inventory, I then refilled my bag with the necessary supplies, including saline bags and IV kits, as well as gauze pressure bandages, in preparation for the patrol I was going on later in the day. Normally, I wasn't assigned to them, but they were short a man, and I had the skills, so my commander had asked me to go, and I had said yes. I was always willing, as were most in the squadron I was with, to jump in when needed. That's just part of who I am as a person, I guess.

"You ready to go, Cross?" Branch asked.

"Yes, sir. Just making sure I'm prepared," I responded, grabbing a few more things before I zipped up my bag.

"Let's hit it."

---

*I heard a click that sounded out of place, and without thinking, turned and yelled, "**RUN!**" to the five other men with me. The subsequent blast had me flying through the air, and I felt pain immediately start to radiate through my lower back, and hip region.*

Despite the excruciating agony coursing through me, I was able to assess my teammates, and with Branch's assistance, got IVs started with saline and used every single one of the pressure bandages I brought. Branch insisted on treating me as well, despite my insistence that I'd be fine; but I saw the look on his face, one of pity and terror, as he was doing what he could to take care of me until help arrived. Considering he was the toughest, most no-nonsense person I had ever met, his expression prepared me somewhat for what I would hear once we were safe and being treated.

Later in the hospital, lying flat on my stomach due to the injuries I had sustained to my low back and hip, as well as my upper thigh on the left side, I cried, letting out all the fear and terror I felt during the long ninety-minute wait I'd endured before the next troops arrived, bringing us much-needed help as they got us transferred to the hospital. Thankfully, none of us were killed, but in reality, we were all hot messes with burns and broken bones. Mine were, unfortunately, some of the worst based on what the doctor had described.

My parents, and Jonas had flown in as soon as they were able to get a flight, and keeping positive in the face of Mom's tears and Dad's stoic expression wore me out. They had just left to go back to their hotel, but I saw the revulsion on Jonas' face when he saw where I was injured, and I knew in my soul that it was only a matter of time before he broke off our engagement. It wasn't as if I was exposed to the room or anything, but the special-ized bandages they had covered my left side in, from my waist to my knee showed enough to where it wasn't too difficult to imagine the possible damage that I'd incurred.

"Cross? You okay?" the nurse asked as she walked into the room to take my vitals, and swap out my empty IV bags for full ones.

While my pain meds were injected straight into my IV, I had bags hung for the fluids and antibiotics I was being given to stave off any infection, and keep me as hydrated as possible. I wasn't all that thrilled having a catheter, but realized the impracticalities of me being up and down to go to the bathroom, so I dealt with it. It wasn't like I was awake all that much; the doctors had decided against a medically induced coma, but they were keeping me 'under' more often than not to aid in the healing. The longest I'd been awake since we arrived was today when my parents and Jonas were visiting.

"I'll be fine," I replied, wiping the tears from my face.

To prevent bedsores on the front of my body, and blood clots from inactivity, the nursing staff would get me upright, give me a shot of Lovenox in my abdomen which helped prevent clotting issues, give me a sponge bath, then gently lay me on the clean bedding. I was 'covered' in the sense they'd rigged up a blanket that enveloped me without touching my skin, and to say I was always chilled was definitely an understatement. The one thing driving me absolutely crazy besides the damn catheter, of course, was the inactivity I was facing, but I understood the reasoning since the skin grafts already done needed a great deal of time to heal. The whole situation sucked balls, but this was the hand I was dealt, and at the end of the day, all of us were alive, so I'd suck it up, and make the best out of an absolutely shitty situation.

"How's your pain level?"

"On a scale of 'oh I stubbed my toe' to 'holy shit a bear is trying to tear me apart' I think I'm at the bear level, possibly two bears at this point," I admitted.

Nurses and healthcare workers make the worst patients, and I knew that from the years I'd been in the field, but in this instance, I was doing what was asked, and definitely taking the pain meds because holy fuck, did I hurt!

"Let me get you some more pain meds then. You've got another surgery scheduled in the morning."

"Great. Can you hand me my phone, please?" I asked, trying hard to keep the sarcasm out of my tone. It wasn't her fault I was here or injured; no, the blame lay solely at the feet of a bunch of terrorist fuckers who didn't value any human life.

The nurse handed me the phone that had been just out of reach, and I checked my messages. Seeing one from Jonas, I took a deep breath.

Jonas: Sunday, you deserve more than I can give. I'm sorry, but I can't do this anymore.

Sunday: I'll send the ring back with my folks.

Jonas: No, keep it. I'm sorry.

I took another deep breath, then another, while I chanted to myself to take the high road. I knew why he was breaking it off. My injuries would leave me permanently scarred, even with surgery, and he was all about the appearances. I knew that about him way back when, so part of the heartache I was feeling right now was on me.

Sunday: Take care of yourself. Please don't come back.

CHAPTER
ONE

SUNDAY

PRESENT DAY

"Sunday, c'mon, you gotta come with us tonight!" Bria pleads. "You haven't really been out since you've been home. Cut loose a little."

I look at my oldest friend and smile. "You know that's not fair. I've spent most of the past two years having surgeries, and doing the recovery rehab work. Makes it hard to go out when your ass is covered in a protective bandage, and you're wearing those 'lovely' compression garments. Besides, who the hell is going to want a freak like me? Even with all the surgeries, my left ass cheek, and thigh are horrible looking."

"The right guy isn't going to give a fuck," Bria states. "Jonas was a pussy."

Bria's comment has me laughing out loud. "Oh my God. Tell me how you *really* feel," I tease, the laughter evident in my tone.

"Well, he was! I mean, let's get honest for a second, okay? If you had married him and stayed the course, eventually, shit would have started sagging and wrinkles would have formed. And if you had kids, you'd have that pooch thing going on with stretch marks, too. You might have gained weight or hell, I don't know, lost a limb due to some obscure thing. He obviously didn't have what it takes for the long haul, honey. I look at pictures of my grandparents when they got married, and they were both skinny and young. Now, my grandma is short and round, but my grandpa? He still worships the ground she walks on. He sees her inside, not the outside that doesn't stay firm and youthful."

"Fine, I'll go, but only because it'll get you off my ass."

"We're gonna have a blast and you know it," Bria cheers, going to my closet. Thirty minutes later, I'm decked out in skinny jeans, an emerald green silky tank top, and my tan boots. Bria corralled my hair into a French braid, and I had applied a light coat of makeup. "Alright, you're good to go, let's blow this popsicle stand," Bria advises. "If you get any prettier, I won't have a shot at catching myself a man."

"Whatever. You know you get your fair share of guys."

"Not when you're around, I don't," Bria retorts as we close and lock the doors, then head down to my car.

"Where are we going, anyhow?" I ask once we're in the car, and buckled up.

"Ike's."

Shit, I like Ike's, but sometimes, Jonas is there, and the last thing I want is to run into him. He married someone I knew from school, and now, lived in the same fucking town. If it weren't for the fact I own my home outright, and my parents lived in the same town as well, I would have packed up and moved.

"What if... fuck... what if he's there tonight?" I ask my friend.

"You ignore him, just like the other thousand times you've seen him around town."

"It's just that any time I do see him, it brings all of that pain back to the forefront."

"I know..."

I cut my friend off, saying, "No, you have no fucking clue. I was lying in a hospital bed on my fucking stomach, my ass and leg pretty much open to the world when he came with my folks once they were notified. I *saw* the revulsion on his face. He looked like he wanted to puke.

Then to break it off like he did? Yeah, no. No one knows how I fucking feel about him, or the situation. I know he probably wants to apologize, but I don't want to hear it, or see him. *Ever.*"

Bria reaches her hand over and squeezes mine hard. "I'm sorry, Sunday. I don't know about the physical pain you've endured, although I suspect it was far worse than what you've shared. I do know, though, that not all men are like him."

"Let's just have a great time, okay? Don't think I'll be meeting my Mr. Forever tonight, anyhow."

"You never know," she says, suggestively wiggling her eyebrows.

"From your mouth to God's ear."

JETT

Sitting at a table that's in the back, hidden in the shadows, I'm sipping a beer when she walks in. Fuck, she just gets more gorgeous with each passing year.

No way she'll wanna get involved with you, asshole, you're a single dad, and a loser.

Shaking my head at my negative thoughts, I raise my hand for another beer. I can still watch, and maybe, just maybe, get a dance or two from her to store in my memory banks.

Sunday Cross was a breath of fresh air in high

school. Her outgoing personality, and kindness toward others even when they were mean, was admirable. I grimace remembering how Stacey used to treat and mock her. God, what a fuck-up that was, staying involved with Stacey for all those years.

I should have broken it off with her, and gone after the woman who still consumes my thoughts, still to this day.

Only, I was young and dumb. Now, I have a child and am a single father trying to make it on my own. What woman would want to be involved with someone like me? My baggage alone from all the shit Stacey pulled is enough to have anyone running away, screaming in fear.

Face it, Jett, Stacey sucked you dry in more ways than one, then left you holding the bag.

Growling at my inner voice, who hasn't shut up since I saw Sunday walk in, I down the rest of my beer. If I keep this shit up, I'll need to get a sober ride home. Dusty deserves one parent who gives a fuck about him. I smile, thinking of my tow-headed little guy. At nearly eleven now, he's sturdy, like I was at that age, according to my mom, and so curious about every-thing. Raising my hand, I catch my waitress's attention and once she comes over, I ask for a glass of water for myself, then tell her to get whatever the two women are drinking, and put it on my tab, once I point out Sunday and Bria to her. Hopefully, it'll start a conversation.

"Jett, thank you for the drinks," Sunday shyly says, once she makes it over to my table.

"You're welcome. Do you want a seat?" I ask. "It's kind of crowded here tonight."

She pulls out a chair, and sits down so we're able to look at one another, which is good because that means I'll be able to hear her when she says something.

"Right? Normally I'm not up for something like this, but Bria insisted, and you know she always gets what she wants."

I can't help it, I start laughing, because even though they were several grades lower than I was, in this small town, everyone knows everyone else, so Bria Chandler and her escapades are well-known.

"She forced you out, huh?" I ask in response.

"Yeah, she said no one remembered what I looked like, or some shit," she teases. "Shit, I'm sorry I swore. Dammit, I did it again."

My laughter erupts again, because now she's got a very becoming blush staining her cheeks. "Sunday don't apologize for swearing. Hell, Dusty's first word was *not* 'dada'!"

Her laughter rolls through me, causing my heart to beat a little faster. I know from the newspaper articles that she was severely injured while deployed, and since she's been home, her focus has been on getting better, so she hasn't been out and about all that much.

"My vocabulary definitely increased significantly while I was in the military," she confesses, grinning at me. "Not like I can be mistaken for a guy, but I was one of a handful of women in our unit, so I got used to it."

"I hate you got hurt," I convey. "That any of you were injured, to be honest."

A look I can't decipher crosses her face before she takes a deep breath and responds. "Thank God none of us were killed. I just wish we had seen the signs ahead of time."

"From what I understand, it was your quick thinking that kept all of you from that fate."

She shrugs, then takes another sip of her drink. "True, but even still, it's not one of my fondest memories."

"I can't imagine it is. Are you okay now?"

"They've done all the surgeries they can to make the repairs, now, I just need it to completely heal so I can decide what to do next."

"What do you mean?" I ask.

A flush crosses her face before she replies, "I'm thinking of finding a tattoo artist to see about covering the scars. The only thing is it would be a huge piece."

"What are you thinking about getting?" My curiosity

about her is all-consuming at this point; I want to know everything about her down to the smallest detail.

Instead of answering immediately, she pulls her phone out of her pocket, and opens up her pictures before sliding it in my direction. "I was thinking about something like this," she states, as I start flipping through her photo gallery.

"Damn, these are spectacular," I murmur, my eyes captivated by the flowing vines and flowers. Interspersed are dog tags, denoting the others who were on the mission with her. "These are the men you were with?" I ask.

"Yeah. I wanted to turn that shit storm into something beautiful."

"Have you reached out to the tattoo artist yet?"

"I have an appointment next week for him to see the area. I know I can't start on it yet because the skin is still healing, but I want to know what it's going to cost, plus he'll have an opportunity to create the design."

"It's going to look awesome when it's done." Hearing the music change, I ask, "Would you like to dance?"

I feel like I'm in ninth grade again, waiting with bated breath for her response.

"I'm not as swift on my feet as I used to be," she admits.

"That's okay, I'm no Fred Astaire."

She giggles before nodding. "Since I'm no Ginger Rogers, we should be okay then."

CHAPTER
TWO

JETT

As I get ready for bed, I replay the rest of the evening at Ike's. Dancing with Sunday was a fucking dream come true. Since neither of us knew the newer line dances, we stuck to the slower songs. Having her in my arms, and breathing in her light, floral scent, I knew I had to push through my baggage in an effort to be the kind of man she'd be proud to call hers.

Once I'm in my flannel lounge pants, and have brushed my teeth, I head to Dusty's room. Walking inside, I again wonder how a mother could walk away from her child. I grin seeing him in his bed. It's shaped like a race car, complete with racing stripes down the side, and working headlights which let off a soft glow in his room. I asked him recently if he wanted to change it up since he's getting ready to be a preteen, but he declined since his second love is NASCAR.

"C'mon, little man, that can't be comfortable," I murmur, gently repositioning him on his bed, and straightening his covers. Leaning in, I lightly tussle his hair and kiss his forehead. "Love you, Dusty. Gonna keep being the best dad I know how to be for you."

He doesn't wake up, but I hear a slight snore come from him as he settles into his pillow.

"See you in the morning, son."

After grabbing a bottle of water, I head back into my bedroom, and flop down onto my bed, grabbing the remote. Finding a movie that will eventually lull me to sleep, I set my alarm, then put my thoughts to Sunday.

Her years in the military have changed her, which is to be expected, of course, but it's more than that. She's more watchful, observing everything around her, and while she still smiles easily, it doesn't always seem to reach her eyes.

"She's got her own demons, apparently," I murmur to the television, "just like I do. The question is, can we slay them together, or will I never know how my lips feel against hers?"

Shaking my head at where my thoughts have veered, I decide to focus on myself first. If Sunday and I are meant to cross paths, as more than high school acquaintances, I need to eradicate the shit that Stacey spewed. Now, that's one woman who could be the poster child for what not to do in a relationship, that's for sure.

"You were young, dumb, and full of come, asshole," I grumble. "Head cheerleader and starting quarterback, you fell into all those stupid fucking cliched romances, that's for damn sure." I may be repeating myself but, in my mind, it definitely bears repeating. Something for me to make sure Dusty knows about when it comes to girls. Don't let the small head do the thinking; look at the whole picture.

Grabbing the notebook, I started using as a journal of sorts, something the therapist I saw right after she left so I could get my shit straight, in order to raise Dusty suggested I do, I read over some of my 'stinking thinking' as it's called.

"You'll always be a has-been, Jett. I need more excitement in my life than you can give me. You owe it to me, dammit!"

"You could've been a coach for the NFL, Jett. Why did you turn it down, and take on teaching kids?"

"Look what having that brat did to my body! No one is ever going to want me like this!"

Yeah, I was offered the chance to move up the ranks as a coach once my own career ended thanks to a crippling knee injury, but my heart wasn't in it, so when I was offered the opportunity to take over the head coach role at my old high school, I jumped at the chance, wanting to follow in my dad's footsteps.

He was my first coach, teaching me from the time I could hold a ball how important sportsmanship was, how learning the fundamentals and practicing them over and over again would give me muscle memory when needed. I owe my own career to him, and being able to teach my team what he gave me might not get them to the pros, but it'll hopefully give them the life skills and tools they need to achieve their own personal goals. I just wish Dusty could've known him better before he passed away, but it wasn't meant to be. Thankfully, I've got a ton of videos of the two of them out on the football field, my son toddling around in his football uniform as my dad's team 'taught' him how to play. They're fucking priceless, and I'm glad I have them.

"You're not a has-been, what you do has value and worth," I say out loud while jotting it down. "As far as what having Dusty did to that bitch's body, well, I honestly thought it showed how much of a warrior she was, carrying our child and keeping him safe until he was born. Stretch marks are a badge of courage as far as I'm concerned. I'm sure she wouldn't be able to handle the scars I know Sunday has, she'd probably think she would be better off dead or something."

For the next hour, as the movie drones on in the background, I write, pouring out my fears and frustrations. I worry that Dusty not having any real maternal involvement in his life will hurt him somehow, since my mom is gone as well, and Stacey's parents cut off contact once she split and we divorced. He gets some from my sister, who loves on him as though he was her own, but it's not the same. I dread the day he asks me why he wasn't enough for his mother to stay, and pray it doesn't happen for a few more years at least.

What the hell can I possibly tell him? I guess, depending on how old he is at the time, it'll be the truth, or as much of it as I think he's able to handle.

Tiredness begins to seep in, so I put everything away, get up and take a piss, then check to make sure the house is locked up for the night before I peer in on Dusty one more time.

"Night, little man. Your dad loves you more than all the stars in the sky."

Bouncing against my full kidneys has me opening one eye to see my boy grinning down at me. "Wake up, Dad!" he squeals. "You said we're going to the park today, remember?"

"Let your old man up, son," I mumble. Once he's moved off of me, I roll out of bed and stretch to get all the kinks out. I may not be all that old, but the years of punishment I took on the field mean that every morning I snap, crackle, and pop as though I'm nearing my geriatric years.

"I'm ready for breakfast," Dusty says. "Want me to get it started or what?"

"Give me a few, little man, okay?" I ask, moving to my bathroom. "I'll be out in a few minutes, go ahead and head into the kitchen." Hell, he's no longer a toddler, but my habit of calling him little man persists. I expect it'll be his nickname, or one of them, at least, until the day I draw my last breath.

I waste no time going through my morning routine, tossing on clean jeans, a t-shirt, and my socks before I make my way to my son. He already has our bowls and spoons out, so I hit the button on my coffee pot, then head to the pantry to pull out a box of cereal. "How about a banana this morning to go with your cereal?" I ask, handing him the box once I've filled my bowl.

"I'd rather have strawberries, please," he replies, bouncing in his seat, a byproduct of his ADHD. Ruffling his hair, I grab the milk and juice from the fridge, set it on the table so he can start eating, then set about cutting up some strawberries. Once he's taken care of, I pour myself a cup of joe, then quickly fry up a couple of eggs, and make some toast to go along with my cereal.

"We've got to do our chores before we head to the park, Dusty," I remind him once I'm seated at the table.

"Then, after the park, we'll grab some pizza, how does that sound?"

"I like pizza," he says, grinning at me.

"So do I, little man, so do I. Should we get wings tonight too? There's a game on."

"Football!" he exclaims, now bouncing in his seat.

"Yeah, bud. Are you ready?" I tease, playing off the old commercial, even though he's far too young to catch the reference.

"Yes! I'm done, Dad. What now?"

"Go ahead and put your stuff in the sink, then you can get dressed."

He tries so hard to be independent, which is fine, but he still needs direction from time to time. Time is flying by so damn quickly; it seems like only yesterday he was dependent on me for everything, and now, for the most part at least, he's handling things on his own with some oversight from me. Sighing, I finish up my own breakfast, then make short work of cleaning the kitchen.

Finally satisfied that everything is spic and span once again, I start the dishwasher, then walk to Dusty's room to see how much progress he's made. Typically, he gets sidetracked by one of his games or a book, but today, I'm pleasantly surprised to see he's dressed and is picking up his room. He's already got his clothes hamper out of his closet, his books are back on their shelf, and even though it's crooked as hell, he's made his bed.

"Great job, Dusty," I praise as I grab an errant sock from underneath the bed. "You get better at this all the time, don't you?"

"From watching you, Dad," he replies, grinning at me. He already looks like he's going to be as tall as me, and it's honestly like looking in a mirror sometimes.

His words nearly send me to my knees, a reminder that everything I do or say is being monitored by my kid. We've already had to have a talk about some of the words he's used, thanks to my own inability to stop swearing. I chuckle when I remember that first one happening, the second day of kindergarten. Damn, does time fly.

"Well, you're doing a fantastic job."

Seeing my boy running around the park, without a care in the world, loosens something inside. He's got such a pure, gentle heart, which guts me when I realize his own mother didn't want him. I don't understand why, either. I mean, even though I ended up having to retire from playing pro football, I made enough while still an active player to lead a good, financially stable life. The only reason I took a coaching job at my old high school was because there was no way I could sit on my ass the rest of my life while doing nothing. No more, and no less. Well, health insurance, too, of course, because I had to make sure I could get Dusty seen by his physician if he got sick. It's also one of the reasons I changed my career path from what I had planned to do; become a paramedic. Working as a teacher and coach gives me the ability to be with my son at night, whereas, if I had gone into that field, I'd work day-long shifts. I wasn't willing to miss that much of his life, so pushed that dream to the back of my mind, and focused on being the best dad and teacher possible instead.

We've already tossed the ball around, and now, I'm sitting on the bench as he burns off more energy. Even with the medicine he takes to help him focus, he's still like a live wire most of the time. I figure age and maturity will tame that a little bit, and as long as he knows how to treat other people, I don't care if he jabbers a mile a minute in my ear.

"You ready to order some pizza and wings?" I call out.

He stops what he was doing, and jogs over to me. "Yeah. Can we get some ice cream for sundaes after the game?"

"Why else do you think we have the chest freezer?" I tease.

"For the meals Aunt Cissy makes for us during football season," he retorts, grinning at me.

"And for ice cream. You gonna want me to get root beer?"

He plops down next to me, and looks over my shoulder at the grocery list.

"Yes, please. Can we get some beef jerky too? And I need more deodorant, can't be smelling funky around the girls."

"What girls?"

He grins at me, the freckles across the bridge of his nose the only thing different from me. "Dad," he says, drawing out my name until it's more than a single syllable. "Girls, Dad. They think I'm hot."

"You're too young to be hot. Maybe, just maybe, you're lukewarm," I tease.

"Well, eventually lukewarm turns to hot, so there," he sasses.

Damn, I love this kid.

"Okay, let's head to the grocery store and stock up. I'll call for the pizza and wings when we're almost done, so it'll still be nice and hot by the time we get home."

"Race ya!" he yells, jumping up from the bench toward my truck.

"I'll let you have this one," I call out. My knee's been giving me fits, and I don't want to spend the rest of the weekend doped up when he's out of school. I'll ice it once we're home, and take something for the swelling before bed. Maybe it's time to dig out my brace, since I've been spending a lot of time on the field, showing my players various moves.

"Okay, showers are done, let's settle in and watch some football," I decree, grabbing the pizza and wings in one hand. I've kept them warm in the oven while we both showered off the dust from and sweat from the park, and got dressed in more comfortable attire. "You grab the drinks, paper plates, and napkins."

"Got them," Dusty replies.

"Two games today, think we'll do it? It's going to be a late night," I caution as we get situated in the family room.

My huge television is one of the few excesses I splurged on when I retired from playing, and I'm not even a little bit sorry. I reach into the pizza box, grab two slices, then add four wings before I sit back, and start eating while listening to the commentators announce their picks.

"Do you think you'll stay single forever, Dad?" Dusty asks around a mouthful of pizza.

"What?" Where the hell is this coming from?

"Well, I mean, you're still young, you could get married again, you know?" he casually replies, sucking down some of his root beer. I'm sure there's a professional out there somewhere who would cringe if they saw our normal weekend fare which typically doesn't include vegetables, but for the most part, we eat relatively healthy, a byproduct of my years in the pros. But when it's time for a game, we eat pizza and wings. Sometimes, barbecue. But unless there are pickles involved with the sandwiches, no veggies are in sight.

"Maybe, I don't know. I mean, I need to find someone who can put up with not only me, but my lukewarm son, after all," I tease.

"Dad, in a few years I'll be off to college, then probably moving out on my own. Are you saying you'd be okay living here all by yourself?"

A memory of Sunday from the night before flashes through my mind.

"First of all, you're going on eleven, not eighteen, so I've got a good seven years or so before you head off into the wild world," I reply. "Second, like I said, I've not really dated all that much, so if you're hoping this is something that's going to occur next week, sad to say, but you're out of luck, son."

"How can you meet anyone though if we're always together?"

"I met someone last night when I went out," I tell him.

"Really? Who? What does she look like? Is she

pretty? Do you think she'd like me?" He tosses questions at me left and right, causing me to laugh.

"It's a girl I went to high school with, Dusty. She's a nurse now, but she served in the military until she got hurt. I think she's very pretty, but just so you know, looks aren't everything."

I feel as though I have to remind him of that fact because his mother was the quintessential blonde-haired, blue-eyed cheerleader. Pretty face, banging figure, but sour disposition and soul. She hid it rather well, though. I mean, I saw glimpses of it from time to time, but whenever I'd call her out on it, she would just say I was imagining things.

"Does she like football?" he questions.

"I think so. I mean, she used to come to the football games when we were in school."

"Cool. Because you have to find someone who has the same interests."

Jeez, this kid.

"Why?"

"So you have things in common. You should know this stuff, Dad, you're older than me."

"Been out of the game for a long time, Dusty," I remind him. "Things might've changed."

"Naw," he confidently replies. "Aunt Cissy says couples who stay together do stuff together, but they also have things that they do on their own. Something about mystery. I don't understand that part, though. Shouldn't the person you're spending your life with be your best friend or something?"

"I think so, yes," I slowly state. "Although, couples should have their own interests as well, so they have other things to talk about, being able to share common likes is very important."

"Good. So you need to find out if this woman likes football, then how she feels about pizza and wings, and if she likes kids or not."

The laugh that bursts free at his comment has him glaring at me before he shrugs, and gets himself another slice of pizza.

"Suit yourself, Dad, but if you don't, you'll get stuck with someone like my mother again."

Looks like he already knows what his mom is like, and we won't have to have the conversation I've been dreading his whole life.

CHAPTER
THREE

SUNDAY

"Are you blind, ref?" I yell at the television after my team gets another flag thrown at their play. "He was obviously *not* holding, for fuck's sake!"

"Anyone listening to you would think life and death hinges on this game," Bria teases, handing me a full glass of wine. "So, I saw you dancing a lot with Jett Blake."

I can't help the flush that rises, heating me from the inside out.

"He's just as nice as he was in high school, Bria," I quietly state, taking a sip of my drink.

"And he's single again too," she sing songs, nudging me with her shoulder. "Couldn't ask for a better guy for my best friend in the whole wide world."

Brows raised, I glare at her. "Trying to marry me off already? Have you forgotten my ass and thigh look like ground meat?"

"They do not, dammit! Yes, you can tell you were hurt and have had surgeries there, but the areas are smooth thanks to the grafts. Get out of your own damn way, Sunday, and let whatever's gonna happen between you two happen for heaven's sake!"

Sighing, I put my glass down. "Bria, now that everything's done, it's time for me to focus on my job."

I just got hired at the local hospital as an emergency room nurse. While a lot of my friends in school preferred to focus on one area, like surgery or labor and delivery, I wanted the adrenaline rush from trauma that handling different cases would give me. I suspect my stint in the Navy, where every day was never the same mundane routine in the medic tent, drew me to emergency medicine. I've gone through my orientation, and start working the eleven to seven shift in three days, which is one reason I'm staying up late. I have to change my whole schedule, something I think will be consuming, but I've never backed down from a challenge in my life, and I'm not going to start now.

"Bullshit," she retorts. "Most people successfully manage working and maintain a relationship, Sunday, and you're no different."

"Whatever," I reply, anxious to change subjects.

"Mom said Jonas stopped by the dealership today to buy a new vehicle."

"Oh, really?" she asks, grinning at me.

"Yeah, and as soon as Dad saw him, he told him to leave, his money was no good there."

"Your dad let a sale go?"

I snicker because she sounds shocked. My dad's not a hardass, but after Jonas broke up with me the way he did, he told anyone who would listen that he would never sell him a vehicle. And if what Mom says is true, he's kept his word.

"Yep. Now, he has to go two towns over to buy a car, and I know for a fact they raise their tag prices higher than Dad's dealership."

The only reason I know this is because I was shopping around for a new car, and went there first to see what I wanted, before I turned around, and came back to my father's dealership. The same vehicle with the same options was almost four thousand dollars less and that was before using the company discount I get for being family.

"He just doesn't get it, does he?" she questions, clicking her tongue in criticism. "I'm surprised they're still living here because most folks who know you won't give them the time of day."

"I've never asked anyone to do that, Bria," I say. "Besides, should he have stayed with me when what happened to me in the field repulsed him? Thanks, but no thanks. I don't need any man's pity."

"No, I think it's because of *how* he did it. He could've manned up and told you to your face, but instead, he sent you a fucking text like a coward. Trust me, your folks dropped that information in the right ears, and you know what happened after that! *Everyone* knew he was a piece of shit, so when he and his wife decided to move here, they chose you. Although, I kinda hate it for their kids, because they've got a shitty father, but regardless, he made his choice and now he gets to wallow in it."

My best friend is nothing if not loyal. Since I was finally able to come home, she's been by my side through countless surgeries and rehab. She and my mom took turns changing the dressings, even though by her own admission, she can't handle blood and guts without squirming and getting choked up. I giggle thinking of all the times she gagged while my mom threatened her with a beatdown if she puked in the sterile field.

"At least he didn't string me along, Bri."

Do I want to run into him and his perfect wife? Absolutely not. He knew he couldn't handle less than perfection in his future spouse, so even though how he broke up with me was downright shitty, I'm glad I wasn't dragged along further only to be dumped when I was wholeheartedly invested in our future.

"Don't put him up for sainthood, Sunday," she warns.

"Now, back to Jett. You know he didn't have to work but he took the coaching job at the high school."

"Really? I didn't know that," I say. "Of course, he was always busy back in the day too, and if that's the case, I can't really see him just sitting around on his ass like a bum while life goes by."

"True. His kid is freaking adorable. He's at that awkward phase, all gawky and shit, but he's an absolute hoot to be around. Funny but smart, and definitely kind, like his dad was back in the day."

"I haven't seen him in years. Bet he looks a lot like Jett."

At least, I hope he does because Stacey, while beautiful, is a straight up bitch.

"He does, nearly his mirror image, except for a spattering of freckles on his nose."

"How do you know this?"

"Oh, Dusty's in one of my class periods for math," she supplies. "He's smart like his dad was, too. Keeps me on my damn toes, always asking questions that make me feel unfit to teach, or needing to pull out a book to research the answer. Both options are embarrassing."

"That shouldn't take much," I tease. "I'm still unsure how you ended up teaching *that* class when you hate numbers like you do!"

"Shut it!" she exclaims throwing a pillow at me. "Weren't you wanting to watch the game?"

"I'm sure I'm forgetting something," I murmur as I look through the stuffed bag I've packed for my first shift. One of the longtime nurses suggested I bring an extra pair of scrubs and shoes in the event I needed to swap my outfit for a clean one, so I've got two sets because I'm extra cautious like that sometimes. I also have protein shakes, bottles of water to drink so I stay hydrated between traumas, protein bars, and a cache of loose change to put in my locker. My lunches for the next three days are all prepped, and two are in the fridge, while one is in my insulated lunch bag. I have a stock-pile of water to store in my locker, juice, and one soda, along with a tumbler to fill up when I'm able to take a few minutes to update my charts.

I'm currently scheduled to work in the emergency room department, which should give me the adrenaline rush I crave. I just hope I'm able to keep up; the weather has me a bit more rigid and my muscles tighter than normal.

Grabbing a bottle of Tylenol, I shove it in my bag along with my ID, a pack of gum, and my lip balm. Hopefully, I have everything I need, but if I don't, I'll just write out a note of it and bring it for my next shift. My goal is to have my locker crammed with enough necessities that all I have to bring is my lunch. We'll see how that works for me.

I check my place one more time, ensuring doors and windows are locked, then turn the light on over the stove so I'm not coming into a pitch-dark house. Once I'm positive everything is closed up tight, I grab my tote and lunch bag, then head out to my car.

"Here goes nothing," I whisper, starting my car to head out to the hospital and start my new adventure.

"Doing well, nurse," the doctor says, as I hand him another instrument, so he can finish suturing up the patient.

"Thank you," I reply. He's an older man, somewhat gruff, and the other nurses had warned me about his mannerisms, but I've had no problems with working beside him.

Maybe because he reminds me of Branch? I don't know, and won't look at it, or over-analyze it too closely. I watch him tie off the stitching, then snap off his gloves, and toss them into the hazardous trash bin since they had a trace of blood on them.

"Go ahead and clean it thoroughly with saline, then get him bandaged up while I get his aftercare instructions and discharge paperwork taken care of." To the patient, he gives him the verbal instructions by saying, "Keep it clean and dry, change the bandages daily, and make sure you finish the whole round of antibiotics I'm prescribing."

"Yes, sir," the patient confirms. Once the doctor has left the room, he looks at me with wide eyes. "How is it you have no issues with Dr. Crane? Nobody likes working with him."

I smile as I reply, "He reminds me a lot of my commanding officer. The man was brusque, and to the point in everything he said, and did. It's almost like being with him without the sand, and sweltering weather, of course."

By the time I'm finished with the patient, Dr. Crane has returned, handed him a prescription to keep infections at bay, and his discharge paperwork, then left once again without a single word uttered.

"You have a good night, Sunday," the patient says, looking at my lanyard which has my name prominently displayed. "Hopefully, it won't be too crazy."

"From your mouth to God's ear," I tease, removing my own gloves, and tossing them. "On to the next one," I state. "Don't take this the wrong way, but I hope I don't see you again any time soon."

"I'll see what I can do."

"Cross, I need you in here," Dr. Crane calls out, as I

pass one of the rooms on my way to the nurse's station to complete his chart with what services I provided.

"Coming, sir," I reply.

Looks like charting will be done when I can get to it. Probably about the time the next shift nurse clocks in to take over.

"I swear I've never been more tired than I am right now," Moira, one of the other nurses on duty, complains as we grab our purses from our lockers.

"The shift was definitely hopping," I reply, slipping off my Crocs, and replacing them with my tennis shoes.

"You did really well. Dr. Crane was impressed," she states, complimenting me as we walk out to the employee parking lot.

"Just did my job, Moira," I rebut. "You guys were doing the same."

"Yeah, but he's never requested any of us to work alongside him, like he did you tonight," she insists as we reach our vehicles.

I shrug, unsure what to say in response as I hit my key fob to unlock my car.

"See you tonight," I call out.

"Get some rest, we're almost to a full moon, and

that's when all the crazies come out!" She hollers as I crawl into my driver's seat.

Shaking my head, I just shut my car door, crank it up, then head out to grab some breakfast to take home. I'm too damn exhausted to cook, so a drive thru it is.

After picking up a breakfast sandwich and some orange juice, I drive home, thankful I survived my first shift. By the time I pull into my driveway, my food is consumed, and I'm ready to soak in a hot bath to soothe the ache in my leg. I know I'll get stronger, but until that happens, I suspect I'll be investing in a lot of Epsom salts.

With everything finally gathered and organized for the next day, I collapse into my bed, eager to sleep until I have to get up, get ready, eat, and leave. "Let's see if I can make it through an episode or two before I pass out," I muse, grabbing my remote, and opening up my recordings list. I'm hooked on a first responder show, but I prefer to binge watch several episodes at a time, instead of waiting impatiently each week for the next one to air.

As I drift into dreamland, my show forgotten, and my e-reader idly laying by my side, Jett comes to mind, consuming my thoughts.

"If only..." I murmur.

CHAPTER
FOUR

JETT

"Get the lead out!" I yell as my players lackadaisically run their laps. "I've seen senior citizens in wheelchairs make better time than you guys are right now!"

"Christ, Blake, they're all acting like they just got up from the Thanksgiving dinner table or something," my defensive coordinator mutters.

"Right? Something must be going on. Call them in, we need to get to the bottom of this shit."

I stand there waiting as Collins gets the team over to me, crouching down while taking a knee to wait on me, and anxiously waiting to hear what I'm going to say. This isn't the same group of kids who slaughtered Penn Holley last week, and if they don't put some pep in their step, they're going to get dragged through the mud and lose their hard-earned ranking. Not to mention, if their attention doesn't shift back onto the plays, they'll end up injured or worse

"The easiest way for a player to get hurt is to be unprepared and lax in their plays," I state. "During our summer camps, you boys gave it your all during two-a-days and three-a-days. You learned new plays, and worked hard to ensure the existing plays were committed to memory. Last week, you led the region in rushing and passing yards, touchdowns, and possession. Yet today, you all look as though someone killed your dog. So, tell me, what the hell is going on?"

Junior, who is the only sophomore on the varsity squad, raises his hand. "Go ahead, Junior."

"Well, Coach Blake, none of us are feeling all that well."

"What do you mean you're not feeling well?" I inquire. I'm unaware of any stomach bugs going around, and while I know teenage boys will push the envelope with drinking, most of the team has chosen not to go that route. I have a few who will occasionally indulge from what I've heard, but only after a game, and for sure none of them do drugs.

His shoulders drop and I notice he's got sweat beading on his forehead that wasn't there a few minutes ago. Gazing at the rest of the team, I see most of them look the same.

"Coach, we all ate the school lunch today," Timmers states when Junior fails to speak further. "Not gonna lie, I'm not sure if I'm going to puke my guts up or shit my pants."

Fuck. Sounds like good old fashioned food poisoning. "Any of you go to the nurse?" I ask.

"Jameson did because he threw up in sixth period," Cordell calls out.

I look at the team again and realize Jameson is absent from practice, one day before our game. "Did he check out and go home?" I question.

"Yeah, Coach, he did," Timmers replies.

I mutter under my breath, cursing the fact that if the rest of the team ends up as sick as it sounds like Jameson is, we're going to end up forfeiting the game. But my boys come first because at the end of the day, this is just a game.

"Okay, boys, I suspect you all have food poisoning and it's only going to get worse from here on out. Let's head over to the clinic so we can get the rest of you checked out, so I know how we need to proceed."

"What do you mean, Coach?" Junior asks, wiping at his mouth. I note he and several others have moved spots from where he was originally, and realize I need to move this fiasco along, or the staff that keeps the field in pristine condition is going to be cursing all of us.

"Thinking tomorrow's game needs to be called off, Junior," I reply. "Let's move it, boys."

"Coach, they're our biggest rival," Timmers ghastly states with a forlorn look crossing his face. "We can't forfeit!" he protests.

"We can, and we will. None of you boys are in any condition to play football, and the nausea and cramping is only going to get worse," I inform them, preparing them what they're facing while remembering my own bout with food poisoning several years ago. I thought I was dying, and at one point, was positive I had thrown up food I consumed in my earlier childhood years. I even swore I was seeing my stomach lining at one point, but my mom told me it was hallucinations from the fever.

"While you're getting checked over, I'll see if I can snag a bus to take you guys home. No way are any of you who drive getting behind the wheel in your condition. Your folks can come back later this evening and grab your vehicles for you."

"Sorry, Coach," Timmers mumbles as I drop him off.

"Not yours or anyone else's fault, buddy," I reply.

I only ended up taking a handful of the kids home because several ended up being transported to the hospital from the school's clinic, and a few of the boys called their parents who came and picked them up from the resource office. Once I get done taking the bus back, I'll be heading to the hospital to check on my boys.

Tonight's gonna be a long night; I've already called the coach from the rival school, as well as the division officials. At the end of the day, I'm not worried about one loss because to date, we're undefeated, so our team should still make the county playoffs at the end of the season.

Apparently, not only my team was impacted; it seems that anyone who ate the school lunch has taken ill. The last I heard, the principal was in communication with the superintendent to see about closing school tomorrow, and possibly Monday, to allow the kids to get better while the kitchen is completely cleaned and disinfected.

"See you Monday, Coach," Timmers says before walking up his driveway, shoulders slumped in defeat.

"Hopefully so, man," I whisper before heading back to the bus depot.

Time to head to the hospital. Right now, I'm glad Dusty is spending the night at my sister's house. We do that a lot during the season since practices run so late; that way he's able to keep to a schedule. I've found with his ADHD that those are a must, otherwise, he devolves, and things get ugly fast. Other than that, he's a good kid and I'm grateful he's mostly easy going.

Once back at the school, I turn the bus keys into the bus barn, then head to my office to grab my duffel bag before driving up to the hospital. Morris, the school janitor, is carefully mopping the floor outside the locker room.

"Coach, heard about your boys so I've already cleaned and disinfected the locker room and showers, and have pulled all the towels from the shelves. The ladies got them running through the wash now. Can't be too careful."

I'm blown away by his initiative. Hell, I never even really thought about it being transmitted further, but it's better to be safe than sorry in case it's a stomach bug and not food poisoning.

"Morris, appreciate that a lot because it never crossed my mind."

"Wouldn't have mine either, Coach, then I remembered when this happened while I was in school. No one thought to sanitize, and we kept getting reinfected because boys will be boys and share every last thing, you know? Water bottles, snacks, so it kept transferring back and forth."

"Need any help, Morris?" I question, ready to assist the older janitor with this thankless task.

"Naw, Coach, but I appreciate the offer. Just about

finished, this was the last little bit, unless you want me to hit your office too."

"It might not be a bad idea for the simple fact I think Jameson stopped by earlier. I don't claim to understand how any of this stuff gets transmitted, you know what I mean?"

He chuckles while nodding his head. "Definitely. I know folks probably think I'm just a lowly janitor and don't know shit, but if they knew I've been able to raise a family of five kids on my salary, they'd think again. Sometimes, the thankless jobs like this are the ones where money can be made. But with that being said, none of them have ever thought to ask me if I had a higher education or a degree, and I'm not one to share that information with others unless I'm asked."

"I knew there was more to you than just a mop and broom," I jest, pointing to two of his tools of trade.

"Was on track to go into medical school, Coach," he confesses. "Fell in love with my Millie, we got hitched, then she started popping out our babies."

"Surely, you were familiar with how that happens," I state, grinning.

"Well, yeah, of course, but those babies needed food and residency is hard enough without having a family in tow, which is where I was at in the program, but after you add in a wife, two little ones, and all the bills they come with, left us financially spiraling, and suddenly, I had to find something else. I don't regret it either," he emphatically announces. "Best parts of me are now grown and living their best lives, while me and Millie reap the rewards with spoiling the grandbabies."

"Why don't you retire?" I question.

"And do what? Sit on my ass all day watching daytime television? No thanks, Coach. My granny always said you don't start dying until you stop living. I never understood what she meant by that until my last baby got married, and it was just Millie and I again, rattling around in our big old empty house. Millie found a little part-time job down at the hospital in their gift shop, and I kept on working. We take vacations during the school breaks, visit our kids who've moved hours away, and we are both involved in several different charities in town. We're still living, Coach, and I don't see that changing for me until I draw my last breath."

"I'm the same way. When I got injured and couldn't play anymore, my manager couldn't understand why I applied for the job here. He said I had enough money at my disposal that I could rest on my laurels for the rest of my life. Only, what would that teach my boy? Nothing I wanted him to know. I don't mind being busy, and he's learning to work for what he wants."

"Seen your boy around, Coach. He's a good kid."

"He is and so are the boys on the team. Gonna let you get back to it, Morris, so I can head up to the hospital and see how they're all doing. Thanks again for thinking of doing this."

"Any time, Coach. You let them boys know me and my Millie will be praying for them, and if any of them need anything, they can get a message forwarded to me, and I'll take care of it."

"Will do, Morris. Have a great night."

He shoots me a wave while heading into my office as I jog out to my truck. Time to check on my boys and make sure it's not worse than I predicted. Once I arrive at the hospital and am brought back to the treatment area after I explain who I am, and why I'm there, I find that all of the affected kids on the team are now signed in, and have been admitted to the emergency room. My pulse accelerates tenfold when I see Sunday bustling around, as parents ask questions while waiting to see the doctors.

"Mrs. Timmers, what have you heard?" I probe, going over to where she's standing next to a gurney holding her son, an IV already in place while two different bags of fluids rehydrate him, and drips into his veins. Controlled chaos reigns as my boys are in what appears to be an open area, spread out on multiple gurneys, with several nurses moving around tending to all of them.

"From what the nurse has been able to determine, they're going to be admitting the team," she states, her tear-filled eyes looking at me. "They're running blood-work on all of them right now, and have got all the boys hooked up to anti-nausea medication and saline fluids while they wait to find out what strain of food poisoning they're dealing with."

"I know there are some pretty bad strands out there, so hopefully, it's one of the more easily treated ones where the boys will all be miserable for a few days, but will bounce back quicker," I reply, trying to sound as encouraging as possible while I mentally think about our upcoming game schedule.

Not trying to be a dick about the situation, but if I have to appeal to the state and ask for them to adjust things so my team has a chance to recover their strength, I need to know all the facts around what I'm facing. The priority, of course, is them and their welfare. Always has been, and always will be.

"Most of the kids at school have either been here, and are either already admitted, or had to go to the next town's hospital, because they've run out of rooms," she admits. "We're fortunate that you sent the kids home when you realized what was happening, Coach, so we could get them seen."

"Haven't heard the final word yet, but Principal Waystein is checking to see about closing the school for a few days to give the kids a chance to get better, while also thoroughly bleaching and sanitizing the kitchen.

The lunchroom manager has also been in contact with the school's vendor. She's been hounding them to find out if the food they delivered has any product codes they can trace, and is searching to see if they've had any type of recalls for the meals on the market, which will help the medical professionals better diagnose and treat everyone that's been impacted," I reply, passing on the little information I know.

"I think he's going to be packing his lunch from now on," she professes, laughing slightly before breaking into a small sob when Timmers moans in pain.

"I'll leave you to him, I'm going to check with the other parents and their boys," I tell her, nearly bumping into Sunday. "You or any of the others need anything, send me a message and I'll take care of it," I state.

"What! Oh, I'm sorry, Jett," Sunday sputters, barely managing to keep hold of the fluid bags she's holding.

"The fault is mine, Sunday, I'm in the way," I reply. "Just wanted to check in on the boys."

"It's bad, Jett," she whispers, leaning in close enough that I catch a whiff of the light, clean scent she's wearing. "I can't say anything more than that, of course, due to HIPAA, but I'm sure your own eyes can tell you that much."

Glancing at the overflowing triage areas where most of my team, and quite a few of the other students from school are moaning in agony, I nod. Taking a moment, I send up a silent prayer that the kids recover quickly, and their suffering lessens soon, before looking at her once more.

"You look run off your feet, I thought you worked a later shift?" I question. I don't really want to delay her, but curiosity wins out right now.

"I got an 'all hands on deck' phone call, and when I heard what was going on, I couldn't *not* come in, Jett. The principal has to be freaking out," she replies.

"He might be, but he's educated and trained for these scenarios. It's why he's earned the position and title he has, so I'm sure he'll be just fine." Seeing her glance over her shoulder, I say, "Go ahead, Sunday, I won't keep you. Thanks for taking good care of my boys."

"Always, Jett."

CHAPTER
FIVE

By the time my actual scheduled shift is done, I'm beyond toasted. As I slip my Crocs off and my tennis shoes on, I bag them up to take home and run through the washing machine, along with the other two sets of scrubs I've gone through and exchanged thanks to all the projectile vomiting that occurred in the ER. Thankfully, some of the kids didn't have to be admitted because they didn't eat their whole lunch, but there are still enough who were that our hospital is temporarily closed to any incoming traumas. I'm sure it won't stop the emergency room from hopping when I'm on shift again, but I'm off for the next two nights.

"I definitely need it, too," I mumble, grabbing my

stuff and pulling out my keys. My goal is to hit up the Tasty Chick drive-thru, buy a family-size bucket of chicken along with the sides, then spend the next two days recovering. Hopefully, they'll be open since it's still early for fast-food operating hours, but if not, I'll figure something else out. With all the charting I had to complete before I could officially clock out and leave, I'm starving since I had to skip several of my breaks, and my belly is rumbling in protest even as my feet drag, and my eyes droop.

Once inside my car, with the bag of dirty scrubs and my Crocs tucked inside the trunk, I head out of the parking lot toward restaurant row so I can order some of the best chicken I've ever had. As my phone syncs to the Bluetooth in my car, I hear the pings of all the missed calls and texts. Hitting the message icon, I listen to each one, grinning when I hear the robotic female reading my mom's message, which is a play by play of what she's taken care of for me since I was called into work before my shift began.

"You're the best, Mom," I state once given the option to reply. "I'm grabbing food for the next few days then holing up in my bed. Hopefully, there won't be any emergencies come through the hospital that get me recalled into work, because I'm not gonna lie, I'm in a lot of pain."

My phone immediately rings, and her concerned

voice reverberates from the other end of the line. "Honey, I grabbed some Epsom salts when I was out and about running my daily errands. I stored them in your bathroom's medical supply cabinet for you, be sure you take a long soak and use some please."

Laughing, I remark, "Definitely, they've been a lifesaver."

I'm sure my surgeon would frown on how much I moved around during the influx of students that walked in needing to be seen. From what Moira said when I was caught rubbing my aching limbs, shifts aren't normally that bad and raucous. The situation with the school, however, was something completely unprecedented. I do know the trauma response team plans to implement an emergency protocol should something like this ever happen again.

"I also hit up the grocery store and stocked you up on the things I know you like, sweetie," she reveals.

"Mom, I'm all grown up now, remember? Plus, I live on my own," I state.

"You may be an adult, but you'll always be *my* little girl. When I heard what happened, I figured you'd be working overtime, so took one of your chores on. That's all, no more, and no less," she retorts. "If I can't help my own daughter, who else can I help?"

"Thanks, Mom. I do appreciate it because I'll be doing laundry until I return to work," I grumble. "I'm kinda glad I'm a bit over the top about some things though, because at least, I had clean scrubs to change into."

"It's always a good idea to have a backup set. Your grandma told me that trick when I first started working in the nursing field."

"I went through both pairs of my backups," I admit, snickering. "And my Crocs get to go into the wash as well."

"Good heavens, it was that bad?" she asks. "You know I don't want the particulars because you can't tell me, but I must have misheard the rumors because I didn't think it was too horrible and outrageous."

"Well, we had a large group in one room since the parents and kids all knew each other, and before the anti-nausea meds took hold, there was quite a bit of projectile vomiting going on," I disclose to her, snickering when she makes a gagging noise. "What? It's not like you haven't had people do the same to you when you were working on the floor."

"Yeah, I know, and it made me gag then, too," she sasses. "Get yourself home, take a good, hot soak, then make sure you take some of your pain meds, honey. That's what they're for, and I know you're probably hurting like hell."

"I almost feel like I did after my first few surgeries.

But I'll be sure to do what you suggest once I inhale half of my chicken that I'm about to order," I tease.

"You and your chicken. I swear you're going to grow feathers one of these days. You let me know if you need me to do anything else. I saw the reminder notice that Princess Pudge is due to go to the vet for her shots on your refrigerator."

"Yeah, she's due for her next round, then, I'll get her spayed. She had no clue what she was in for the day she showed up on my back porch, did she?" I question, giggling.

"She's definitely spoiled, but I'm sure she's lonely when you're gone. Have you considered getting a second pet to keep her occupied?"

"Already planning on me being a crazy cat lady, Mom?"

"Not at all, but during your shifts, they'll keep each other company, honey. Besides, I heard you were seen talking to Jett Blake last weekend at Ike's."

I roll my eyes, even though she can't see me, as I pull up to the drive-thru. "Hang on, Mom, let me place my order." Once I've done so, and pulled around to wait for my delicious yumminess, I continue where I left off before pausing our conversation. "He was there when I went out with Bria, and he bought the two of us a round of drinks. I went over to thank him."

"I see."

Hmm. Those two words hold a wealth of 'Mom' in them, so I wait patiently to see what else she's going to come up with, grinning like a lunatic which probably has more to do with how tired I am, than the fact she mentioned his name.

"I think you should let him know you're interested, Sunday," she finally says.

"Mom!" I exclaim. "How does *one* simple conversation over a drink translate to me being interested?"

"Sunday Marie Cross, you can lie to yourself, but you can't lie to your mother," she admonishes me. "You've always liked that boy, so why not show him?"

"Maybe because he has more to consider than just himself? He's got a kid, remember? Plus, who's to say he'd want to get involved with me anyhow? I definitely don't look the way I did in high school."

"Sunday... really? You're going to go there with me? Your daddy hasn't said or even acted like my mastectomy scars bother him."

"Daddy's one of the good ones, Mom. Not all men are like him," I retort, thinking of Jonas and his reaction when I was first injured and hospitalized.

"Not all men are like that good-for-nothing ex of yours, sweetie. I suspect Jett's more like your dad in that regard than you think. What would it hurt?"

Nothing except my heart shattering into a gazillion pieces if I'm rejected by him.

"Fine. *If* the situation presents itself, I'll let him know I'd be interested in seeing him as more than friends, okay?"

She sounds almost giddy when she confesses, "That's all I want, sweetie."

The clerk knocks on my window, and I roll it down to take the bag and thank her for bringing it out to me. "Mom, gotta go, hot, fresh chicken is now onboard."

"Heaven forbid I come between you and your food. Love you, Sunday. Be careful and I'll talk to you later on when you wake up."

"Love you too, Mom. Bye!"

"Okay, Pudge, now that we've got the clothes going, let's go take a hot bath while I eat some chicken," I say to the kitten who's been purring at my feet. Leaning over, I pick her up, and cuddle her as she licks my face with her sandpapery tongue. "I love you too, fuzzy butt."

I make a plate of food, then store the rest for later, before heading into my en suite. Once I've stripped off my work clothes, and tossed them into the hamper I use strictly for my scrubs, I start the water in the tub, then go into my closet where my dresser is, and find a comfy nightshirt to wear after I'm done. As I slide into the water, I groan. My body aches letting me know I've done too much.

"Can't be helped, Pudge," I tell her as she curls up on the wide ledge to watch me eat. I'm pointing a chicken leg at her, but she doesn't grab for it, which I'm impressed by. Instead, she meows as though she's agreeing with me. "Your grandma thinks you need a companion, what do you think?"

She meows again and I nod. "You're right. You will be lonely when I'm at work. How about I check the shelter to see if there's anyone you might like?"

Moving closer to me, she nudges my head then trills before she takes a running jump and leaves the bathroom behind. "Yeah, I'm kind of done with myself too, little girl. Time to focus so I can take some meds and get some much-needed rest."

CHAPTER
SIX

JETT

With the school on lockdown for a few days while they sterilize the rooms, and the students affected have a chance to recover, Dusty and I are taking care of some necessary yard work, which translates to he's picking up the weeds I've pulled, and placing them inside the extra-large garbage bags, he has been chattering my ear off. The mowing and trimming are already finished, leaving this particular job left to do, which I hate.

"Dad?"

"Yeah, Dusty?"

"You gonna ask that lady friend of yours out if you see her again?"

"The one I told you about? The one that I saw last

weekend, right?" I query, sitting back on my heels to look at him. "Does it really bother you that I'm single?"

"I just don't want you to be alone, Dad, like we talked about. I mean, how many times have I seen my own mother since she left? Once? Twice? She wouldn't even recognize me if she passed me on the street, I bet."

I highly doubt that since he's the spitting image of me, but I keep those thoughts to myself. Instead, I consider what he's really saying, and warmth courses through my body. He's a good kid, just looking out for his old man, is all.

"If the situation presents itself, I'll see if she's willing to go out with a single dad, who comes with a lukewarm kid, how's that sound?" I tease. His sigh is sufficient to have me laughing. "C'mon, let's wrap this up so we can enjoy the next few days off since you're caught up on homework."

Later that day, while I work on game plans for the upcoming week, hoping we'll be able to cobble enough of the kids together to even play, and Dusty is destroying zombies or some shit on his video game, my phone rings.

"Hello?"

"Um, hi, Jett. It's Sunday. Sunday Cross."

Her voice washes over me, making me wish she was right in front of me instead of on the phone.

"Hey, how are you?" I ask.

"Well, I've got a bit of a problem, and I'm hoping maybe you can help?" The last part comes out unsure, posed as a question instead of a statement, and it has my interest piqued.

"What's going on? Are you okay?"

"I'm fine, but a few weeks ago, a kitten showed up on my back porch and I took her in. I'm getting her vetted and all that stuff, but that's not the problem. Apparently, she has a sibling, only it's stuck in my bushes, and I can't quite get to her. I thought maybe you might be able to help me get her out."

"Give us a few minutes and we'll head on over," I reply, already setting my team binder to the side. Dusty, without any prompting from me, saves his game and stands, practically vibrating with excitement as he listens to my half of the conversation.

"Thank you. I didn't know who else to call since Bria's away on a trip for work, and my dad's allergic to cats."

"We're on our way, Sunday," I promise.

"She looks just like the other one almost," Dusty says, once we finally untangle the other kitten and he compares the two. "Except Pudge is heavier and doesn't have black spots on her back."

"I think I'll call this one Smudge," Sunday says, grinning at him. "Thank you both for helping me with this. I was actually going to look at the shelter to see about getting another kitten so Pudge wouldn't be by herself. Now I just need to take Smudge in and get her started on her shots, I guess."

"Go ahead and call the vet, see if we can come and get her looked over now," I suggest. "We'll go with you."

"Oh, I couldn't impose like that," she says.

"We're not doing anything else, Miss Sunday," Dusty replies. "We already did all the chores, and were just sitting around."

I hide my smile, because ever since we got to her house, Dusty has been *Team Sunday*, and when he figured out she was the one I mentioned, he's ramped up his efforts to hang around and delegate. Pushing us closer together... the little matchmaker. When she looks at me for confirmation, I merely nod, then watch her pick up her phone to call the vet.

She already has the kitten in a carrier to keep the two separated, which is smart since one has been living as a stray.

"Dusty, while she does that, why don't you grab her trash can, and take it down to the curb?" I ask.

Before she can protest, he's up like a shot and running over to the corner of her garage, where her trash can is sitting. I watch as he maneuvers it so it's not going to fall over, then he takes it to the end of her driveway, and puts it to the side by the curb so it's not hit from her pulling in or out, like we do ours.

She hangs up the phone, and says, "He's a good kid, Jett."

"Yeah, he really is. Are they able to see you today?"

Her smile is radiant as she nods. "I just need to grab my purse then I can take her. Thank you both for your help."

"We can drive you, if you want," I offer, not quite ready to leave since I'm enjoying the time we've spent together.

"You don't have to, Jett. I feel bad enough I had to pull you away from what you guys were doing to help me get her untangled."

"Not an imposition for either of us, Sunday. In fact, because I promised my boy I would, if the situation presented itself, ask if you would like to go out with me the next time you're off?"

Shit, I feel like I'm sixteen again, asking a girl out for the very first time. I almost want to bounce in place like Dusty does in an effort to rid myself of the nerves.

"You want to take me out?" she softly asks. "Really?"

"Yes, really," I reply.

"Yes, I'd like to go out with you the next time I'm off, which is Saturday night."

"Then it's a date."

The small glances she keeps giving me, as we come back to her place from the vet's, has me wishing we weren't at the beginning stages of a relationship, but I can be patient. Once we pull into her driveway, Dusty quickly undoes his seatbelt, then jumps out, before carefully getting the carrier out and heading up to Sunday's porch.

"I was going to heat up some homemade spaghetti sauce I made, if you and Dusty would like to join me for dinner," she announces. "I just have to cook the pasta, and I might have the fixings for a salad, too, because my mom hit up the grocery store for me the day I got called in for the extra shift when the kids all got sick, and she knows how much I like them."

"Not too sure about Dusty eating a salad, but if you're sure, we'd love to join you."

Anything to stay a little longer, I think to myself. Because she's captivated me for a long time now, and I'm grabbing onto this opportunity with both hands.

CHAPTER
SEVEN

SUNDAY

Dusty keeps up a running commentary that ranges from the video game he's currently playing, to how the two kittens are snuggled together sleeping in the cat tree that's set up in my living room. He's currently helping me cut up tomatoes and cucumbers for the salad, which he swears he'll try.

"Dusty, give her a break, little man. You're going to talk her ear off," Jett says, grinning at his son.

"She doesn't mind, Dad. Do you, Miss Sunday?" Dusty asks.

"No, sweetie, I don't. And you can call me Sunday, if it's alright with your dad."

"Great! Um, can I watch your tv? Unless you have a game system?" he eagerly asks, making me laugh.

"No game systems here, unfortunately, but you're welcome to turn on the tv. The remote's on the end table."

"Thank you," he replies, hurrying out of the kitchen while Jett laughs.

"He's liable to put on the sports channel or something like that on," Jett warns.

"I don't mind, Jett, I promise," I reply, grinning at him. "What do you think I watch when I'm home?"

"No clue. The Hallmark Channel?" he teases.

"Oh, I definitely watch that when the Christmas movies come out. I guess I'll set my DVR to record the new ones, so I don't miss any of them. But I also like a few dramas, and sports wise, I follow a few college teams, and a few pro teams."

"You do?" he asks.

"Yeah, I spent so much time watching high school football, it carried over when I went into the military. I got hooked on a couple of college teams then and my squad loyally watched them play whenever we were able to. Unless we were out on deployment, we would have the games on from the time the first scheduled game came on, until the last bit of discussion on ESPN," I state, giggling. "Who knew, right?"

"Dusty's going to fall in love with you," he mutters,

chuckling. "That kid is all about football. During the off-season, he catches old games on the tube, and watches them like they're pre-game film or something."

"Does he play?" I question, finishing up the salad and putting it into the fridge to chill while the water heats up for the pasta. I already have the sauce warming; I've found that making it, then waiting a day to actually eat it, causes all the flavors to blend better. The garlic toast is on a baking tray so I can pop it into the oven once the pasta is almost cooked.

"At the rec league level right now. I'm still debating whether or not to let him play in middle school."

"Why?" I'm genuinely curious because I would think he'd want his son to play as early as possible.

"I don't want him to burn out."

"You didn't," I remind him. "In fact, you came back here to coach the team and I seem to recall you played when we were in middle school. Maybe you should ask him what he wants to do? I mean, I'm obviously not a parent, and you're his dad, and know him best, but it seems to me if you talk to him about it, he'll tell you."

Dusty was definitely a fountain of information while helping me; chattering about school, the classes he liked and didn't particularly care for, what he thought of about various town activities. He may only be eleven, but it was obvious to me he isn't afraid to voice his concerns or opinions.

"He's not shy about letting me know how he feels, that's for sure," Jett murmurs, chuckling. "It's one of the reasons we have 'no veggies' weekends."

"What do you mean?" I question breaking the spaghetti and adding it to the boiling water.

"I was all about making sure he had vegetables of some sort for every meal, like I grew up, you know? Well, he was about eight when he looked me in the eye over his paper plate that had a slice of pizza and a helping of green beans, then said, 'Dad, I get more than the recommended daily requirement of fruits and vegetables. I think if I don't eat them on the weekends, especially when we're watching football, I'll still grow up big and strong'," Jett replies, mimicking his boy.

I can't help it, I burst out laughing because in my short exposure to the little boy, I can picture the earnest look on his face while he pleads his case. As Jett watches, a soft smile stretching across his face, I try to get myself under control. Finally, when I feel as though my face is a thousand degrees of hot, I manage to stop giggling.

"Yeah, that was about my reaction as well," he drily teases. "Needless to say, when I thought about what we normally eat, I decided he was right. On the weekends when we're watching games, vegetables aren't required."

"He's got strong negotiation skills, obviously. Maybe he'll be a lawyer or something someday down the road."

I watch as Jett does a full body shudder as if in horror, which almost causes me to lose it again. "Not a fan of attorneys?"

"Most don't go into the field for the right reasons," he replies. "But ultimately, it'll be his choice."

We continue to chat while the spaghetti finishes cooking, and when it's done, he carries the pot over to the sink so I can drain it, then helps me get it set down on the table before telling Dusty to go wash his hands while I fix us all drinks.

Dinner is a boisterous affair, and I find myself putting the memory of having Jett and his son sitting at my table in my memory banks. I know we're going out on a date in a few days, which still seems so surreal, but that doesn't mean anything. We could find we have nothing in common, or that we'd be better off as platonic friends than anything that leads to a romantic relationship.

Although... I've definitely caught him staring at me when I'm talking to Dusty with a look on his face I can't quite decipher. I decide I'll call Bria later, once they leave, so I can get her input on the whole situation.

As we clean up the kitchen, I put most of the left-overs in a large container while also preparing two smaller ones. The bigger one I hand to Jett and say, "This will end up going to waste here, but based on how well Dusty eats, you might get another meal, maybe two, out of it."

He chuckles and replies, "You're probably right about that. I swear he's going to eat me out of house and home."

Taking a chance, I lean closer and state, "I'm glad you two were able to stay for dinner, Jett."

His smile warms and he cups my face with his hand. "I am too, Sunday. Looking forward to our date on Saturday."

"So am I."

"Dusty, go ahead and turn off the television, we need to get home, son," he calls out. Once the plates were cleared from the table, he went back into the living room to 'catch up' on the sports channel.

"Okay, Dad!"

"Do you want a bag for that to make it easier to carry?" I ask, pointing to the bowl. "Just in case?" I've seen one too many Tupperware mishaps and would hate for dinner to spill all over his interior and stain it.

"Naw, it'll be fine."

As we walk to my front door, Dusty heads to Jett's truck, yelling, "Thanks for dinner, Sunday!"

I giggle because his stride is so reminiscent of his father's, and his voice, while it's still the higher-pitched timbre of a child, seems like when he goes through his vocal change it'll be as deep as Jett's is, which means he's gonna be another heartbreaker once he inherits Jett's gravelly, husky tone. Jett turns and smiles down at me, causing my heart to flutter in my chest.

"Six good for Saturday?" he asks.

"Perfect. Do you know where we're going to eat?" I question, wanting to figure out my outfit.

"Well, we're doing a movie first, so what if we go to Logan's Roadhouse? The dress there is more casual, since I'd rather we both be comfortable while watching a movie. We'll save the dressy stuff for another date."

Another date.

With Jett Blake.

Be still my heart.

"Okay. Jeans it is," I tease.

"Works for me. See you then," he whispers, lightly brushing his lips across my cheek before he heads to the truck, and hops inside. As he's backing out of my driveway, he lightly beeps the horn as if to tell me to head inside. I wave at them both before going back inside, and locking the door behind me.

Time to fill Bria in on my current status.

CHAPTER
EIGHT

JETT

I wasn't surprised when Dusty was enthusiastic about my date with Sunday. What did surprise me were all the questions he's asked in the ensuing days. Does she like kids, or was she just pretending? If we got married, would we stay in our house, or move into hers? Would we have more kids? Does she like dogs, or only cats?

His list of inquisitions was endless, and since I had no answers, I finally told him when I knew, he'd know, which seemed to satisfy him, at least temporarily. Now, as we go through the grocery store, I watch as he adds some odd things to the cart.

"What are you doing?" I question, glancing at the list on my phone.

"I noticed Sunday likes these when we were over there, Dad," he replies, his hands now hovering protectively over the drinks he put in, guarding them so I don't put them back on the shelf. "She'll be coming over at some point, right? We need to be ready."

"She will, yes, but I don't think we need two twelve-packs, Dusty," I gently tease. "She can only drink one at a time."

"I know, but if she likes us a lot, then she'll be at our house more often, so she'll drink them then."

"Eventually."

"Dad." He draws my name out as only a kid can do, causing me to chuckle.

"It's fine, Dusty," I say. "Now, how about you go and grab the cereals while I pick out the meat packs?"

Divide and conquer. It's the only way I can handle coming into the grocery store. I'm just glad my son is still willing to be seen in public with me. I remember once I hit my teen years, I did whatever I could to avoid 'hanging out' with my own parents. Now, of course, I wish I had spent more time with them, considering they're both gone, but they understood.

"What do you say we make sure you've got everything gathered that you're going to need to take to your aunt's tomorrow?" I ask once we've gotten home, and put the groceries away. "I've got pizza and wings ordered, so we should have enough time to do that before we settle in for a movie."

"I wish I could go with you tomorrow night," he complains as we head to his room.

"Yeah, not happening on the first date, bud," I retort. "I'm sure if things go the way I want them to, we'll do things together."

"Like what?"

"Oh, you know, the museum, botanical garden, maybe the center for puppetry arts?" I tease.

"How about the amusement park, zoo, or the arcade?" he counters, giggling.

"Let's see where things go. Now, while you're grabbing your clothes, let me have your hamper. May as well get ahead on the laundry."

He snickers as he grabs his duffel bag from the floor of his closet, and tosses it on his bed. "Can I take my game?"

"You know your aunt will probably have things planned to do for you guys," I warn, since my sister is notorious about scheduling 'fun activities' for the cousins to do when they're together. Since that happens frequently during football season, and it keeps me from having to go to every small-town carnival or pumpkin patch, I don't put up much of a fuss. I love spending time with my boy, but prefer sports instead. It works for Dusty because he gets the best of both worlds; physical activity with me, fun stuff, and occasionally things that are educational with his aunt.

"I know, but she usually gives us an hour before we go to bed."

"Just don't forget it when you come back home because I'm not going out at midnight to pick it up. If you do, you'll have to wait until the next time you go over there to grab it."

Not really, but I know he tends to forget his stuff over at her house, and with school starting back up on Monday, I want an early night for the both of us.

"I promise," he replies, crossing his hand over his heart.

"Don't forget your toothbrush. I'll meet you downstairs."

Later that night, lying in my bed, my thoughts drift to the next night and my planned date with Sunday. I know for her it may seem soon, but I hope I'm able to lay out what I foresee for the two of us, and our future.

A future that includes more kids, lots of laughter, and more love than either of us have ever known.

"Patience, Jett," I mumble to myself while watching

the day's highlights in sports. Not like Dusty and I didn't spend several hours in front of the television seeing them in real time.

As I feel sleep beckoning, I smile, knowing that in less than twenty-four hours, I'll be with her.

CHAPTER
NINE

SUNDAY

Bria was absolutely no help whatsoever when I called to give her the latest news. I'm still experiencing a bit of hearing loss from her shrieks of excitement, quite truthfully. At the same time, she did come over while I was working, and brought several shirts she thought would work with my jeans and low-heeled boots. As I stand in my bathroom waiting for the water to heat in the shower, I mentally go through everything I need to do in order to get ready before he arrives.

"You've been out on a date before, silly," I say out loud. "Granted, it's been a few years, but the concept's still the same. If you like someone or they like you, you spend time with each other, and go from there."

But I like him so much, always have, even as a teenager when he was out of reach because he was dating Stacey. Plus, even though I'm scared to talk about my scars, they are a part of who I am now, and I need to know right from the start if they're going to be an issue or deterrent for him or not. When Jonas broke off our engagement, I was devastated because I knew it was due to my injuries, and the fact that even with extensive surgeries, my body would always reflect the damage. However, looking back with clearer eyes, I now realize we probably wouldn't have even made it to the altar.

Jonas expected perfection in every little thing, from my appearance, to what I did for a living. He never made it a secret that he didn't think much of my career in the Navy; but those years, regardless of the outcome of my last mission, not only helped pay for my degree to become a nurse, but they also forced me to grow up and mature.

Because the day I stepped foot on the grounds at NAS Great Lakes up in Illinois, Uncle Sam owned me. I'm proud I served my country and was able to work with such a wide variety of people. I developed solid communication skills, which definitely helps me when I'm at work in the challenging, often exacerbating, emergency room in our little town of Possum Run.

Sighing, I push thoughts of Jonas into the abyss of my mind, determined that he will not be a dark cloud on something I've longed for. Stepping into the shower, I shampoo my hair then put conditioner on the layers to keep my hair from tangling, while at the same time, making it appear shiny, and feel smooth by leaving it in for three to five minutes as the directions state. The next step in my routine is to start the process of carefully washing and gently debriding the healing area on my thigh. The initial grafts done after my injury got infected, which caused my body to reject them, so once I was home, my parents sought out the best plastic surgeon they could find to treat the damage.

Dr. Barnard is probably the reason I still have a leg, and it didn't have to be amputated because he wasted no time to start a course of aggressive treatment once he saw me at my appointment. I was in surgery the following day, then in ICU while he closely monitored everything. The worst part of it all were the compression garments I had to wear, much like a burn victim. They were hot and uncomfortable, plus they chafed. So, even though it's obvious I had surgery, the skin is smooth, and as long as I abide by the instructions I was given, every-thing should be just fine. I still wear a lighter compres-sion garment under my scrubs and jeans simply because of the tactile issue. The surgical area's skin is still a bit thin and needs the extra layer of protection.

I take my time exfoliating, then shaving my legs, before applying the lotion I have to use to ensure the skin on my left side remains supple. I grin because I ended up with a 'butt lift' of sorts since most of my left cheek was ground up like hamburger due to the blast. Since Dr. Barnard is all about symmetry, he matched the right side, so I've got the perfect, shapely ass for any pair of jeans now.

Snickering at my musings, I finish my shower, then wrap a bath sheet around me so I can air dry, which my team of doctors prefer me to do, while I blow dry my hair. As I sit down at my vanity, and pull out my detangling brush, Pudge comes waddling over to me, meowing in greeting.

"Hello, sweet girl, are you coming to watch Mama get ready?" I ask, spritzing some heat protectant on my hair.

Her meows make me laugh, especially when she jumps up and proceeds to sit on the top of the vanity while looking at herself in the mirror. When she touches the reflection with her paw and hisses, I lose my battle and almost double up laughing. I make a mental note when cleaning to get the nose prints I'm sure will now be present on my mirrors around the house.

"Silly girl. I bet this is going to scare you," I murmur, turning on my blow dryer.

With everything all spic and span, I sit in my living room waiting on Jett to arrive. I've talked to Bria three times, my mother twice, and considered canceling once. Only... I can't, because despite my fear of rejection, I have to take this chance with him. I decide to read while I wait, glad I downloaded the reading app to my phone as I settle in to read about an alpha shifter rejecting his mate.

I'm so engrossed in the story that when my doorbell rings, I startle and cause both kittens to meow in protest. While I was engrossed with the story, they had come onto my lap, and burrowed into it to take a nap since I was just sitting there. Setting my phone down, I go to the door, check through the peephole to make sure it's really Jett, then open it with a smile.

"Hey," he says. "I'm a few minutes early, but didn't want to hit any traffic along the way and end up being late."

"It's okay, I'm ready to go. I just need to grab my purse and a jacket."

Once I've got everything, we head out after I admonish the kittens to behave, and lock up. He helps me into his truck, and while he's going around to get in the driver's side, I breathe in deeply, inhaling his scent so I can commit it to memory.

Our conversation is easy as we head to the movie theater, although I have to laugh when he tells me about

Dusty's inquisition. "He's something else, isn't he?" I ask, glancing over at him.

He's got such a strong profile, but I watch as it softens when he thinks about his son. "He really is a good kid. He's got ADHD, did you know that? It took me some time to wrap my head around the fact he would always struggle to a certain degree with impulsiveness. It's one of the reasons he enjoys sports so much, I think. He can burn off that energy in a positive way."

"None of us are perfect, Jett. I would term him precocious if I had to pick one word. He's been raised in a family where it's okay to be who he is, so he's confident enough to ask questions when he doesn't know things."

"I like your perspective," he softly replies, briefly smiling over at me as he reaches for my hand.

We walk hand-in-hand toward the ticket booth after a brief debate on where to park. He wanted to park closer so I wouldn't have to walk as far, but I reminded him I would always let him know if I needed any kind of accommodation. Today is a good day, so I'm okay to walk. After the teenager tears our tickets and hands the stubs back to me, I carefully tuck them into my pocket to save.

"So, let's hit the concession stand," he says, leading me to the left.

"But we're going to eat after the movie," I reply.

"It's not a proper movie date if we don't have

popcorn, sodas, and maybe some M&Ms," he retorts, grinning down at me.

"Ah, I see your plan now," I tease. "We'll end up getting full here so at dinner, we'll only want the salads."

His chuckle sends shivers through me as we step up to the counter. "Well, surprisingly enough, they have these neat inventions called to-go boxes, so if we get full, we'll just take what's left home, Sunday. Now, tell the nice lady what you want."

Like me, he prefers to sit high up, in the middle, and I'm not surprised when he lifts up the divider between our seats. As we settle in with the popcorn in between his legs, he grabs my hand and laces our fingers together, smiling down at me.

I return his smile before saying, "I hope the hype about this movie is true, don't you?"

"It doesn't matter to me, I'm right where I want to be."

"This has been one of the best dates I've ever had," I confess as we walk out of the restaurant, him carrying the bag with our to-go boxes. We still managed to eat real food despite our gluttony at the movie theater, but we've both got leftovers for later.

"For me as well," he replies, grinning down at me.

After helping me climb into his truck, the bag securely nestled at my feet, I watch as he maneuvers around the front of the truck to get inside. When his phone pings, he glances down, and I see him grimace.

"What's the matter?" I ask.

"Seems someone hit a transformer on my side of town and the power's out until sometime tomorrow," he replies, starting up the truck.

"Jett, you can't stay at home! It's dipping into the low thirties tonight," I protest. "Dusty's at your sister's overnight, right? Why don't we run by your place so you can get whatever you need, and you can stay at my house tonight."

"Are you sure?" he asks.

"I'm positive."

It's time to embrace the future, regardless of my fears.

CHAPTER
TEN

JETT

With her hand held in mine, and our fingers laced together, I drive us to my place. After parking, I turn to her and say, "If you want, you can stay out here where it's warm. I'll only be inside for a few minutes."

"Okay, I'm not keen on being in a dark house," she teases.

"Be right back," I promise, practically vaulting from my truck. I have no expectations for tonight, other than sleeping, but my mind is racing over the fact it'll be with her in my arms. It doesn't take me long to get into the house, and using my flashlight app on my phone, I go into my bedroom and grab my duffel bag from my closet.

Right now, I'm glad I had laundry caught up thanks

to the impromptu break we had due to the school being closed for those few days, because I'm able to put my hands on laundered clothes for the next day, as well as a pair of clean sleep pants and T-shirt. A quick trip into the bathroom garners my toothbrush, deodorant, and comb, which I put into the travel bag Dusty got me one Christmas. Actually, it holds a variety of the products I use, and while we don't take a lot of trips, it's come in handy on the away games because I'm able to freshen up before we hop back onto the bus and head back to the school.

Once I'm sure I have all of my essentials, I zip up the bag, then take a few minutes to turn all the faucets in the house on so they're lightly running since frozen pipes are not something I want to deal with ever. I also unplug the computer as well as the television because even though they're on a surge protector, I refuse to take any chances with my electronics. Confident that I've done everything I can to protect the house from any damage due to this outage, I grab the bag, then lock up the house before heading back out to the idling truck.

"That didn't take long," she observes once I've tossed my bag into the back seat, and jumped back into the truck.

"Would've been out sooner, but I went ahead and made sure the water was dripping, and everything important was unplugged," I admit, putting the truck in gear.

The ride to her house is comfortable, but quiet, and I wonder what she's thinking or if she's regretting her impulsive decision to have me stay with her.

Parking in her driveway, I turn to her and state, "Sunday, I don't have any expectations, even though I *am* attracted to you and hope things progress with us."

Even in the dim light, I can see her face flushing. "I didn't ask for that reason, Jett. I think it's obvious by now that I like you and am attracted to you, but I'm not going to lie, I'm nervous about anything physical."

"How about we go in where it's warmer? We can talk, okay?"

I'm pretty sure her scars are where her insecurities are coming from, and need to share my own.

Her kittens are happy to see us, and we spend several minutes playing with them before she heads into the kitchen to make sure they've got plenty of food and water. While she does that, I go ahead and make sure the house is locked up for her.

"Should I let my water run too?" she asks, coming back into the living room.

"Probably wouldn't be a bad idea," I muse. "I mean,

you've got electricity right now, of course, but there's a freeze warning so even with that, your pipes could still burst if they're not well-insulated."

"Okay, I did in the kitchen, so I just need to do the guest bathroom and mine," she says.

I follow her, stopping in the hall while she makes sure the water is running in the spare bathroom before we walk through the door of the master bedroom where I'm completely taken by surprise.

She's got one of the biggest beds I've ever seen; definitely larger than a king size, with an identical headboard and footboard which compliments the decor. The room is painted in a soft gray, while the comforter is in shades of green, purple, and white. A matching triple dresser, two nightstands, and a wardrobe barely fill the room.

"Your room is huge," I say, setting my bag down on the side that doesn't appear to be used.

"It was one of the selling points of the house for me," she admits. "Wait until you see the walk-in closets, and its his and her bathrooms."

Closets.

Plural.

She motions for me to follow her which I eagerly do only to see a small hall, for lack of a better word, with *two* closets, one on each side. While that's impressive in its own right, there are actually two bathrooms. The tiled shower is in the middle and appears to have multiple shower heads, as well as a bench. She waves me into the one on the right, and I can see a huge garden tub, plus the closet itself with shelves and racks neatly organized with her clothes neatly stacked and hung. A built-in vanity is off to the right before the closet door, along with a sink.

"The other side is empty, but you're welcome to use it. Make yourself at home," she encourages, turning the water in the shower on so it's slowly running.

"This is fantastic, Sunday," I murmur. "I'll be back in a few minutes."

"Take your time, Jett, I'm going to go ahead and change for bed since I'm already in here."

"Oh my God, those are great," she manages to say between her giggles once I breach the bedroom. She's not in bed just yet, and I see her flush slightly when I glance in her direction.

Looking down, I grin. "These? Another Dusty gift. My sister takes him shopping at Christmas, and he always manages to find the craziest sleep pants." Right now, I'm wearing flannel Grinch ones, but I've got a pair that has red lips scattered all over them. I just didn't think they were appropriate. Yet.

"Well, he's got great taste. It's one of my favorite movies. Um, I wanted to show you my scars, Jett, and while I know nothing will happen tonight, you deserve to see them beforehand so you can decide whether or not you can handle them."

Before I can utter a word, she reaches underneath the longer sleep shirt she has on, and slides the matching pants off. At first glance, I can see there's a slight difference in the muscle tone from one leg to the other. It's minimal, which is a testament to how hard she's worked to recover. My gaze is drawn to her thigh, where it's obvious she's had surgery; however, whoever did it was a fucking genius, because other than the slight lines, it looks smooth and unblemished. My breath catches in my throat when she turns, and I'm presented with her ass. The damage there is more noticeable, but still, it's not as bad as I thought it would be. Light pink lines criss cross her lower back, down the cheek itself then toward her thigh, but both sides are perky, for lack of a better word.

I move closer and cup her face with my hands so she'll look at me since she's avoided my gaze once she dropped her sleep pants. While I'd love to trace each line, first with my fingers, then with my lips and tongue, we're not there yet, but she needs to grasp how *she* affects me.

"Sunday, I'm not sure what you're thinking right

now, but I gotta tell you, nothing about what I'm looking at is a turn off, at least not to me," I confess, feeling my dick grow hard with her naked flesh within reaching distance. "In fact, I suggest you put your pants back on or we're going to find ourselves in a predicament that we're not ready to act on just yet."

She whips around, and I can see a spark of hope igniting in her eyes as she quickly pulls her pants back up. "Really?" Her tone is unsure, and I want to break her ex's nose for making her feel like she's less than ideal.

"Yeah, really," I reply, motioning to the front of my tented pants, where it's obvious my dick is trying to escape. Her giggle has me chuckling. "We've all got scars, sweetheart. Some are just more visible than others. Here, let me show you mine." When her eyes grow even wider, I can't help but laugh. "I don't need to strip down, sweetheart." Because if I did, there's no way we would stop until I was buried inside of her.

I roll up the bottom of my own pants to my thigh so she can see how fucked up my knee and calf are. The surgeon did his best, but I had multiple infections set in, so the scar tissue is raised and puckered in some areas because I had to have additional surgeries.

"Oh, Jett, that had to hurt like hell," she murmurs, moving closer, then crouching when she's directly in front of me. I hold my breath as her hand lightly traces the scars that have lightened with age, but are still noticeable.

"It still swells from time to time," I admit. "Mostly when I do too much on the field with the boys. That's when I dig out my compression brace."

"But that doesn't stop you, which is another reason you're such an honorable coach," she replies, standing.

"If you say so. I just try to teach them everything I was taught."

"It's made you a good man," she states. "I'm going to grab a bottle of water, would you like one?"

"I'll get them, you go ahead and crawl into bed, sweetheart."

"If you're sure."

"Positive, Sunday. Now scoot."

Her giggles follow me as I head out of the bedroom toward the kitchen to retrieve our waters. I'm hoping I can calm my dick down but realize it might be an impossible task since I'll soon be in the bed with her nearby.

CHAPTER
ELEVEN

SUNDAY

While I wait for him to return, I try to calm my nerves at the fact that Jett Blake is in my home, soon to be in my bed *with me* no less. Never in my wildest dreams could I have predicted how this date would go, that's for sure. But thanks to a reckless driver, a cold front that's causing freezing temperatures, and the fact his house is shrouded in darkness until the transformer is replaced, something I never dreamed would happen is soon to become a reality.

I can't help the giggle that emerges when I see him striding through the door, both kittens following behind him like little stalkers. As he sits down on his side of the bed, they jump up and immediately start wrestling, making him chuckle as he hands me my water. I watch him slide beneath the covers while sipping some water before placing the bottle on the nightstand.

"So, I was thinking," he starts, rolling over to face me, his head propped up on his hand.

"About?"

"You. Me. *Us*."

"What conclusion did you come up with?" I ask. I'm tempted to hold my breath, but he smells so delicious, I realize I can't and don't want to.

"We both have a past which has given us excess baggage. I'm willing to unpack mine with your help, Sunday, and hope you're willing to do the same with me at your side. We're stronger together, don't you think? The badass Navy medic, and the former pro football player?"

His earnest face has me biting back my smile; it's endearing because I know we've each got our own demons, but what he says makes sense.

"You mean the ER nurse, and the hot high school football coach?" I tease, moving closer. "You know the downside to your power being out?" I ask. When he shakes his head, I continue. "I was looking forward to you bringing me home, because I was going to let you kiss me before you left."

"Well, instead of goodbye, how about good night?" he murmurs, his voice husky.

I pretend to think about it, although in my head, it's a no-brainer. "I think that would work just as well."

His hand cups my cheek as he leans in closer. As his lips ghost over mine lightly, and I sigh, moving my hand over his shoulder to curl around his neck. When he deepens the kiss, I completely surrender, eager to get a taste of something I've always wanted.

Long minutes pass as our lips stay locked, until we eventually break apart, both of us breathless. With his forehead pressed against mine, he whispers, "Good night, Sunday. Sweet dreams."

"Good night, Jett. I'm sure they will be with you here." He turns out the light on his nightstand, prompting me to switch off mine too, grinning like a lunatic as the room plummets into darkness.

Once I turn onto my side, he moves closer, throwing his arm over my waist so he's snuggled into my back. I feel him kiss my shoulder as he settles in and before long, the steady rhythm of his breathing lets me know he's fallen asleep.

***

I wake up the next morning, and can feel his erection pressed into my low back and ass. Feeling feisty, I wiggle it lightly into his erection, until a gentle swat lands on my skin. "Keep it up, Sunday, and you'll get more than you've bargained for," his husky voice warns. "Been lying here, breathing your scent in for an hour now, trying not to be impulsive and act on how I'm feeling."

"What if I want you to?" I ask, feeling bold since I'm still facing away from his line of sight. His arm bands tightly around my waist, wrapping me in his embrace like he's afraid I'm going to move. I'm somewhat surprised, simply because Jonas wasn't a cuddler, so I'm not used to the intimate act, but apparently, my subconscious was perfectly fine having Jett spooning me the whole night.

I hear the hitch in his breath at my brazen words. Is he surprised I'm being so forward? Or regretting what he said. Doubt starts to crowd my mind until I find myself whipped around, so I'm flat on my back with him hovering over me.

"Do you?" he questions, his eyes dark and dilated with desire.

Slowly nodding, I verbally respond as well. "Yeah, I do, Jett," I whisper before his lips crash onto mine.

The passion that's been simmering all night long while we slept ignites, and I find myself moaning as his hands lightly skate over my body while we continue to kiss. My blood heats, my core clenches, and I realize I've found the missing piece that's been hiding when it comes to physical intimacy.

Jett.

He makes the difference as he undresses me, dropping kisses and touches along each section of exposed skin. His touch has me writhing, and I can feel how wet I am every time I twist my legs. As I watch my pajamas sail over the side of the bed, I grin up at him and say, "Seems one of us has too many clothes on now."

His chuckle is earthy, before he pulls his shirt over his head, doing that crazy move only men seem to know how to do. I gasp, seeing his well-formed chest on display, each ab delineated as if it was carved from stone. He has a smattering of chest hair; not too much and not too little, which has me raising my hands to run across his pecs, causing his nipples to pebble, much like my own have already done.

"You're fucking gorgeous, Sunday," he murmurs, staring down at me with heat in his eyes. I roll my eyes at him, and he lightly tickles my side, causing me to squirm. "You are and always will be that way through my eyes."

"Still too many clothes," I tease, my eyes honed in on his straining erection. He's bigger than I've ever had, which isn't saying much since Jonas is the sum total of my experience, and I briefly wonder if he's going to fit, then decide it doesn't matter.

If I die while we're making love, I'll go happy and that's that.

When he stands up after getting off the bed, I'm

treated to a sight that has me praying this is the first of many times we're together like this; his toned, tanned physique, slightly trembling, with a hardon that's jutting toward me.

Yes, I wouldn't mind seeing that every day for the rest of my life.

"I wouldn't mind either, sweetheart," he whispers, once again hovering over me.

"Shit, did I say that out loud?" I grumble, closing my eyes to avoid his.

"Yes, you did, Sunday, and all you just said confirms how I feel as well," he replies. "Now, where were we?"

Seconds turn into minutes until time becomes fluid as he licks, kisses, and sucks his way down every inch of my body. Both breasts are treated to an exhaustive examination, which has me nearly coming as pings of desire shoot to my clit. When he settles between my thighs, I unconsciously try to close them, to no avail.

"I need a taste, sweetheart. You gonna deny me that?" he questions, looking up at me.

Seeing his beautiful face, flushed with desire, I shake my head. There's nothing I wouldn't give him right now; I'm a goner for him. He flashes a grin at me before his tongue swipes through my folds.

Holy fucking hell! As he continues his ministrations, suckling my clit, thrusting his tongue deep into my sheath, all while stroking my thighs with his fingers. I realize I've been missing out and decide to enjoy this particular ride to its conclusion.

The moan that escapes when he inserts his index finger has him peering up at me through his lashes. "You good?" he asks, his voice slightly muffled because of where he's at, and what he's doing.

"Mmhm," I reply through a hum, shockwaves of pleasure coursing through me as his digit moves in and out of my core while his mouth and tongue continue their own sweet assault.

As my release builds, I struggle not to pull his hair out from the roots, and instead, settle with gripping and twisting the sheets between my fists. But when he adds a second finger, I'm done for and I detonate, keening his name out as my back arches away from the bed.

Long moments pass as I ride out my orgasm while he slows his actions down until I start to wiggle and squirm, moving from his diligent attention when it becomes too sensitive.

"Jett, I need you," I plead, gripping his biceps as he raises up.

"Gotta protect my girl," he replies, leaning over to the nightstand where I notice he apparently laid his wallet. He flips it open, and slides out a strip of condoms, which has my brow raising. "Not what you think, sweetheart. Carry them because of the boys on the team and have never been happier that I keep them stocked." He rips off one, quickly opens the package between his blunt teeth, and sheathes himself before notching his head at my entrance.

Our moans mingle as he slowly enters me with gentle thrusts until he's fully embedded. As my nails lightly score his skin, he starts to move; long, sure strokes that have my desire ramping up again.

Sex was hit or miss with Jonas. He didn't like performing oral, and I sometimes didn't climax, which I realize now shows just how selfish and shallow he truly was, because Jett has barely begun moving and I'm already close to orgasming for the second time.

"You feel so good," I moan out, clutching his shoulders.

"You're so hot and tight, Sunday," he manages to say. "I can feel you tightening on my cock, and if you keep it up, this won't last long."

"Not doing it intentionally, I'm going to come again," I admit, my eyes wide in wonder.

As his pace quickens and becomes erratic, he slides one hand between us to lightly stroke my clit, which has me calling out his name as he pumps his hips twice more before stopping. I can feel him pulsing inside as wave after wave of pleasure crashes through me. Then, he does something that endears him to me forever; he leans in and gently kisses my lips before pulling me into his arms and rolling us, so I'm splayed over him. His hands stroke up and down my body, and he doesn't avoid the areas where I was injured, but is instead, extremely gentle there as we both return from the stratosphere.

I'm nearly catatonic. I'm so sated when he lightly taps my hip that I bury my head deeper into his pecs, my body refusing to accept what I know he's fixing to convey. "Need to take care of the condom, sweetheart," he reluctantly tells me, eliciting a moan of protest from me.

"No, I don't wanna move," I mumble, still enjoying the residual high from my astronomical orgasm.

"Okay, so you might not remember, but seeing as you're a nurse, you should understand biology. I'm going to go soft, the condom will slip, then everything *inside* will be left in you. Not sure how you feel about having babies, but since we haven't had that conversation yet, I'm erring on the side of caution and thinking you aren't planning on having one just yet."

"Spoilsport," I grumble, sliding off him and flopping heavily to my side. He chuckles, which turns into full-out laughter as I cross my arms over my chest, and do my best to mean mug him.

Of course, the glare changes as I watch his taut ass

stroll across my bedroom toward the bathroom, but I'm not going to confess that little secret to him.

"You're going to have to add more supplies to your wallet," I tease as he gathers his stuff. His electricity is once again back on, and even though I hate that he has to leave, I have to work tonight and will need to get some sleep, plus he has to pick up Dusty from his sister.

"I'm going to get a box for here, and one for my place," he promises, smirking at me. "The only reason I carry them for the boys is sometimes, when they're hanging out with friends or partying after a win, they're ill-prepared for the situation, and quite honestly, I don't want any of them going through the hell I did with Stacey if I can help it."

"I didn't say anything against it, Jett. They should carry their own, too, though."

He gives me a rueful look then rebuts, "They do, but sometimes they forget to 'replenish their stash' as I've been told by them a time or two."

I can't help giggling because it sounds like something a teenage boy would use as an excuse.

"I hope they're all feeling better." They were in so much pain and terribly sick that my heart felt saddened for them.

He grabs my hand and leads us into my living room, dropping his bag by the door, and pulling me into his arms. My head is resting against his chest, and I hear his heartbeat steadily beating, lulling me into a contented state. "I've been getting regular texts from either my players or their parents. All are feeling better and ready to hit the field on Monday, which is good because we're heading into the playoffs for the state championship in our division, and I need them all ready. Now, you're on duty for the next three nights, right?"

I nod. "Yes, three on, two off, then four on, three off."

"So, we might have to be creative in order to see each other."

"I always eat before I head into work, usually around six or so. Granted, it's breakfast but who doesn't like eating that for dinner?" I ask. "You and Dusty are welcome to join me any one of those nights you'd like."

"Or we could grab a family chicken meal and bring it over. I understand you're a sucker for their food any time they're open for business," he replies, grinning at me.

"Aha, I see small town gossip is still alive and well in Possum Run," I retort. "I love that place, though. They have great portions, the chicken has a good flavor beyond what they season it with, and their prices are affordable."

"Maybe we can grab drinks at Ike's on one of your off nights," he suggests, changing the subject.

"I'd like that, Jett."

A ping from his phone has him pulling it out, then bursting into laughter. "Dusty says to hurry up and kiss you so I can come get him, because he's figured out how to beat the next level of his game," he reveals, reading me the message.

"Then you better go so he's not kept waiting," I reply, smiling up at him.

"Oh, I'll go, but not before I get my fill of you to last until we see each other again." Pulling me tighter into his arms, we spend the next ten minutes making out much like teenagers, although I have no personal knowledge or experience of that, much to my chagrin. My high school years were lackluster compared to the young adult romances I've binged on during my read-a-thons.

"Bye, Jett," I murmur against his lips as he pulls back slightly.

"Bye, Sunday."

I watch as he walks out my door to his truck, then wave goodbye as he honks his horn before pulling out of my driveway, idling in the street until I step through the threshold where I close and lock the door. Only then does he drive away.

Best. Date. Ever.

CHAPTER
TWELVE

JETT

The past two weeks have been hectic between practices to get ready for the playoffs, ensuring Dusty does his homework, and spending time with Sunday... but I wouldn't have it any other way. I grin thinking about last weekend when we went to Ike's. While it's a bar, they have some of the best burgers and onion rings around, so we placed an order of those, grabbed our drinks, then found a table to settle into since the waitress would handle serving us our food once it was plated.

We were laughing over something one of the kids had done at practice, when a male voice called out, "Sunday? Is it really you?"

Her gaze slid sideways, and I saw her pale slightly, but

her nervousness never showed in her voice. "Hello, Jonas," she replied.

"Wow, I knew you lived here too, but since I hadn't run into you, I just figured you were avoiding me." I held back my snort of amusement, that man was a moron. He watched her like a boy who lost his puppy. I waited for his tongue to lop to the side and drool.

"What's to avoid?" she asked. "Have you met Jett Blake? He's the head coach at the high school."

Begrudgingly, and only because I ended up with the girl that he foolishly let go, I held my hand out and shook his. My woman definitely has manners because I wouldn't have given the fucker the time of day. But that's just me.

"Well, I mean, you know," he stammered, making me smirk.

"No, I really don't, Jonas. If you're referring to breaking off our engagement when I was in the hospital, after nearly dying, I hold no ill-will at all."

"Y-y-you don't?" He seemed almost shocked at her words while his wife looked appalled as she gave her husband a 'what the fuck?' look. Yeah, sweetheart, he's a real charmer. You might wanna listen to what comes out of my woman's mouth so you can grasp how shallow your man truly is, and know if you slip off the pedestal, he'll end up ditching you too.

"Absolutely not. I mean, at first, I was hurt, of course, but I've come to realize we weren't really suited for each *other in the long run, and it probably wouldn't have lasted long enough for us to get married. Congratulations to you two, by the way," she replied, nodding to his wife.*

He seemed to bow up a bit at her words, and I knew I was right when he asked, "What does that mean?"

"It means that I was never going to be good enough for you, Jonas. No one is perfect, and that's what you were looking for, so the minute I became scarred, I ceased being important to you and lost my standing on your pedestal. And that's okay, because Jett doesn't give the first fuck that I've got visible reminders of my service to our country. Do you, honey?" she asked, glancing at me.

"Nope. Not at all," I answered, smirking at the asshole who was now glowering down at my woman. If he kept it up, I was gonna owe Ike some money for the damages I was about to cause.

"I see your language is still that of a sailor and unlady-like," he sneered.

"I represent that wholeheartedly, because I was a sailor, remember? Words are just words, Jonas, and I don't have time to censor my vocabulary for anyone, least of all you. Now, if you'll excuse us, we're on a date and waiting for our food to arrive."

I'm now laughing, which has Collins, one of my assistant coaches, looking at me in bewilderment. "You okay, Blake?" he asks.

"Yeah, just remembering something that was funny."

"So, you and the hot nurse, huh?" he teases. When I glance at him, my brow raised, he puts his hands up in pacification. "It's not like that, Blake. But with all the extra practices, your boy's been around, and he's been singing her praises to everyone who'll listen. I'm seriously happy for you, man. If anyone deserves a good woman, it's you. Sunday Cross is one of the best, hands down."

"She really is," I reply. "Been thinking about the future," I confess. "I know it'll seem too soon to a lot of folks, but we all know about opinions."

"They're like assholes, everyone's got 'em," he retorts, chuckling. "Honestly? I was just starting out when you two were in school, and I remember how you both would watch the other whenever you were in the same place at the same time. Y'all's eyes were like two magnets drawn together. Even though you were dating that witch, which I still don't quite understand because she was horrible to everyone around her. However, you seemed to have a soft spot for Sunday."

It's true; seeing how Sunday interacted with everyone, from the janitors to the lunch ladies, I always wished Stacey had some of those gentle qualities.

"You know how it is when you're a teenage boy and ruled by your hormones," I ruefully reply. "But I'll never regret staying with her because I got Dusty out of it," I remind him. "And he's worth all of the hell I went through."

"He's definitely a damn good kid," he remarks, his eyes now on the field where the boys are goofing off as they pick up the equipment.

"Best of all, he adores Sunday." My admiration of her is profound, and I would shout her praises from the rooftops if it was necessary. But the town seems to adore her like I do, so it's not needed.

"Kind of important since she's going to be his mom, don't you think?" he questions, smirking at me. "Some folks might think you're moving too fast, others not fast enough. The important thing for you to keep in mind is that it's not about them, it's about the two of you. As long as you guys are happy, and Dusty's okay with it, in the end no one else matters."

"Good point, Collins. Thanks."

Sunday: Kinda wishing you were here right now. This big old bed is lonely without you.

Me: Oh really? And you had to bring that up now when it's too late for me to foist my kid off on my sister?

Sunday: LOL just teasing, honey.

Me: Mmhm. You just wait, sweetheart.

Sunday: I don't have a choice, thanks to the extra shifts I picked up to help out. I hate that I'll miss the game!

Me: I'll see if Cissy can keep Dusty after the game, and be there waiting for you when you get home, how does that sound?

Sunday: Like a winning plan to me! Okay, I'm going to get some sleep so I'm ready for the next twelve hours. Good luck to you and your boys, honey.

Me: Sweet dreams, Sunday. See you in the morning.

"And with the final whistle blown, the Possum Run Polecats are off to the state championships!" the announcer screams enthusiastically as we make our way to midfield, shaking the other team's hands while saying, "Good game."

"Great game, Coach," the other coach says, shaking my hand. "Your guys never gave up."

"Appreciate that, Coach," I reply. "It's how I was taught, so I teach them to keep playing until the final whistle."

"Well, it worked tonight, that's for sure. We'll be rooting for you at state, Blake," he says.

"Gonna be a tough game, but we'll be as prepared as we can possibly be, and I hope my boys are ready to practice their tails off," I tell him.

Seeing my team is done shaking the hands of the other team's players, I blow my whistle to bring them in close. "Alright guys, hit the showers because I'm sure some of your girlfriends are waiting on you in the parking lot." Wolf whistles fill the air as several of them blush.

"Dad! Are you staying longer?" Dusty asks, coming up to stand in front of me.

"Was going to meet with the coaches to set up a game plan of sorts to get ready for state," I admit. "Why? You got a hot date?"

"Dad," he drawls out, smirking at me. "No, I was hoping you weren't so I could maybe go to Aunt Cissy's early is all. I know you and Sunday have a date when she gets off work, and don't want to be in the way."

"Since when are you in the way?"

He doesn't reply, just rolls his eyes at me, making me laugh. "I know I'm not, Dad, but I also know you've both been busy. I really like her," he leans in to whisper. "And I know she likes cats but also likes dogs, loves her house, and wants kids."

This kid.

"How do you know all of that?" I ask. While we've both seen her during this time, he hasn't been alone with her long enough to ask those questions.

"Because I texted her."

"You text her?"

"Well, yeah, I mean, you're not all that good with science, Dad. I know you think you are, but she's a nurse and has you beat, hands down! When I said something about my science grade, she gave me her phone number and told me to call or text her if I had any questions," he replies in a 'duh' tone.

"I'm sure she meant if you had any *science* questions," I retort, holding back my smile, because I know my woman doesn't care why he reaches out, she just wants to be there for him. But *he* doesn't know that, so I need to give him some hell.

"Huh, well, I asked her the stuff I wanted to know, and she answered me, Dad."

"How often do you text? Do I need to worry about you trying to steal my girl?" I tease, chuckling.

Again, he rolls his eyes at me, making the players who have been close by, and overheard our bantering, start laughing. He glares at all of them which makes them snicker even harder. Seems my boy might have his first crush, and of course, it's on my damn woman. Sighing, I pull him close for a hug, and lean down close to his ear and whisper, "She's mine, little man, but if you can keep a secret, I'm planning to ask her to marry me the next time we have more than ten minutes together."

He whoops out loud, and breaks free to do some sort of weird dance, which I hope to never see again. While the boys pester him about what I said, I smirk when he doesn't give in and disclose our secret. Instead of answering them, he ignores their taunts, and acts like he's zipping his lips before tossing the imaginary key he used to lock his lips with, launching it over his shoulder.

"Hey, Coach, uh, I overheard Dusty asking about you taking him to his aunt's house. I'd be happy to drive him over for you," Timmers says. "I wasn't planning to go out and celebrate tonight with the rest of the team. Wanna ice my leg, you know?"

Timmers has taken Dusty over to my sister's quite a few times when I couldn't, and I know he's a safe, cautious driver. Still, I feel I need to warn him, because I know how my son is as well, and don't want him to egg on Timmers and cause him to do something dumb.

"Speed limit, no assing around, seatbelts," I bark out, making him smirk.

"Same thing you tell me every single time I take him for you, Coach. I promise, I drive like he's my grandma who has a full pitcher of sweet tea sitting on her lap."

The visual has me laughing as I clap him on the shoulder. "Hit the showers, then you two can go, alright?"

"Gotcha, Coach. Hey, Dustman!" he yells out. "I'm your ride to your aunt's house, so don't go anywhere."

"Thanks, Timmers!" Dusty bellows in response, while I grin at my son's nickname.

———————

As Timmers walks over to where I'm standing with Dusty, his duffel slung over his shoulder, I grin seeing the girls who stuck around staring at the handsome teen. He doesn't seem to notice, keeping his focus on the two of us. Once he's directly in front of us, I hand him two twenties.

"Stop by the Burger Shack and grab some food for the two of you. Keep the rest for gas," I instruct.

"Sweet! Let's go, Timmers!" Dusty exclaims, his mind already on the greasy food he plans to order.

"Thanks, Coach. Can you let your sister know it's me dropping him off?" he asks.

"Already done. Thanks, Timmers. See you on Monday, be ready to work hard."

"Definitely. We're gonna win state, Coach!"

Dusty gives me one last hug, then sprints to keep up with Timmers' long-legged stride, making me grin. A few more years and my boy's going to be just as tall if not slightly taller than I am. Wonder how Sunday will feel being the shortest person in our family?

CHAPTER
THIRTEEN

"They won!" Moira exclaims, coming into the meds room where I'm updating the ER's inventory. Thankfully, tonight has been blissfully silent, allowing us to catch up on the gazillion tiny chores we never seem to get done during our shifts. I grin, because it means when I get home, Jett's going to be in a *very* good mood and looking to celebrate, with me being the lucky beneficiary.

"I bet Jett's ecstatic," I reply, smiling at her.

"I just hate you couldn't go to the game," she laments, scanning over what I've already done before she begins opening up boxes with gauze pads, and stacking them on the shelves.

"No, it's okay. Sandira couldn't help having emergency surgery." Sandira, the nurse whose shifts I'm covering, ended up having an emergency appendectomy earlier in the week. Since most of the staff are married and have kids, it's not as easy for them to pick up the slack as it is for me. "I don't mind, I'll just put all the extra money on my paycheck into my savings account."

"Pssh, you've probably got enough in there already to buy a brand-new house."

I snicker but don't reply because she's right. I've got a hefty nest egg saved, plus a money market account, since my expenses are minimal. I bought my house while I was still enlisted, after my mom found out it had come up on the market, then because I got wartime pay and hazardous duty pay, I was able to pay off the mortgage long before I got injured. Then, once I was home, I stayed at the rehab facility during the times I had surgery, or with my parents, so I was able to do all the renovations I wanted, which weren't all that many. Mostly cosmetic items, like paint, although I did add bidets to all the bathrooms. It was something I got used to when I was overseas, and I had the money to add them, so I figured why not?

"Well, hopefully, I'll be off for the state finals, because I don't want to miss it," I admit.

"Girl, if you're scheduled and I'm not, I'll switch

shifts with you," she replies. "No way you're gonna miss that one if I can help it!"

We're nearly finished when Dr. Crane pops his head in the door and points at the two of us. "Need you both at the bays. A multivehicle accident with life-threatening injuries is enroute."

As a unit, Moira and I rush after him, once I check to ensure the self-locking door is closed. The last thing either of us need is a disciplinary report because someone got into our supply room, and stole a bunch of stuff. When we reach the bays, which are already open in preparation for the pending ambulances, I glance over at Dr. Crane to assess his mood so I can determine how urgent this upheaval is going to be.

He's one of the best trauma surgeons in the region, although his gruff personality puts a lot of folks off, his dedication to giving his all to each patient is admirable. While I have no issues, thanks to working alongside my commanding officer, Branch, for years, many of the others do. Right now, he looks worried, which is concerning because I've never seen that formidable expression on his face before.

"Dr. Crane, do you know the severity of what we're getting?" I question, grabbing some latex gloves to put on when I hear the sirens roaring in the distance and moving closer.

He glances at me and tensely replies, "Two vehicles, three occupants in total. One driver was DOA on the scene, the other appears to have minor bruising and lacerations. However, it's the passenger in the other car that has me feeling concerned. In fact, I need one of you to page Dr. Patel to be on standby. I have a feeling I'm going to need him for this patient."

"Got it, Dr. Crane," Moira says, running over to the 'house phone' to request an urgent page for Dr. Patel.

"Is it that bad?" I whisper, my mind running rampant. "I mean, tonight was a big game at the high school, and I know the kids usually celebrate by hitting up the Burger Shack."

He leans in, which is uncharacteristic for him, and confides, "From what was reported, one of the players was driving a juvenile home after going to the Burger Shack. The second vehicle ran the red light at a high rate of speed, broadsided the teen's vehicle which shoved them into the power pole. They had to cut the juvenile out of the car but have stated he's got multiple traumas, and it's been difficult to stabilize him in the field. That's why I wanted Patel to be on standby because he's the best thoracic surgeon I know."

I start praying, worried it's one of Jett's players, and know the parents of the deceased teen will be devastated. This news is going to change their lives. Death of a child is inconceivable to parents, and most struggle with depression afterward. As a matter of fact, the suicide rate for those who've lost their kid is high. All they want is to be with them, even if that's only possible through death.

As the ambulances arrive, I notice the one with no lights or sirens goes to the first bay, then watch as a sheet-covered gurney is wheeled inside, so a doctor can make the official loss of life pronouncement. I hope whoever it was, they didn't suffer needlessly. Dying on impact may be a cruel thing to wish for, but in my opinion, no one should have to endure horrific pain as they pass away.

A second and third ambulance are pulling in, and I mentally shift gears so I'm ready to handle whatever results may occur. When our patients are younger, it's hard not to get attached, even though we're encouraged not to do so. I see another team take the gurney, with what looks like a woman, back into the treatment rooms. Getting ready for what lies ahead, I take a deep breath as the doors of our ambulance open, and the paramedic on board starts rattling off vital stats while rolling the gurney toward us.

"Male, approximate age estimated to be between ten and twelve, sustained a hard hit on the right side of the body when the vehicle was crushed into the power pole," she says, pushing the child to the back.

"Curtain three," Dr. Crane commands, handing out a room number. Looking at me, he informs me, "It's got the most openness for us to work."

The paramedic continues relaying her report. "He was unconscious at the scene, has sustained multiple facial and upper body lacerations due to flying glass. The power pole entered the passenger compartment upon impact, causing several compound fractures which we've stabilized with field splints. C-spine collar in place due to likelihood of him taking a hit to the right side of his face. Blood pressure is now stable, but was erratic when we arrived on the scene. We've notified his father–" Her litany doesn't pause, but my brain refuses to process anything past her last comment.

We've notified his father.

Not his parents, his *father.* Glancing at the gurney as we finally make it into curtain three, and have quickly, yet efficiently, transferred him onto the hospital bed, my heart stutters to a stop.

Dusty!

My Dusty. The little boy with the infectious laugh, who has become so important to me in such a short amount of time. Seeing the usually rambunctious preteen lying there so still, almost buckles my knees and I sway, but there's a job to do. None more personally linked to me than this one, but I still force myself to keep things professional. Quickly sending up another prayer, I start to assess and catalog his vitals while Dr. Crane begins his exam, barking out orders which Moira and several other nurses with us in the triage room rush to handle.

"Is Patel here?" he questions, directing it to the room at large.

"Right here, Crane," comes the male voice. "What do we know?"

"Need X-rays and multiple CAT scans, as well as an abdominal ultrasound, but based on his abdominal bruising and rigidity, I suspect internal bleeding," Dr. Crane barks out, his eyes never straying from Dusty, while I work to cut and remove his clothes.

Without warning, alarm bells sound off, indicating that Dusty has stopped breathing. I don't think, I just react, jumping onto the bed and digging my knees into the mattress next to his body where I begin chest compressions as Moira grabs the Ambu bag, and begins breathing for him. Dr. Crane and Dr. Patel grab the railings on the hospital bed, take off the brakes, and start running toward the prepped and waiting operating room.

"Don't you give up, little man. Keep fighting like I'm fighting for you right now," I chant as I continue CPR while tears stream down my face.

CHAPTER
FOURTEEN

JETT

"Thank God that didn't take as long as I thought it would," I mutter as I enter my truck. While the adrenaline is still coursing through me, all I want is a shower, a few beers, then to kick back and rest until Sunday comes home.

I can't help the smile that crosses my face when I think of her. We might only be in the first month of our relationship, which is probably stretching it a bit by some folks' estimation, but I don't care, however I can see forever when I'm with her.

"Now to help her see that as well," I say out loud just as my phone rings. Seeing it's my sister, I answer quickly. "Hey, Cissy, what's up? Dusty get there okay?"

"J-j-j-ett, oh my God, Jett," she cries out, her voice trembling.

"Slow down, Cissy. What's going on?" I ask, dread rushing through me.

I hear my brother-in-law in the background before he takes the phone. "Jett, it's Larry. There was an accident and Dusty's at the hospital. You need to head there ASAP," he states while Cissy sobs in the background.

"How bad, Lar?" I question, making the turn out of the parking lot that will take me to the hospital. Possum Run may not be a huge town, which is part of its appeal, but we've got one of the best trauma hospitals in the area, so I'm not really concerned. Especially since Sunday's working; she'll take good care of my boy.

I hear a deep sigh on the other end of the phone and brace myself since this sounds like more than just a simple fender bender, especially with the way Cissy is nearly hysterical in the background, hollering out instructions to her kids so they can 'get up there right away'.

"Bad, Jett. The guy who was driving died at the scene, apparently on impact," he quietly states.

Timmers. My mind sees his grin, how he is with his teammates, as well as with my son and I refuse to believe what I'm hearing.

"You're saying Michael Timmers is dead?" I whisper. "What the fuck happened? They were hitting up the

Burger Shack before he brought Dusty over to you. Tell me what you know," I demand, fear making my tone sharper than normal.

"I don't have all the pieces, just what is already going around the gossip mill, but I heard the accident on the scanner and went to the scene to see what I could find out," he says. Since he's on our local police force, it makes sense he would show up. "Saw the car, recognized it as one of your boys' rides then asked the responding officers if there were any passengers. He knows Dusty from the baseball league, Jett, and told me while they worked to get him out of the car, I needed to notify you."

"That still doesn't tell me what the fuck happened!" I exclaim, my distress morphing into anger.

"Getting to that, Jett, trying to keep everyone calm right now. Your sister's losing her shit, the kids aren't much better, and not gonna lie, I'm fucking holding on by a thread myself," he growls out.

"Sorry, sorry. He's my boy, Larry," I moan out, holding back my tears. Gotta be strong for my little man and my woman, no matter what happens.

"Yeah, he's ours too," he whispers. "Family, Jett. My boys got Blake blood running through them too. Anyhow, it seems some woman ran the red light and plowed into Timmers and pushed him into the power pole. The pole came into the passenger compartment which is where Dusty's injuries came from."

"That bad?" I whisper, no longer able to think.

"Just get there, Jett. We're on our way as well. You won't face this by yourself."

I'm in the hallway headed to curtain three where I was told they had Dusty when I see the hospital bed come flying out from behind the curtain, my woman straddling my son while doing CPR as another nurse holds something over his mouth, rhythmically squeezing it as Sunday continues her compressions.

When I hear her say, "Don't you stop fighting, little man. Keep fighting like I'm fighting for you right now," I hit my knees, especially when I catch a glimpse of the tears steadily flowing down her face.

"Dusty!" I bellow, tears now falling freely.

I'm led to a waiting room while he's in surgery. At least, that's what the nurse who helped me up said. Other than that, I don't know anything and right now, I'm still all alone.

Memories flood my mind as I allow the fear to course through me.

The ultrasound picture of a tiny little blob.

Holding him right after he was born.

Learning to care for an infant when Stacey decided to leave.

His first step, wobbling over to where I was sitting in my recliner, a wide toothless smile covering his little face.

The first time he lost a tooth, and then didn't want to put it under his pillow for the Tooth Fairy.

Walking him to his class on the first day of school.

Finding out he had ADHD, then learning everything I could so we could successfully manage it together.

Teaching him how to swim, fish, and play football.

Videoing him with my parents as often as possible.

Watching him grow into a responsible young man.

"I wish you guys were here right now," I whisper, looking up. "I sure could use you both." I miss my folks all the time, but right now, in this moment, it's so real and all I want is to have my parents' arms wrapped around me. Instead I say, "Since you've got a line to Him, put in a few good words for my boy."

The door opens and I glance up to see Sunday coming toward me. She's a mess, her eyes are swollen nearly shut even as she continues to cry, and I can see dried blood covering her scrubs. As she falls into my waiting arms, I'm not sure which of us is comforting the other as our tears mingle.

Finally, she pulls back, swiping at her face. "We got

him back, Jett. I heard you yell his name when we were heading to the operating room. But he's hurt, honey, so we may be waiting for a while to hear any news."

"I love you," I tell her. "Some may think it's way too soon, but I was already falling, and seeing you doing everything you knew to do to help my son, solidified it."

She cups my face in her hands, her smile radiant through her tears as she replies, "I love you too, Jett. *Both* of you. When I realized who we were working on, I started praying for the medical team, you, him, even me. Because I wanted to make sure I was doing everything I could to help him."

"From what I saw, you did," I murmur, capturing her lips in a gentle kiss. "Now, we wait."

CHAPTER
FIFTEEN

SUNDAY

"Thanks, Moira," I mumble through exhaustion, taking a pair of clean scrubs from her so I can change. "I'll get them washed and back to you on my next shift."

"Girl don't even worry about it, they don't fit me anymore thanks to my addiction to Ben & Jerry's," she teases.

Despite the solemnity of the situation, I can't hold back the giggle that slips through. She hugs me tight and whispers, "You guys need anything, let me know. I know waiting sucks."

"I think we're good right now," I quietly reply, looking back at the group of people who have arrived since finding out about Dusty being wheeled into surgery.

It's a testament to how well thought of Jett is in our town, because while not everyone has stayed, several stopped by with food and even blankets for comfort, knowing there was no way we will be leaving until we hear the prognosis. Even then, I suspect Jett will badger the doctor to let him stay in the recovery room with Dusty, at least until he's alert. And if he has to be admitted, I'll make sure Jett has the best cot we have in storage.

"Dr. Crane said to pass on that he's putting you on leave."

"I don't have much time accrued right now, it hasn't been that long since I started."

"Honey, you don't understand how we work here. Every one of us has chipped in hours to cover you while you're out," she replies.

Tears well in my eyes once again at the kindness extended to me by proxy. "Really? But I don't understand."

"Do you honestly think none of us have noticed how you readily pitch in to pick up shifts when someone's sick or, like with Sandira, out unexpectedly? It's the least any of us can do for you," she explains. "Now, go get changed and dry your eyes, missy," she instructs, making me giggle. "I'll go see if I can get any kind of an update for you guys."

"We'd appreciate it."

"Coach?" As Jett and I turn, we see Mr. and Mrs. Timmers standing there, their eyes red-rimmed from crying, and their faces lined with grief.

"Mr. and Mrs. Timmers, I didn't expect either of you to stop by," Jett says, standing and hugging both of them. "Words can't express how sorry I am for your loss. Michael was one of the best young men I've ever met. I feel terrible that, because he was taking Dusty to my sister's for me, he was in an accident. If not for that, he'd still be alive."

"Coach, you can't think like that," Mrs. Timmers argues. "Michael thought of Dusty like a younger brother, and he loved it when he was able to help you 'haul him around' as he used to say." Her smile is slight, but the sentiment behind it has me reaching for her hand. "We wanted to see if you had heard anything yet."

"Not yet," I interject since Jett seems to be at a loss for words. "He's still in surgery, and one of my coworkers just went to check to see if she could get an update."

"Then we'll sit and wait with you for a while," Mr. Timmers decrees. "Is there anything you need?"

"Not that I can think of," Jett murmurs. "Besides, that should be my question for you two."

"We have an appointment in the morning with the funeral home. Coach, if it's not too much of an imposition, we'd like to ask you to be one of his pallbearers, as well as several of his teammates."

"I think we'd all be honored to do that for him," Jett quietly replies, tears slowly coursing down his face.

"Mr. Blake?" Dr. Patel's voice breaks through the silence in the room, although at this point, as late as it has gotten, the only ones here are me, Jett, and his sister. His brother-in-law, who I met for the first time tonight, took their kids home.

Jett grips my hand in his as we walk toward where the doctor is standing. It's evident he's exhausted, which is unsurprising since we've been waiting nearly six hours since he went into the operating room. "How's my little man?" he asks, his voice breaking slightly at the end.

A small smile graces Dr. Patel's face as he replies, "It's going to take some time, and a lot of patience on both of your parts, but I believe he's going to be perfectly fine. The main reason the surgery took so long is while we had him under, we decided to repair the fractures in his arm and leg, as well as the aortic dissection which is what necessitated CPR. He does have a concussion as well as an orbital fracture, so we have a call out for an EENT surgeon since we couldn't do anything with the significant swelling. The EENT doctor will be able to assess whether or not there's any vision changes, as well as determine if surgery will be required. He's currently being transported up to ICU, and I want to warn you ahead of time, he's in a medically induced coma to allow his body to heal."

"He's alive," Jett whispers, his knees buckling. Both the doctor and I manage to keep him upright as his tears begin to fall. "Thank you, thank all of you who made sure my boy is going to be okay."

"You're welcome. A nurse will be down shortly to take you up to him once they have him settled into his room. Dr. Crane has advised that he will have his parents staying with him," he states, looking at the two of us.

"There are no words to express my gratitude right now," Jett says.

"Well, his mother gave him that shot," Dr. Patel advises, looking at me. "If not for her quick thinking, the outcome might have been completely different. She continued with CPR until we were able to use the defibrillator."

"I was doing what I've been trained to do, sir," I reply, blushing under his praising perusal. Neither Jett nor I correct the doctor's misconception that I'm Dusty's mom; the facts wouldn't change and at the end of the day, it doesn't matter what others think, we know the truth.

"Crane was right, you're too modest for your own good. Both of us will be checking on him daily, but if you have any questions at all, please let his nurse know, and they'll get a message to me."

"Thank you again, doctor," Jett calls out as Dr. Patel leaves the waiting room.

We slump into the chairs as Jett wraps his arms around me, and his sister as we cry once again, this time in relief.

I grin walking into Dusty's room two weeks after the accident. It took a week before they decided to wean him off the medications keeping him in a coma, but since awakening, he's been a model patient. It's hard not to be, though, when one leg is in traction, your dominant hand is in a cast from your fingers to your shoulder, and your other side has all the wires and tubes to ensure you get what is needed.

Still, he's been as good as can be expected.

"So, how's it shaking?" I ask once I'm next to his bed. "You been giving anyone any problems today?"

He snickers, but shakes his head. "Naw, why should I? If I did, you and Dad would be upset with me because anything they ask me to do is only to make me better. At least that's what I think, anyhow."

"Wish more patients were like that," I murmur, opening up my lunch bag to pull out two sandwiches. "Thought I'd come up and eat with you during my break, that okay?"

"Beats eating by myself until dinner. Thanks, Sunday!" he exclaims before he begins eating.

"You should get to come home at the end of the week."

"Just in time for the big game, huh?"

"Yeah, you excited?"

His face grows serious as he turns to me. "I'm gonna miss Timmers, Sunday. He was a really neat guy, you know? Called me Dustman, and treated me like I was more than just the coach's kid."

I nod in understanding. Jett's been having a hard time dealing with his emotions, especially since he feels he needs to be strong for his team, as well as Timmers' parents, who are beyond distraught over the loss of their son.

"I didn't really know him, Dusty, just from that time when almost the whole school ended up in the emergency room, but your dad has talked a lot about him. He was well-liked from the sound of things."

"He was, but he wasn't a jerk about it if that makes sense," he replies, moving to his pudding cup. It amazes me that he's doing so well eating with his opposite hand because I'd be making the biggest mess.

"It does because that's how your dad was when we were in school," I reminisce. "He was super popular, the school's star quarterback, great student, but he was nice to everyone whether they were a friend or stranger."

"That's how I'm gonna be when I grow up," Dusty vows, grinning at me. "Sunday? Can I say something?"

"You can say, or tell me anything, little man."

"I wanna say thank you for helping to save me. Dad says it wasn't easy for you to do it knowing it was me, but I'm good with a few broken ribs since it means I'm still here to hopefully get a baby brother or sister down the road," he quietly says as he takes another bite, subtly giving me a hint.

"A baby brother or sister, huh? Does your father know your master plan?" I tease, blinking quickly so the tears that want to fall dissipate.

He snickers while shaking his head. Then he stops and looks up as though he's in deep thought. "I think he might because I've heard him tell you he loves you, and you tell him the same thing. Don't people in love get married and have kids?"

I shrug, holding back my grin. "Sometimes, they do. Right now, we're both focusing on you getting better, okay?"

"Sunday? Can I tell you something else?"

"Anything, little man," I reply.

"I can't believe my mother was the one responsible for the accident." This time, his voice is barely above a whisper as his head drops in shame. "So, it means Timmers dying is kinda my fault."

"What the fuck?" Jett explodes, having apparently come into the room without either of us noticing. "No, nuh-uh, no fucking way you're going to carry that load of horse shit, bud. No way. She might have given birth to you, but she's not your mother by a longshot. In fact, since she's facing prison time for purposefully causing the accident, I have my lawyer drawing up the paperwork to terminate her parental rights."

"What does that mean, Dad?" Dusty asks.

I'm still sitting here, horrified that he knows it was his birth mom who caused the wreck in the first place. When we found out, Jett went ballistic, then reached out to her family who had tried to come and see Dusty where he told them in no uncertain terms that they were *not* welcome, and especially not Stacey, who had wailed out her anguish over 'almost killing her baby boy'. Jett put them all in their place without allowing the drama to spill over onto Dusty.

"It means, little man, that according to the law, she would no longer be your mom."

"Does that mean I can be adopted?"

The look on Jett's face is priceless, and if the subject matter wasn't so serious, I'd be laughing my ass off. "Well, I mean, I suppose you could be, say, if I got married. The woman would be able to make that decision herself to become your mom," he slowly replies, slyly glancing in my direction.

"Cool. So someday, Sunday will be my mom, since she's been more of one to me than my birth mother ever was," he announces rather matter-of-factly.

CHAPTER
SIXTEEN

JETT

My fucking kid. I'm not sure how to answer him, but I can see the blush covering my woman's face. We've had several heart-to-hearts about our future, so she knows where I'm at, and thankfully, we're on the same page. However, right now, the priority is Dusty's recovery which is what she insisted on getting through first when I wanted to move ahead. We'll be staying at her place since the doors are wider, which will make it easier for him to maneuver in the wheelchair he's going to be using for a few months.

Instead of answering him, I move closer to Sunday and lean down to brush a kiss across her temple. "You decided to hang with him during your break?" I ask, grinning at the two of them.

"Yeah, it was either that, or cramming it down while I counted out supplies," she teases. "No, seriously, I figured he would enjoy 'real' food compared to what he's been getting, so I brought him a sandwich. If I had known you'd be here too, I'd have made an extra one for you."

"I'm good, sweetheart. Just swung by to see what he wants me to pick up to eat later."

"It doesn't matter, Dad," Dusty replies. "You pick, okay?"

"Well, you two, I've enjoyed it tremendously, but I need to head back to work," Sunday announces, picking up the trash and throwing it away.

"I'll walk you down," I offer, grinning at her.

"Thanks, Sunday!" Dusty exclaims.

"Anytime, little man."

Between the rollercoaster ride of Dusty nearly dying, us all feeling the aftereffects of losing Timmers, and getting plays mapped out for the state championship game, I feel worn out, but despite that, I can't help the smile that I'm sporting as Sunday wheels Dusty around her house while her two kittens ride on his lap.

In typical fashion, he's chattering a mile a minute while I unpack his stuff in the spare room that Sunday set him up in. Walking out of the room once I'm done, I find them in the kitchen where he's regaling her with stories about the nurses he had during his stay.

"They're all good, Dusty," she chides, sliding a tray of fries in the oven. "Some have been there longer, of course, but they know their stuff, I promise."

"Yeah, I know, but one of them was really young, and every time I'd ask her a question, she'd run out to the desk and talk to the person behind it, then she'd come back to answer me. I don't think she knows all the stuff yet, Sunday," he states, sipping on his glass of chocolate milk.

"Could it be because you asked her stuff that was totally unrelated to your care?" she teases, handing me a beer.

"I don't know, maybe," he huffs out. "But grown-ups should know stuff that kids don't, right?"

She shakes her head and replies, "Dusty, you asked her if she knew how to operate a forklift!"

I snicker, because when he's bored, like he was the past few days, he tends to think up bizarre scenarios. "What was her response?" I ask, curious now about how she handled my son.

"She said that she actually did because she worked in a warehouse as a teenager and even had her certification! I think that's pretty cool," he says, grinning at me.

"Well, I think we need an early night because the game is tomorrow and it's going to be a long day for all of us," I retort as Sunday brings plates to the table.

"Ladies and gentlemen, please direct your attention to the scoreboard," the announcer requests.

I take a deep breath, knowing what's about to happen; a tribute to Timmers, which I suspect will have many in the audience weeping. He was a phenomenal kid and I know I'll miss him. Collectively, the people in the stands swivel their heads up to the board, where pictures of Timmers throughout his playing seasons flash on the screen in succession.

"Several weeks ago, Michael Timmers, number eighty-five on the Possum Run Polecats, was involved in a fatal accident that cost him his life, and critically injured his head coach's eleven-year-old son. Timmers was an all-state wide receiver, and already had numerous colleges vying for him to commit to their school. In addition to his impressive record on the field, he was an Eagle Scout, held a grade point average of 4.0, and had other colleges wanting to give him a full academic ride. While the Falls Ridge Red Devils and the

Possum Run Polecats may be rivals between the lines for four quarters, the loss of this young man is felt within our football community. Both teams are wearing his number on their helmets in remembrance of this fine young man, and the Falls Ridge Alumni Association has set out a donation jar at the concession stand to help his family with anything they need."

Knowing everyone's attention is now on me and my team, I call them in and say, "This game, regardless of the outcome, will probably be one of the most important ones you ever play. Let's honor your friend and team-mate, Timmers' memory, and give it everything we've got. Just know that no matter what the final score ends up being, I'm beyond proud of each and every one of you boys. You've stood tall, come to practice even though you're all hurting, and been there for his family. Small towns are sometimes given a bum rap because everyone seems to know everything about what's going on, but in this case, the tragedy we suffered has brought this team closer and has united us, giving us a purpose. Now, get your minds set on what we've gotta do, which is play hard until the last whistle blows."

"For Timmers!" Junior yells, putting his hand in the middle of our circle.

One by one, each of the boys, as well as all of us coaches, put our hands in to join theirs, then in unison we shout, "For Timmers!"

As I walk over to the fence where Dusty is set up, I see my woman has given him a warm blanket to ward off the chill, along with a goofy hat which has him grinning. "You good to go?"

"Yeah, Dad. Sunday said if I needed anything, to text her and she'd take care of it so you can focus on the game."

"She did, huh?" I tease, loving how she mothers him.

"Did you see this hat? When she found out Timmers used to call me Dustman, she said she went online and found this for me because it would've made him laugh. I think she's right, don't you?"

I look at what he's wearing and chuckle. She found him a Pigpen hat with dust motes floating all over it, reminiscent of Timmers' nickname for my boy, Dustman. "It's perfect, little man."

"Yeah, now go win, Dad!"

"He would've loved this," Collins says as we watch the team celebrate on the field after winning the game. In addition to the players, the parents are out there, as well as the other team, who have been congratulating each one of the boys.

"Still kind of shocked we pulled it off," I murmur, my mind replaying the game. We were behind at half time, then when the game picked back up again, and the announcer mentioned that so far, over five thousand dollars had been collected for Timmers' family, the tide changed in our favor. The Falls Ridge Red Devils fumbled twice, which we recovered the ball, and ran in gaining touchdowns, then their quarterback, who has the best accuracy in the state with respect to completions, lack of interceptions thrown, and overall yardage, threw an interception which put us over the top.

"Not sure why, Coach. We've taught them to take advantage of missteps, which they did."

"I know, but even though I *am* proud as hell of all of them since the accident, you know good and well they've been all over the place during practice," I retort.

"Maybe so, but regardless, we're state champions, and I know we worked hard to get here."

"You're right. I'm going to see if I can find Sunday so we can get Dusty home."

I walk off the field while the kids and parents continue to celebrate, and head toward the concession stand because that's where she said she was going earlier. When I see her standing up ahead of me, her arms moving wildly while her body is tense, I take a closer look at who she's talking to and feel my blood freeze in my veins.

Stacey.

My strides lengthen as I get to where they're

standing only to hear Stacey insist, "I need to see my son."

"No. Absolutely not," I state, my voice short and clipped. "You have no business even being here, Stacey. What the hell are you thinking?"

She turns her tear-streaked face toward me and replies, "It's my fault Dusty almost died, and the other kid did. I wanted to pay my respects."

"The time to do that was at the funeral for Michael," I retort. "And *my son* doesn't want to see you. Do you know he was blaming himself for the fucking accident? Because you're his birth mother."

"That sounds so harsh, Jett," she sneers.

"As far as he's concerned, that's what you are, Stace," I reply. "Sunday has been more of a mother to him in the short time we've been together than you've been his entire life. What does that say about you?"

She glares at Sunday, and I see her open her mouth, likely to say something scathing and mean so I throw up my hand nipping that in the bud before she has a chance to spread her venom. "No. You don't talk to her, you don't talk to Dusty. In fact, you should be getting paperwork from my attorney at any time."

"For what?"

"To terminate your parental rights. It's what he wants, and I try to give him that whenever possible within reason. This definitely falls under that umbrella as far as I'm concerned. Now, leave. Because trust me, the Timmers don't need to see you walking around as though you don't have a care in the world."

"He wants that?" she whispers.

"Yes, he does," Sunday replies. "And I agree with Jett. Michael's family doesn't need to see you here, Stacey. You need to leave."

Surprisingly, where she was all set to argue with me, once Sunday says her piece, she turns on her heel and leaves.

"Come on, sweetheart, let's get our boy and head home."

"Sounds like a plan to me. I have a special celebration in mind for you," she teases, winking at me.

My laughter rings out as we walk back down the track to where Dusty is being pushed toward us by Collins.

CHAPTER
SEVENTEEN

SUNDAY

Hearing the front door open, I call out, "Did you guys get the pizza and wings?"

"Yeah, Sunday," Dusty replies. "Pudge, no, you can't have any chicken just yet."

I giggle, grabbing the paper plates and napkins, then walk into the living room where they've got two boxes already sitting on the coffee table. It's been a month since the team won the state championship, and we're now watching pro football. I can't every weekend because of my schedule, but thankfully, I'm off this weekend, because our two teams are rivals and they're playing one another.

"Why don't you go ahead and make our plates, I'll

get the drinks, and Dusty, you go wash your hands," Jett orders.

It's playoff weekend, and my guys and I are going to enjoy yelling at the television while we eat our weight in carbs, something I enjoy more than I can express. As the two of them move to take care of their tasks, I set the plates down, and open up the lid of the box then gasp.

"Will you marry us?" is spelled out in pepperoni slices, with a green bell pepper serving as the question mark.

All the memories we've made so far flash through my mind; from the weekend camping trips to the solo dates with just Jett and me. While it's only been a few months, I know beyond a shadow of a doubt I want to spend the rest of my life with him by my side, along with Dusty, and any children we might have further down the road.

"Well, will you?" Jett asks, causing me to turn my head to see him bent down on one knee, a ring box opened in his hand, with a gorgeous diamond sparkling at me.

"Yes, yes I will," I whisper, tears slowly rolling down my face.

He slips the ring on my finger just as Dusty war whoops from beside the couch, causing us both to laugh before his lips gently kiss mine.

"I love you, Sunday Cross," he murmurs against my lips.

"I love you more, Jett Blake," I reply. Then, pointing to Dusty, I continue. "But I love our son even more."

"Yeah, I'm a pretty good kid, and very loveable," Dusty says, giggling.

"Modest too," Jett retorts. "Okay, so have you guys decided on what you're betting on for the first game?"

"A week's worth of doing laundry," I state.

"I'll take care of the cats when Sunday works," Dusty tosses in.

"And I'll do the grocery shopping for a week," Jett pledges.

"Then let's watch some football," I reply, getting the plates set up while Jett passes out our drinks.

Later that night, as Dusty sleeps, I come back to the bedroom from cleaning up, and crawl into bed, curling up in Jett's arms. "I don't want to wait a long time to get married," I confess, my hand stroking across his pec.

"You don't want the big shindig?" he asks, looking down at me.

"Nope. Because that's not what makes a marriage. What we've been doing, day in and day out, that's what does, Jett. I'm perfectly okay with going to the courthouse with your sister's family and mine as witnesses. We can always have a huge reception after if that's something you'd like, but at the end of the day, as long as I'm Sunday Blake, I don't really care, do you?"

"Not at all, sweetheart. We'll let everyone know and see when we can do this," he agrees to my wishes, kissing me. "Now, let's get some sleep. Seems I have to go to the grocery store, and I suspect Dusty is going to put everything he can think of on the list."

Even though I'm tired, I can't help the giggle that escapes. "Good night, Jett."

"Night, sweetheart."

EPILOGUE

JETT
ONE MONTH LATER

"It was nice of your folks to take Dusty," I say as we pull out of the courthouse parking lot.

"Are you kidding me? Mom's been beside herself since she found out she was getting a grandson," Sunday teases. "I'm pretty sure there will be minimal vegetables eaten while we're gone as well, because they're going to spoil the hell out of him."

"He was so young when my folks passed, he doesn't really remember them," I reply. "Stacey's folks wanted nothing to do with him when she split, so he's past due for some grandparent spoiling."

"Don't say I didn't warn you." I suspect those words

are due to the fact her mom has clued her in as to the plans they have with our son.

"It's okay as long as it's not an everyday thing, sweetheart," I tell her as I make my way to the tattoo shop.

Manual Alvarez, or Manny as he prefers to be called, was finally able to get Sunday in to check out her scar and see if they'd need to wait any longer for her to get the area tattooed. Apparently, he's a whiz with scars, having apprenticed under some guy named Loki, who told him when he reached out that he'd be available to help. Kind of intriguing to me, since Loki is part of a motorcycle club over in St. Mary's, which isn't exactly all that close. But I keep my thoughts to myself since this is something my wife wants.

My wife.

When the Justice of the Peace pronounced us man and wife, then introduced us as Mr. and Mrs., those two words embedded themselves in my heart. Not only did he marry us, but he signed the adoption paperwork afterward, so Sunday is now officially on Dusty's birth certificate as his mother.

After parking, I help her jump out, then we walk hand in hand to the shop, which is just off of Main Street. Walking inside, I hear the chime of the bells announce our entrance, then a male voice yell out, "I'll be right there!"

"Are you nervous?" I ask.

"About needles? I don't particularly like them, but I'm sure the minimal discomfort from getting a tattoo will be nothing. At least, nothing like the surgeries I had, that's for sure," she replies, smiling up at me.

"Hey, I'm Manny," the guy says, introducing himself as he walks through a curtained-off area. "You must be Sunday?"

"Yes, this is my husband, Jett," she announces, standing.

"Come on back and let's see what we're working with," he invites.

I grit my teeth knowing he's going to have to get up close and personal to her body, but he doesn't give off a creeper vibe, which slightly allays my concerns. When we breach the work area, he points to a door and offers, "There's the bathroom so you can slip into something more comfortable."

While she goes to change, I sit in a chair that's been pulled next to the table I presume he uses when working. I watch him gather a sketchpad and pencil, along with his phone. "Sunday says you've worked with a guy who is a rockstar tattooist when it comes to covering up scars."

"Loki's one of the best," he replies. "He does a lot of work on women who have had mastectomies, as well as burn victims. While all skin isn't able to be worked on, from what your wife indicated, her skin grafts took well, so we shouldn't have any problems."

I hear the door open and watch her cross the room, her stride confident even though she's now in a one-piece bathing suit. Manny has her stand straight, and I glance over his shoulder, observing him take several pictures of her thigh before he motions for her to turn around.

"You good with lifting the fabric?" he asks, which I find respectful as hell.

"Yeah," she murmurs, grabbing the bottom of her suit and pulling it over her ass cheek. I can see her blush, but she doesn't say anything else while Manny again takes several pictures.

"Okay, go ahead and get redressed, then we can talk about what image you're wanting to use as a cover up design," he instructs.

"What do you think?" I question as soon as she's in the bathroom again.

"Doesn't look like we're going to have any problems. Whoever did her surgeries should do everyone's surgeries, because I've worked on some seriously fucked-up scars since I started," he admits.

"That'll make her happy," I reply.

"Just putting this out there, but there won't be a charge for her tattoo," he states.

"What? Why? We're prepared to cover the cost."

"Several reasons, actually. One is that both Loki and I were in the Navy, so she's part of our brotherhood in that respect. Even if we hadn't served our country ourselves, she did, and those scars are because of it. The second reason is because I have that discretion and I can tell, even though she comes across as very confident, they bother her."

"They do."

"Well, I have the skills and abilities to change the way they look," he retorts. "So, I'm going to do so."

"Do what?" Sunday questions, returning to where we're sitting.

"He was just telling me he won't charge for your tattoo, sweetheart." When she goes to protest, I hold up my hand. "He's Navy, Sunday."

"Still doesn't make it right," she grumbles.

"My shop, my rules," Manny professes. "Now, what were you thinking of doing?"

Thirty minutes later, we're walking back to my truck with Manny having promised to send her some mock pictures of what he designed once he's done adding all of the final touches. After helping her in, I round the front of my truck, and jump in then grin at her.

"Ready to start our honeymoon?"

"Hell yes!" she exclaims, leaning over to kiss me.

Sundays for most round out their weeks and end them. For me, Sunday is the beginning.

. . .

THE END

Author's Note - You may have caught mention of Loki, who is from the Poseidon's Warriors MC series, as well as the tattoo artist, Manny. While Loki's story has been written, you'll be able to read Manny's story (and also see a bit of Sunday and Jett when she comes in to get her tattoo done) in "Starting Over With You" which will release in July in time for the BRAE signing in Columbus, Ohio. I can't wait to bring y'all Ricci and Manny's story but head's up, it's going to be a tearjerker most likely!

ABOUT THE AUTHOR

I am a transplanted Yankee, moving from upstate New York when I was a teenager. I'm a mom of four and grandma of nine who has found a love of traveling that I never knew existed! I live with the brat-cat pack (all rescues) as well as my dog, Bosco, 'deep in the heart of Texas', as I plot and plan who will get to "talk" next!

Find me on Facebook!
https://www.facebook.com/darlenetallmanauthor
Darlene's Dolls (my reader's group):
https://www.facebook.com/groups/1024089434417791/
permalink/1063976267095774/?comment_id=
1063979757095425&notif_id=1539553456785632&
notif_t=group_comment

DARLENE'S BOOKS

The Black Tuxedos MC

1. The Black Tuxedos MC - Reese
2. Nick - The Black Tuxedos MC
3. Matt - The Black Tuxedos MC

Poseidon's Warriors MC

1. Poseidon's Lady
2. Trident's Queen
3. Loki's Angel
4. Brooks' Bride
5. Atlas' World
6. The Warriors' Hearts (novella)
7. Kaya's King

8. Chelsea's Knight

9. Orion's Universe

Writing in the Rogue Enforcers World

Paxton: A Rogue Enforcers Novel

Esmerelda: A Rogue Enforcers Novel

Charisma: A Rogue Enforcers Novella (with Liberty Parker)

Writing in the Royal Bastards MC world (Roanoke, VA chapter)

Brick's House

A Very Merry Brick-mas

Banshee's Lament - releases June 2023

Standalones

Bountiful Harvest

His Firefly

His Christmas Pixie

Her Kinsman-Redeemer

Operation Valentine

His Forever

Forgiveness

Christmas With Dixie

Our Last First Kiss

Draegon: The Falder Clan - Book One

Scars of the Soul

Hale's Song

Mountain Ink: Mountain Mermaids Sapphire Lake

Knox's Jewel: A Dark Leopards MC Novella

Desire: A Savage Wilde Novel

Contraryed: A Heels, Rhymes & Nursery Crimes short story

Sashy's Salvation

Search & Find

Little Red's

Rebel Guardians MC (with Liberty Parker)

1. Braxton

2. Hatchet

3. Chief

4. Smokey & Bandit

5. Law

6. Capone

7. A Twisted Kind of Love

Rebel Guardians Next Generation (with Liberty Parker)

1. Talon & Claree

2. Jaxson & Ralynn

3. Maxum & Lily

New Beginnings (with Liberty Parker)

1. Reclaiming Maysen
2. Reviving Luca
3. Restoring Tig

Where Are They Now? RGMC updates on original 7
couples (with Liberty Parker)
Braxton
Hatchet
Chief

Nelson Brothers (with Liberty Parker)

1. Seeking Our Revenge
2. Seeking Our Forever
3. Seeking Our Destiny

Rebellious Christmas (A Christmas Novella) (with
Liberty Parker)

Nelson Brothers Ghost Team Series (with Liberty Parker)

1. Alpha
2. Bravo - release TBD - will be 2023

Old Ladies Club (with Kayce Kyle, Erin Osborne and Liberty Parker)

1. Old Ladies Club - Wild Kings MC
2. The Old Ladies Club - Soul Shifterz MC
3. Old Ladies Club - Rebel Guardians MC
4. Old Ladies Club - Rage Ryders MC

The Mischief Kitties (with Cherry Shephard)

The Mischief Kitties in Bampires & Ghosts & New Friends, Oh My!
The Mischief Kitties in the Great Glitter Caper
The Mischief Kitties in You Can't Takes Our Chicken

Raven Hills Coven (with Liberty Parker)

1. Rise of the Raven
2. Whimsical
3. Enchantment
4. Prophecy Revealed

Tattered and Torn MC (with Erin Osborne)

1. Letters from Home/War (novella)
2. Letters Between Us (novella)
3. Letters of Healing (novella)

4. Letters from Mom (novella)

5. Letters to Heaven (novella)

6. Letters with Love (novella)

7. Letters from Nanny (novella)

8. Letters of Wisdom (novella)

9. Band of Letters - all 8 novellas in one volume

10. Her Keeper

11. Her One

12. Her Absolution

COPYRIGHT

This is a work of fiction. Names, characters, places, and incidents are either the product of the author's imagination or used fictitiously, and any resemblance to actual persons, living or dead, business establishments, events or locales is entirely coincidental.

COVER MODEL: JESSE SHEPARD
COVER BY AMANDA SHEPARD
EDITORS: MARY KERN, MELANIE GRAY, NICOLE MCVEY, JENNIFER CORBIN, STEPHANIE ELLIS, BETH DILORETO, SYLVIE HOWICK
PROOFERS: NICOLE MCVEY, CHERYL HULLETT, NICOLE LLOYD
FORMATTER: LIBERTY PARKER

ACKNOWLEDGMENTS

Without the encouragement of JoAnna Edger, this book wouldn't have been written. She was the one who showed me the gorgeous cover, then asked, "Do think you could write a story for this for Beyond the Read Author Event (2023)?" I, of course, was like, maybe...ha!

Then, the story started revealing itself, bit by bit and piece by piece. I worried some of the topics might be hard and triggering for some readers (so read the author's note, please), but despite the fact this is fiction, my characters experience "real life" events on a regular basis.

So, thank you, JoAnna. I hope Ricci and Manny's story exceeds any expectation you might have had when you showed me the cover.

XOXOXO

Darlene

DEDICATION

Dedications are hard. But this one may not be as difficult as normal, since the man on the cover, Jesse Shepard? This is his first-ever cover that was sold! His wife, Amanda, is the photographer and cover designer and gotta say, this one picture gave me one helluva story if I say so myself. So, to Jesse and Amanda Shepard. May your journey be as filled with love and joy as Ricci and Manny's eventually is and thank you both for a gorgeous cover!

XOXOXO

Darlene

AUTHOR'S NOTE

While I'm not huge on giving every single thing away in a book, especially when it's geared for ages 18+, this book is one that I want you, the reader, to know may have some triggering situations that may include but aren't limited to: domestic violence and child loss/miscarriage. Because while the characters are purely figments of my overactive imagination, the situations they find themselves in are all to sadly, the way of this world we live in nowadays.

Please know that I tried to handle each and every situation the characters endured with sensitivity and compassion as I've experienced both many years ago. My ultimate goal was to give you, the reader, a story that was initially rooted in despair and sadness which ended up morphing into a love story filled with hope and joy. I pray I've succeeded.

And, if you find yourself in an abusive situation, please know there's hope and healing when you're ready!

Darlene

STARTING OVER
with you

INTERNATIONAL BESTSELLING AUTHOR
DARLENE TALLMAN

BLURB

Manuel "Manny" Alvarez

I will *never* regret my actions that led to me spending five years in prison. Hearing my sister's voice on the phone as she screamed for help, then seeing her vacant eyes staring upward as her body lay sprawled at her boyfriend's feet while he laughed in my face may have made me snap and beat him so viciously, he ended up dying from complications due to the injuries I inflicted, but I don't care. While it cost me a long-time girlfriend, I would do it all over again if only it meant that the outcome for Luci would be different.

Settling back into my hometown is sometimes challenging as the townspeople are now leery about me, but

I'm determined to make a success of my uncle's tattoo shop that I took over, while I also build up my custom woodworking business on the side to combat my loneliness. When I come home from a business trip after delivering some furniture, I notice something is off in my workshop, so I install cameras to see who is breaking in at night. I never expect to find my future rolled up in a sleeping bag, feverish and delusional.

Ricci Addams

My childhood was perfect; two loving parents and a small, fluffy dog, until the night a drunk driver stole my parents away from me, which thrust me into the foster care system. I bounced from home to home and quickly realized that while some homes were good, others were downright terrifying. When I turned ten, I found Mama and Papa B, and life turned good again.

But life is a capricious witch, and I lost them too, moving in with my boyfriend. My days are soon spent walking on eggshells while my nights often end in tears. After enduring my fourth miscarriage thanks to his volatile anger, he tosses me out and I leave town, living out of my car while I search for a job. When I find a large shed that appears to be unused, I sleep there at night and during the day, I pound the pavement in

Possum Run looking for a job, never realizing that my body is carrying a lurking timebomb.

Can two people whose pasts have hurt them push beyond their feelings and find happiness together?

Suitable for ages 18+ due to adult language, content, and situations

PROLOGUE

MANNY, AGE 16

"Luci, it's not right how he treats you," I stated, watching my older sister stir the sauce on the stove.

The left side of her face was puffy and swollen where her boyfriend, Turo, slapped her because she spent too much at the grocery store. I didn't like him for a lot of reasons, but even though my papa had died when I was really little, my uncles and my grandfather had taught me that women were to be protected and cherished.

"It's okay, hermano," she replied, stiffly turning toward the fridge. "I deserved it. He works hard and I shouldn't spend all his pay."

With my fists clenched at my sides I shook my head.

"No, Luci. You didn't deserve it. *No* woman deserves to be hit. Especially when that woman is carrying a baby *and* the man says he loves her. One day, he's going to hurt you really badly or even kill you."

She smiled at me, even though it didn't reach her eyes. "That will never happen, Manny. He loves me."

"Love shouldn't hurt, Luci," I retorted.

I just wish I had been able to see the future.

"Luci, I'm on my way over," I stated. "Mama said she wanted me to bring over the stuff you needed."

When I told Mama what Luci said the last time Turo had smacked her, I noticed that she added 'extra' stuff to the shopping list, then she'd have me take them down to my sister. None of us were happy about the current situation, but if nothing else, Luci was stubborn to a fault. She felt that since she got pregnant, she *had* to stay with the baby daddy, even though Mama had tried to tell her it didn't matter.

"Okay, Manny. Be careful," she teased, knowing all I had to do was walk up a block to the tiny apartment she and Turo shared. I grinned because it was the same thing she always said whenever I'd call to let her know I was on my way over.

She was three years older than me, and I'm pretty sure the only reason she moved in with Turo was because of the baby she was expecting. I didn't much care for him because whenever he got mad, or had been drinking, he was a little too free with his fists as far as I was concerned. But, Luci, my beloved sister, was convinced that because she was now pregnant, he wouldn't be like that any longer.

I wasn't so sure; I knew leopards didn't typically change their spots. He'd been a bit of a bully at school, always eager to engage in a fight, especially against those who were weaker than him.

As I gathered the things Mama wanted me to take over to Luci's, my phone rang.

"Hello?" I asked, seeing my sister's name on the caller ID. "Luci?"

"Don't come, Manny," she whispered. "He's in a mood right now."

I heard something that sounded like flesh striking flesh, then her bloodcurdling scream before the call disconnected. I flew out of our apartment, uncaring that I didn't lock the door behind me, then ran as fast as my legs would carry me to my sister, but I was too late.

And maybe, just maybe, I could've prevented what I did next but as I hit my knees next to my sister's bleeding and broken body where she lay on the ground outside their apartment, her motherfucking boyfriend *laughed.*

Manny, age 17

"All rise," the bailiff called out as the judge entered the courtroom.

Once the judge had settled, he speared me with a look I wasn't able to decipher then called out, "Will the defendant please rise."

I stood next to my public defender with my head back and shoulders tall. I would not feel remorse for my actions. Turo deserved to have his ass handed to him after hurting my sister. I could hear my mama quietly crying behind me while my uncle comforted her, as I waited to hear what the judge's sentence was going to be.

"Manuel Alvarez, you've been found guilty of involuntary manslaughter in the death of Arturo Herrera. You will be incarcerated for a period of ten years, with the possibility of parole after serving a minimum of five," Judge Millano announced. "I realize there were extenuating circumstances behind your behavior on that day, and while I am truly sorry for your family's losses, I cannot condone your actions that caused the loss of another life."

"Mama, I'm so sorry," I said as the guard gave me a few minutes with my family. "I never meant for this to be the outcome."

"Manny, we will be okay. You just stay safe. Jorge will watch over us, mijo."

"I love you, Mama," I whispered as tears fell down her cheeks. "I will make you proud of me someday."

Manny, age 22

"Sign here and here," the bored guard said, pointing to two places on the paperwork I was filling out in order to be released on parole.

Once I had done what he requested, he slid a bag across to me that held my wallet, a cheap cell phone that I was positive no longer worked, and my St. Christopher's medal. Another bag holding the clothes I wore the day I was incarcerated was plopped onto the counter next, causing me to chuckle.

Looking at the guard, I stated, "Don't think those are gonna fit me, do you?"

"Naw, you had a bit of a growth spurt during your stay with us," he advised, chuckling. "Keep your nose clean, Manny. Don't want you coming back in."

He was one of the good ones, always looking out for those of us who were younger, so we didn't find ourselves being sucked into a permanent way of life. "Not planning on it, Rogers," I replied.

"Your uncle's picking you up?" he asked.

"Yeah," I replied. I was eager to get home so I could start figuring out what I was going to do with myself. I knew I'd be apprenticing with my uncle at his tattoo shop, but wanted something else too.

He suddenly looked more serious than I had ever seen him appear before. Leaning in, he said, "It's not gonna be easy, Manny. You live in a small town and people can be real assholes to felons. Even if what eventually happened to Turo wasn't on you, they'll use you as an example to their kids, that kind of shit."

The beating I'd given Turo had sent him to the hospital with a vast array of injuries that required surgery. Unfortunately for me, he developed an infection and had one complication after another set in, until his body was unable to rebound any longer and he died. And maybe it made me a Grade A asshole, but I couldn't find it in me to feel much remorse about the end result.

He killed my sister and unborn niece. We had been told by the medical examiner that the baby that died along with Luci was a little girl, something that devastated my mother.

Ricci, age 10

"It'll be okay, Ricci," my caseworker, Miss Eileen, said, as we walked up some stairs until we were standing on a porch.

I shrugged, unwilling to believe anything I was told at this point. I first heard 'it'll be okay, Ricci' when I was four, almost five, the night my parents got killed by a drunk driver and I was thrust into the foster care system.

It wasn't okay. In fact, it was so far from being okay that I knew at my young age I was already jaded. The first home I went to wasn't prepared to deal with a child of my age who was actively grieving the loss of everything they knew. I didn't understand why I couldn't see my mommy or daddy, or why I couldn't have my doggy, Puff, with me.

So, I was moved. Then I was moved again. And again. And yet again. This would be my sixth foster home and at this point, I was over the whole dang thing.

Miss Eileen rang the bell, and I could hear the chimes inside playing a pretty song as I scuffed my sneaker on the porch. Footsteps were getting louder, and I sighed knowing that it was likely I'd be here only long enough for Miss Eileen to find another house. I was past the 'preferred' adoptable age. Most people wanted either babies or younger kids and I wasn't that any longer.

"Smile, Ricci. I think you'll like the Billingsleys a great deal," Miss Eileen stated. "Not only have they raised a family, but they've done so while fostering many children along the way."

Before I could respond, the door opened and a woman stepped out, a welcoming smile on her face. "Hello, you must be Ricci," she said, crouching so we were at eye level. That one simple act chipped away some of the ice that had encased my heart since the day I found out my parents were dead.

"Hi," I shyly replied.

When she motioned for Miss Eileen and me to follow her inside the house, I picked up my garbage bag full of my clothes and quietly fell in step behind her. I had my backpack on, which held more of my things, but I saw the sadness in her eyes when she spied my bag.

I was totally in awe by the time she showed me the room I'd be staying in, then took us into the kitchen. The house was a farmhouse, with a wraparound porch, and lots of windows, while my room was every little girl's dream, complete with a canopy bed and a huge dollhouse. All of the rooms were large and bright, which felt cheerful to me. As she and Miss Eileen discussed my schooling, and other things like doctor appointments, she put together a snack and set it down in front of me.

"I figured you might like something light right now, since it'll be a few hours before dinner," Mrs. Billingsley said. Then to Miss Eileen she asked, "Is there anything I need to be aware of? Any known food allergies, that sort of thing?"

Miss Eileen shook her head as she slid a folder across the table. "Everything you will need is in there, along with my contact information." With that, she stood up, patted me on the shoulder then said, "I'll check in with you next month. Ricci, you take care."

Ricci, age 12

"Mama B, do you think I can learn to do what Papa B does?" I asked as she brushed out my hair before quickly braiding it.

"What do you mean, sweetie?" she replied, making the face she always did whenever she was concentrating. I was now doing the same thing, biting my lower lip. That made me smile and I briefly wondered if I would've picked up habits from my parents if they had lived or not.

"I want to learn how to work on cars, I think," I mused.

One of the best things that had ever happened to me was being placed with the Billingsleys, or as I now called them, Mama B and Papa B. It took them about six months to break through my shell, which they did with love and consistency, two things I had been lacking in my life for years. Instead of telling Miss Eileen they couldn't handle me when I'd pitch a fit, which was often when I first came, one or the other would actually sit on the floor near me and just talk. They'd tell me about what their kids did when they were little, how much they enjoyed the crazy schedules when one kid was playing soccer while another was dancing.

When I met their kids, two girls and a boy, all of whom were now either in college or living on their own, I met my future best friends, Ivy and Lacie. They frequently took me shopping with them for 'girl's dates' and when I was older, they were going to show me how to wear makeup.

Mama and Papa B opened up a whole new world for me; if I expressed an interest, they got me involved. So, I started taking dance lessons, played soccer as well as softball, and learned how to cook and bake. In short, they loved me like I was one of their own flesh and blood kids, not a foster kid. The only reason they didn't adopt me was because I had an aunt who was my next of kin who wasn't capable of caring for me, but she wouldn't give the state permission for me to be adopted.

"I'm sure he'd be glad to teach you, sweetheart," she stated. "Now, we've got your hair taken care of, are you ready to go shopping?"

After Mama B saw my wardrobe or lack thereof the first day I arrived, she made a special point to take me shopping that following weekend to 'supplement' what

I had, according to her. All I remember is since I walked through that front door two years ago, I've had clothes for *every* occasion. Shoes too. Oh, and most importantly? I had my own set of luggage for whenever we took family vacations. Unlike previous homes, I was taken along and treated like I was part of the family whenever they planned one. Even their son, Stanley, who just rolled his eyes the first time he met me, was okay.

"Yes, ma'am. Can we get the ingredients to make Papa B's favorite cake?" I asked.

"Are you trying to butter him up?" she questioned, grinning at me.

"Maybe?"

Ricci, age 14

"Papa B, will you show me how to do the jitterbug?" I questioned. "We have to know it for our history class because we're learning about World War II. The teacher said we had to write an essay on the popular dances of that time, and also learn one of them."

I was hoping I didn't have to demonstrate the dance in front of the whole class, but if I did, I was pretty sure Papa B would come with me. At least, I hoped he did because I was still somewhat shy. I had a few friends, though, so I had learned about sleepovers and boys, which was a good thing. Even though I didn't think I would ever want to date.

"I'll be glad to teach you, Button," he replied, making me grin. The first day he met me, he proclaimed I was 'cute as a button' and ever since, that's what he'd called me.

"Thank you! Also, Mama B said I should ask you about boys."

"You're too young to date. Maybe when you're thirty," he teased. "But right now, my heart can't handle the thought of you dating."

"Thirty?" Papa B, I'll be an old woman by then!" I exclaimed.

"Hmm, maybe sixteen then, is that better?" he asked.

"I guess so."

I mean, I thought a couple of the guys were kind of cute, but I still had a lot of things I wanted to do and learn, and I definitely didn't want to be like some of my friends in school were, all gaga over a boy. Nope, I knew since I was on my own, I would have to make sure I could take care of myself.

Ricci, age 16

"This is too much!" I exclaimed, looking at the four-door SUV that Papa B had restored for me. As a mechanic, he went to auctions from time to time, and just like he did with his own kids, he found a good, reliable car for me, bought it, then made sure it was in tip-top running condition.

"Button, we know you want to find a little part-time job so you can start saving money. This will let you get there safely, but you're still going to have some rules," he stated.

"I can live with rules."

And I could. I tended to follow rules because that was the easiest way to stay safe and not get hurt. But like I had expressed to both of them, I wanted to go to college for my business degree, and I needed to save money so I could be ready to be on my own once I aged out of the foster care system. I knew I'd have to move out of their house then, which secretly broke my heart, because I'd grown to love them as if they were my real-life parents.

Ricci, age 18

"Sweetie, we know that according to the state, you've 'aged out' of the system, but we have a proposition for you," Mama B said as we sat around the kitchen table eating dinner.

"What is it?" I asked.

For the past two years, I'd worked my part-time job, and also earned an allowance for the household chores I helped Mama B with even though I told them it wasn't necessary. I chipped in for my car insurance, and mostly covered the gas in my car. I say mostly because Papa B would take my car out on Sundays to 'check her out' and he always came back with a full gas tank. When I'd try to give him money, he'd wink and say he had to take care of his girls. So, I had a somewhat decent savings account, plus money in my checking account because Mama B used what the state sent for my care on me without fail every month. She kept a record of it and would hand me whatever wasn't spent, which was actually quite a bit of money, and I'd dutifully deposit it into my account.

"Well, you know as a foster kid, you get assistance for college tuition, plus you also qualify for a few grants as well which will take care of your books and supplies," she stated. When I nodded, she continued. "We have the apartment over the garage which our kids used as they were transitioning to adulthood, and would like to offer it to you if you'd like."

"You'd let me pay rent?" I questioned.

"Of course, of course," she replied. "I'll teach you how to budget and all that kind of stuff. What do you think? You'd be responsible for your own curfew, we just ask if you're going to be out past midnight, you let us know."

"I can do that," I murmured. "Okay, let's do this thing!"

Ricci, age 20

"Congratulations, sweetheart," Mama B said once they were able to reach me. "We knew you could do it."

I had just graduated with my Associate's Degree in Business, and even though I didn't want to walk during the ceremony, she had convinced me to do it since I had done so with honors. I even had quite a few credits under my belt for my Bachelor's Degree, which I would start classes for next semester.

"Thank you, Mama B," I replied.

"We want to take you to dinner to celebrate, will Erik be with you?" she asked.

I thought of my boyfriend, who hadn't come to see me walk across the stage because it was 'just a piece of paper' so it didn't really matter all that much. "I don't know, but I can check with him and let you know."

I was still kind of on the fence about Erik; sometimes, he was controlling, and he didn't like the time I spent with my sisters, Ivy and Lacie. They weren't really my biological sisters, but they'd never let that stop them from treating me like I'd grown up under the same roof they did, and I loved them for that fact alone.

"Do that, Button, and text us, okay?" Papa B asked, before engulfing me in one of his awesome bear hugs.

I grinned up at the man who epitomized what a great father should be; he taught me how to take care of my car, worked tirelessly with me on math when I struggled in tenth grade, and took me to get the biggest ice cream sundae when my heart was broken for the first time.

"I will," I promised. "I love you both so much."

I didn't say that often; my past wouldn't let me dwell on feelings like that because in my experience, everything I ever loved was taken away. But since they took a slightly bitter preteen into their home a decade ago, they had shown me the depth of their love in so many ways, I wanted to verbally tell them I felt the same.

"We love you too, Button," he replied, giving me another squeeze then letting me go. "The kids will be there too, they wanted to help celebrate your accomplishments."

I barely refrained from rolling my eyes; I felt confident that his two daughters, Ivy and Lacie, were happy for me, but his son, Stanley, had always acted as though I had stolen his parents away. He was civil when they were around, of course, but if it was just the two of us, he was surly and sometimes mean. Most recently, he had accused me of taking advantage of his parents since I was living in the garage apartment.

Never mind that he had lived there for seven years before he bought his own house. Guess it was different if you were actually their blood child, but since the arrangement was between the three of us, complete with a rental agreement, I ignored what he said. Most of the time. Because he tended to send his verbal barbs at me when I least expected it, they always struck a nerve and hurt. Not that I would ever let on that they did; no, I was made of stronger stuff, that's for damn sure.

"The Billingsleys were very upset that they were never allowed to adopt you, Ricci," the attorney said. "So, what they did was open a savings account and earmark it specifically for you. In the early days, they put whatever was left from the state stipend they received in there, then they started depositing the whole check. Once you started 'paying rent' for the garage apartment, they included that as well as what you gave them for your portion of the car insurance."

"But why would they do that?" I asked, still stunned over their deaths.

While they were enroute to the restaurant for dinner the night I graduated, someone suffered a medical emergency, ran the light and broadsided them, pushing them into a concrete pole. They were killed on impact, once again turning my whole world upside down. Even a week later, I still struggled to understand how one of the best days of my life could end up being so devastating. What had I ever done to anyone to deserve losing not one but two sets of parents to auto accidents?

"Because they loved you like you were one of us," Ivy replied, squeezing my hand. She and Lacie were sitting on either side of me, while Stanley chose to stand off to the side, his arms crossed over his chest.

"What about the house and property?" Stanley suddenly asked.

The lawyer gave him a look of distaste, but replied, "While they would prefer it be kept for the three of you, they also have a stipulation that indicates if y'all agree to it, the property and house can be sold with the proceeds divided up for all four of you."

"She's not their kid, though," Stanley sneered. "So, why should she benefit?"

"Stanley! You know Mama and Daddy wanted to adopt her, so stop being such a jerk," Lacie retorted. "I'm sorry, Mr. Madison, please continue."

"Their various accounts will be liquidated once I've ensured all their obligations have been resolved, then that money will again be split."

"I want to sell," Stanley advised, glaring at me. "Which means our *sister* will need to find somewhere else to live."

"Well, we don't want to get rid of the house," Ivy said, glaring at him. "So, she can stay there if she'd like. At least until I can get out of my lease, someone would be living on the property to keep a watch on it."

I finally spoke up, clearing the lump in my throat

from all the crying I'd done. "Since I wasn't sure what was going to happen, I told Erik I would move in with him."

It wasn't ideal, but until I could get a job in my field then make sure I had enough money to put down deposits, plus buy furniture and household things, it would have to do.

I just never realized that making that one decision would impact my life so much.

CHAPTER
EIGHTEEN

PRESENT DAY
(MANNY, 32; RICCI, 25)

MANNY

I groan getting out of my truck; my latest trip to deliver some custom furniture had been a bit harrowing due to the extreme weather I drove through. Thankfully, the wardrobe arrived at the customer's home without any damage. After locking up my truck, I head into the house, still marveling over the fact that I now own my grandparents' old farmhouse complete with Granddad's workshop in the back.

Once inside, I take my duffel bag into the laundry room and start a load of clothes before I meander into the kitchen and grab a beer. "Fuck, I'm tired," I mutter after drinking almost half the bottle.

With my clothes now washing, I sort through the mail that my uncle brought in for me, tossing all the junk to one side before I open the bills, snorting when I see the property taxes are due soon. I gather the important envelopes in my hand, grab another beer as well as a bottle of water and make my way to my room.

Ten years ago, when I was released from prison on parole, my Uncle Jorge brought me here for what I thought was a welcome home party. Since Granddad had passed during my incarceration, I just figured either he, my mom, or my Aunt Juanita would move into the farmhouse. Instead, once we got here, the three of them sat me down and let me know that the house and land were now mine. They wanted me to have something to start my life with, and because I was always over here helping in the workshop, they decided giving it to me would be perfect.

"Manny, you gave up five years of your life," Uncle Jorge stated. *"None of us need the house and even Pops was in agreement before he died. He wanted us to do this for you, boy."*

"But y'all are his children, I'm just a grandson. One of many, in fact," I protested, still overwhelmed at what they'd told me.

"And every one of your cousins agrees too. You did the

world a favor by killing Turo," Aunt Juanita spat out. When I tried to protest that it hadn't been my intention to do that, she held her hands up. "I know, I know, it was an accident, but based on how he treated others before our Luci, he would've done it again."

"He's right, Manny," Mama whispered. "Even though we didn't wish death on him, in fact I prayed to the Virgin Mary every night for his healing, he would've hurt another woman like your hermana."

"Well, then thank you. Because I've always loved this place," I finally said.

"You'll start at the shop on Monday," Uncle Jorge decreed. "I need a good apprentice."

I grinned, knowing that he'd been using a lot of my drawings for tattoos while I'd been gone. To keep my mind occupied while I was locked up, I took an art class and quickly found my passion. Now, I was looking forward to learning how to actually ink someone, as well as use some of the designs I'd come up with to make furniture like my granddad. He was well-known throughout the southeast for his custom creations, and I suspected there were possibly some unfinished pieces out in the workshop.

Shaking my head clear of the memories, I toss the bills onto my dresser, then strip down on my way into the master bathroom. A steaming hot shower is definitely on my mind after the long day of driving I just finished. I have no clue how long-distance truck drivers do it day in and day out because traffic was insane today. I spent more time sitting idling while accidents were cleared than I did actually moving.

"Fuck, that feels good," I groan out, once the hot water hits my back. I'm not one to linger in the shower; I typically get in, wash up, then get out, but tonight, I stand there for long minutes allowing the warmth to permeate my tight muscles so I can hopefully get a good night's sleep.

It hasn't come easy lately and I suspect it's because my old girlfriend, Leanna, is back in Possum Run, since she got divorced. While my mind wanders once again, I grab my shampoo and begin washing my hair.

"Leanna, I'll only be in for a few years," I begged, fighting back the tears that wanted to fall.

"Manny, you're a murderer," *she hissed, glaring at me. "I can't be with someone like you."*

"But I didn't mean for him to die," I insisted. "Besides, he killed *my* sister and niece!"

A look I couldn't decipher crossed her face. "I know and I'm sorry that happened. I liked Luci a lot. But you can't really expect me to put my life on hold waiting for you."

"What about our plans?" I asked. "We were going to go to college, then get married and raise a family."

"Plans change."

Shutting the water off now that I'm finished with my shower, I grab a towel and wrap it around my waist, then proceed to brush my teeth, run a comb through my hair, then slap on some deodorant. A quick walk-through of the house to make sure everything's locked up tight and I'm soon back in my room, settling into bed for the night.

***

With my coffee in hand, I walk out to the workshop, breathing in the crisp spring air. One of the perks of now being in charge at the tattoo shop is I can take the weekends off if I want to do so and after the past few days, I need the downtime. Uncle Jorge is still willing to come in and work during those times, but I think it might be time to find one or two younger artists so he and my aunt can truly retire. Unlocking the door, I open both sides wide since I plan to put a coat of varnish on my latest project, a triple dresser with a hand-laid mosaic top.

"Well, that's weird, I don't remember sweeping up before I left," I mutter as I turn on the lights and see how clean the floor looks. I was in such a hurry to get the furniture loaded, I let my uncle lock up so I could get on the road. "Doubt he did it for me either."

My Uncle Jorge is a good man, he truly is, having

stepped up after my dad passed away when me and my siblings were still young, but he's not the cleaning type.

Shrugging, I turn the radio on, then start a pot of coffee in the 'kitchen' area, once again thanking God for my grandfather. His workshop is a work of art, that's for damn sure. It's large, with barn doors that open outward in order to move stuff in and out down a slight ramp that leads to a paved walkway, but the real secret is the inside. He added a kitchenette of sorts, with a smaller sized full fridge, a microwave, and a sink, as well as a functional bathroom, complete with a shower stall. When I asked him once why he did that, he said that my grandma didn't like it when he'd walk through the house covered in sawdust, so he started showering before he came back inside for the night. Although I'm pretty sure based on the cobwebs that were inside the thing when I moved in, he stopped doing that once she passed away.

While the coffee is brewing, I look at the dresser with a critical eye. Prior to my trip, I carefully laid out the mosaic pattern across the top, then glued it down once I was satisfied that it looked good. I also filled the spaces with the resin I found that seems to work the best. Today, I need to smooth down any rough spots, then start varnishing the whole thing so it will look just as good years from now.

"Sure hope whoever ends up buying this likes it," I state to myself before grabbing my fine sandpaper. After

I slip on my safety glasses and turn on the overhead spotlight, I roll my stool over and start working.

Two pots of coffee later, I stand and immediately groan out loud. Seems I'm not as young as I used to be or maybe it's because I spent most of the morning and early afternoon bent over after a long day of driving. Regardless, I can't help the whistle that escapes me when I see the finished product. Pulling out my phone, I take several pictures that I'll upload to my website later. Now it's time to shut it all down and head into the house to get ready for dinner at my mother's house. One quick shower later and I'm pulling out of my driveway to run by the local bakery so I can get something for dessert.

Not that my mom won't make one; she always does. I just grab a sugar-free option since I know my Uncle Jorge needs to cut back on his sweets. Snickering, I signal to pull into the parking lot, park, then hurry inside. "Thanks, Paula," I say to the owner. "You're a lifesaver, as usual."

"I'm just glad your mom is willing to let me do this for y'all," she teases.

"Right?" I ask, taking the bag from her. "She's loosening the apron strings on her recipes a little bit."

"I'm waiting for the day she invites me over so I can sit with her and go over them," she muses.

"I'll put a bug in her ear."

"You're... that would be great, Manny," she whispers, her eyes getting shiny. "I want to be able to make things that others would enjoy."

"You already do, Paula," I advise. "Gotta run, I'm cutting it close as it is."

"Take care."

"You do the same."

Once back in my truck, I continue on to my mom's, my thoughts swirling. A lot of the town treated me like I was a leper when I was first released. They'd go so far as to leave an establishment if I was in there.

However, my family, which is quite large, had my back. Not only did my Uncle Jorge put me to work at his tattoo shop as an apprentice, but he also made it clear to his regular customers that he would fire them, and they'd have to find another tattoo artist if they said one wrong word to me.

My mind is stuck in the past as I pull into my mom's driveway and see I'm the last one to arrive. Uncle Jorge doesn't know we've been substituting his dessert for something that's sugar-free, so I grab the bag and go through the back door which leads into Mama's kitchen.

"You're late," she teases, stirring something on the stove. "Put it over there," she instructs, pointing to where the cake she made for the rest of us is sitting. Leaning in, I kiss her cheek, smiling because she's time-less, at least to me.

When I was younger, she wore dresses all the time. I asked her once why she did it when pants and a shirt would be more comfortable, and she said it was because my dad loved her in dresses. Even after he died, shortly before I turned thirteen, she never stopped wearing them.

That's the kind of woman I need, I thought. *One who I can take care of, but who will also do things because she knows they make me happy.*

"Do you need me to do anything, Mama?" I ask after putting the cake on the counter. While I wait for her to answer, I wash my hands in case I'm needed to stuff something.

She may be protective of her recipes, but she never objects to one of us helping if she needs it.

"Get the enchiladas out of the oven for me, please," she replies. "The sauce is nearly ready to add."

I groan out loud, my mouth already watering for the delicious food I know I'm about to eat. Looks like I'll be adding a mile or two to my daily workout. After pulling the steaming pan from the oven and setting it on the hot pads she has set out, I walk through to the family room.

"Uncle Jorge, look at this," I say, walking over to him and pulling out my phone.

I quickly find the pictures of the dresser then hand it to him to look at. I value his opinion as he has dabbled with woodworking over the years; he just doesn't have the same passion as my grandfather and I have. But he likes to see what I come up with, and I enjoy showing off my work.

"What are you going to do for the knobs?" he asks, slowly swiping through each picture.

"I was thinking of doing a smaller version of the pattern on them," I admit. "It's going to be a bit tedious, but I believe once I get started, it'll go pretty fast."

"This looks fantastic. Do you have a buyer already?" he questions, handing my phone back to me.

"Not yet. Going to put it up on the website once it's completely done," I reply.

"Don't think it'll take long for it to sell, boy," he says. "Because it's beautiful."

"Thank you. I wanted to try something a little bit different."

"Got any clients next week at the shop?" he asks.

"Yeah, Sunday Blake is finally coming in to get her piece started," I say. "I'm a little nervous, but called Loki and we talked about what I was going to do. Sent him pictures of what I'm working on, and he gave me some suggestions."

"It was a blessing for you to meet that man several years ago at the tattoo convention," Aunt Juanita states.

"He didn't care about what you had done, just saw someone who was as committed to helping people cover up their scars."

I shake my head, still amazed by that fact. The man is a highly decorated Navy SEAL for fuck's sake, yet he took me under his wing shortly after I 'earned' my tattoo gun. I spent two weeks with him at his shop in St. Mary's, where we worked side by side on several clients, including one with mastectomy scars.

"I'll probably never be as good as he and Kaya, the woman who works with him, but I haven't had anyone complain so far," I say.

"Let's eat, dinner's ready," Mama calls out.

CHAPTER
NINETEEN

RICCI

The past five years have been... challenging. Even though I got my business degree, finding a job with little to no experience is next to impossible. Instead, I'm a waitress at the diner in town. It's steady work, and the tips are good. Although, I tend to shave money off my tips when I hand them over to Erik since he spends it on beer and weed.

"You need to take a test," Ivy says as we wait for our meal. Thankfully, she, Lacie, and I are still close, and we try to get together at least once a week for lunch. They were in high school and their first year of college when I came to live with Mama and Papa B, and loved having a 'baby sister' to spoil.

Even though Erik hates it, he 'allows' it as long as I'm 'good'.

My eyes well up with tears that I quickly push back. "I know, but it's just going to make him so mad."

Erik mad is a force to be reckoned with, that's for sure. My body and soul have paid for his moods for almost four years now. The first year, he was nice; understanding that I was grieving the loss of the only parents I could remember. Then one day, he came home from work early because it was raining, saw I hadn't done the dishes yet since I wasn't feeling well, and he beat the shit out of me.

I know, I know, I shouldn't have stayed after that first time, but at twenty-one working a minimum wage job, I didn't have anywhere I could go. He apologized profusely the next day when I woke up bleeding and we found out I was having a miscarriage. I know the nurse and doctor were suspicious about how my injuries occurred, but I stuck with my story of falling down the stairs because I tripped over my own feet.

"Honey, when are you going to leave him? You have money in your account, plus you just got the life insurance policies from your parents when you turned twenty-five," Lacie asks, her hand now clutching mine. "Why don't you use that to get away?"

My head drops slightly before I whisper, "I think he's

broken something inside of me, y'all. What if I deserve how he treats me?"

Ivy's face blanches while Lacie looks like she wants to rip her napkin to shreds.

"Listen here, Ricci, and know I'm coming from a place of concern and love. There's *never* an excuse for abuse. Never! Mama and Papa would be so upset to know you feel that way. They loved you, Ricci, and only wanted the best for you."

My tears are now falling, despite my best efforts. These two pseudo-sisters of mine, despite being eight and ten years older than me, are my best friends.

"I don't think I'm explaining it right," I say. "I mean, I've had four miscarriages in four years, y'all. I'm obviously defective."

"You've had four miscarriages because of that jackass," Lacie seethes. "Because of what *he* did, not because you're fucking 'defective'."

We stop talking briefly as the waitress brings our food and promises us drink refills. For a few blessed minutes, the table is quiet except for the scraping of our silverware as we begin eating.

After thinking about it for a few minutes, I look at Ivy and state, "Maybe I should see someone to get my head on straight. I know what he's doing is wrong, but then he'll act so contrite and nice, I just push it away. I guess because I'm worried if I leave him then meet someone else down the line, I won't be able to have a baby. At least with Erik, he knows what he's getting. How could I put someone else through it?"

"Each time it's happened, the doctor has said there's no reason why you can't carry a baby to full term," Lacie reminds me. "Now, let's finish up, go grab a test, and find out if you are or are not pregnant again."

———

"Positive," I whisper, looking down at the two pink lines. I'm not sure how Erik will feel about it, but since he won't let me use birth control, and he never uses a condom, it's bound to happen. "I wonder if he'll be happy this time."

Walking out of the bathroom with the test clutched in my hands, I see Ivy and Lacie standing there, both looking concerned. I can't help the tears that start falling as I show them the test and soon find myself wrapped in their arms as they let me sob.

After several minutes, I manage to compose myself somewhat. "Okay, I'll tell him tonight or tomorrow. And, while I know my head is screwed on wrong, if he touches me again in anger, I'll leave."

"That's gonna have to be okay, sweetie," Ivy says. "Now, clean your face so he doesn't know you've been crying."

I grin, even though I can feel my lips trembling. "Same time next week?"

"Absolutely!"

Despite my promise to Ivy and Lacie, it takes me almost a week before I break the news to Erik. Since he lost his most recent job, he's been volatile, spending his days looking for work and his nights drinking. I have the hidden bruises to prove his mood has been downright awful. Not to mention the stuff he viciously spews at me. He berates me for every little thing, from what I wear to how I fold towels. Although I don't hold out a lot of hope that he'll be happy about this news, I still need to make sure all my ducks are in order just in case I need to leave.

With the house spic and span, I hurry to put the finishing touches on dinner, one of his favorites, before he gets home. Even though I suspect he will be upset, I still hold onto a sliver of hope that this time, things will be different.

He wasn't happy to say the least. As I pick myself off the floor where I've laid for God knows how long, I feel the unmistakable wetness between my legs and cringe. Looks like another trip to the emergency room for them to do whatever it is they do when I'm miscarrying. Carefully standing, I wince when I feel how sore my abdomen is and realize that he probably kicked and punched me while I was passed out.

"Bastard," I seethe, slowly walking toward our room. Once inside, I call out, "Erik, I need you to take me to the emergency room. I'm bleeding."

He rolls over, opens one eye and sneers, "Like they really do anything except baby you. Go clean yourself up, Ricci. There's no reason for you to see them, you've been through this before."

Holding back my tears, I gather some clean clothes then head into the bathroom to clean myself up and see what I can figure out to stem the bleeding. At least while I'm holed up in here, I can plan out my next steps, because he broke the final straw. I just have to wait for Erik to leave the apartment for the day, but he always does, so getting away shouldn't be a problem. I just have to be patient.

Despite the pain I'm still in the next day, once Erik finally leaves, I gather what I want from the apartment, including the tip money I've been stashing, and carry it out to my car, a small smile gracing my face when I see it. Papa B was a mechanic and when I was old enough to drive, he found a decent vehicle at the local auction house, bought it, then we worked on it together to fix it up. I honestly thought it was for someone else, so I was definitely surprised on my birthday when he handed me the keys and told me it was mine.

Jubilee is almost twelve now, but she still looks like she just rolled off the assembly line because he and I kept her up when he was still alive, then afterward, I did the same. She's a smaller SUV, with enough room for me and the few things I'm taking. I don't have much; when I moved in with Erik, I had my clothes and a few special mementos that Mama and Papa B had given me over the years, and I haven't added much in the way of knick knacks. Mostly because I did when we first got together, but he broke them whenever he wanted to 'teach me a lesson'. So, it was just easier not to buy myself anything like that, because it just upset me too much every time he would destroy one of my things.

After I have everything loaded up, I take one last look at the hell I've lived in for almost five years now, shrug, then get into the driver's seat. It's time to blow this popsicle stand and start living life. I may be defective like he's told me for years, but at least I'll no longer feel his wrath on my body.

Hours later, I find myself in a small town called Possum Run. The name makes me smile which is why I stopped. Hopefully, I can find someplace to stay while I look for a job. First things first, I need some food so I can take more Tylenol to ease the throbbing pain coursing through my body. I also need to make sure the bleeding has stopped, or at least slowed down.

As I walk into the diner, a harried looking waitress smiles and says, "Just grab a seat, I'll be with you in a few minutes."

Nodding, I make my way back to a booth and gratefully sink into the seat, barely holding back my yelp of pain. If I wasn't so worried about Erik trying to find me, I would go to the hospital, but I think he's right. There's not much they can do for me that I can't do for myself.

The waitress rushes over with a pitcher of water, pours me a glass then asks, "Do you know what you want to drink? I'll give you a few minutes to look over the menu. The special's your best bet, it's filling." Then, looking closer at me, she says, "Honey, you don't look like you feel all that good."

I smile, sipping at my water. "I'll be okay. Just been driving for a few hours is all and I'm tired."

"Well, you just take a break then and I'll be right back to get your order. What did you want to drink?"

"I'll take a Sprite, please," I reply.

"Coming right up."

While she heads to grab my drink, I look over the menu and decide to get the special. Ivy was right, I've got plenty of money so there's no concern about that, but what I never shared with either her or Lacie was I wanted to use the money in the account that Mama and Papa B set up for me on a house of my own, which is why I haven't touched it. I added most of the life insurance from my dead parents to it as well, leaving some in my checking account. Thankfully, Erik isn't on that, because he's irresponsible as hell when it comes to money. He's lost so many jobs over the years and it's never his fault, according to him. However, his family is wealthy, so they give him an allowance which he blows right through.

"Did you decide what you wanted?" the waitress asks, setting my Sprite on the table.

"Yes, please. I'll take a special. Also, do you know if anyone has any job openings?"

"I might, let me think on it. You planning to stay around these parts? It's a quiet little town, but there are a lot of good people here."

"I think I will," I admit, smiling at her.

"Be out shortly with your food," she replies.

While I still don't feel one hundred percent, when Betty offers me a job waitressing for the breakfast shift at the diner, I take it. I mean, technically, I don't have to worry about money per se, but since I have plans for my savings, I need a job. As I drive around the town searching for a place to stay, at least temporarily, a headache nearly stops me in my tracks. Instead of continuing, I turn down a small dirt road thinking I'll just pull over and rest for a bit. When I come across a privacy fence that's had a section knocked down, I pull over and park.

Why? Because there's a huge shed and I can see an open window that's big enough for me to crawl inside. After carefully looking around, I slip out of my car then through the fence, listening for any dogs that might alert the homeowner I'm on their property. Only, there's nothing but silence. Going over to the window, I see it's right next to the door, so I reach in and unlock the door then go inside.

It's huge, with a small kitchen, a working bathroom if the cleaning supplies inside are any indication, and a ton of shelves across one wall with tools hanging up. Well, most of them are, I realize as I move further into the open space. There's a dresser with a really neat tile design on the top, and several things that are apparently in progress because I can't figure out what they are.

"Well, since I'm technically trespassing, I'll just

sweep up as a thank you," I murmur, spotting the huge broom standing in the corner. It takes me no time, but I find myself sweating profusely and realize I might be getting sick.

"Just what I need when I have nowhere to live," I mutter. I go back out to my car to grab the sleeping bag I stopped and bought since I thought I would be living in my car temporarily, as well as some clean clothes and my hygiene bag so I can clean up before work in the morning.

One shower later, I'm lying in my sleeping bag setting my alarm so I can get up in time to get dressed and get to the diner. I've dosed myself up on Tylenol, sent a message to the group chat I have with Ivy and Lacie that I left Erik, and told them once I was settled, I would let them know where I was, then counted my blessings that I found this place. It might only be temporary, but at least I'm safe and warm.

"Shit, shit, shit," I whisper when I make my way into the shed. I've been sneaking in and out for a week now and haven't seen any evidence that someone lives there.

Until tonight. I can smell the varnish or lacquer that was used on the dresser I admired the first night, and several tools are now on the bench that were hanging up when I left. Plus, the coffee pot has been washed and is upside down in the drainer. Looks like I might have to find someplace else to stay. There's a small hotel just outside of town and I think they allow extended stays, so I guess tomorrow after work, I'll head there and see about getting a room.

I still feel like shit, but go through my nightly routine of a shower followed by dosing myself up with Tylenol before I slip into my sleeping bag. While the situation isn't ideal, knowing I have a plan, I fall into a restless, fever-filled sleep.

CHAPTER
TWENTY

MANNY

For the past week, I've noticed evidence of someone staying in the shed. I haven't yet caught them, but so far, nothing's been taken. Still, it upsets me that my space, one I crave after the years spent behind bars, has been invaded. After my shower, I grab a cup of coffee and head out to the shed. I don't have anything on the books at the shop, so I'm taking the day off to see if I can figure out what's going on, maybe even go into town to grab some of those nanny cam things to set up. Opening the doors, the first thing I see is a small figure curled up in a sleeping bag, moaning as if they're in pain.

Dropping my mug, I rush over, my anger at someone breaking into my space gone as I see whoever is inside the sleeping bag is very ill. I hit my knees and brush back the curls that are covering the woman's face, which I deduce from the shape inside the bag. As her face is exposed, my breath catches in my throat.

Despite the fever that has her skin clammy, she's beautiful. A small, button nose, long lashes that frame cheeks covered in a light dusting of freckles, and thick, curly hair. Her hands are clutched over her stomach, which I lightly palpate to see if I can figure out what's going on.

Not like I'm a medic or anything, but years ago, before my life imploded, I had thought about being a paramedic or something, so I took a shit ton of first aid courses to see if it was something I could handle. Unfortunately, prison stopped that career path, but I still remember the basics, at least.

Her eyes don't open, but she moans in pain and curls into a fetal position. "Shhh, girl, I'm going to get you some help," I promise, pulling my phone from my back pocket.

While I wait for the ambulance to arrive, I look around and spot something through the window in the back. "Well, I'll be damned," I whistle out, seeing the small SUV parked behind my fence. I had no clue a section had come down; must've happened during the last storm. I make a mental note to get it fixed, but first, I need to find out who this woman is and why just looking at her makes me feel things I haven't felt in years.

I had the presence of mind to grab her wallet out of her purse which was sitting on the floor next to her sleeping bag, then pull out her driver's license and insurance card, which I gave to one of the paramedics when they arrived. Normally, I would've never gone into a woman's purse, but with her being unconscious, I pushed my guilt aside. Once they got her onto the gurney, the male paramedic wasn't going to let me ride with her, but there was no way I wanted her to be by herself, so I lied and told him she was my fiancée. Granted, when he asked why she was sleeping out in the shed instead of the house, I had to lie again and tell him she had gotten angry at me. He must've understood the quirkiness of women, because he rolled his eyes but let me get in the back of the ambulance.

Now, I'm sitting in the waiting area of the emergency room where a nurse directed me once we arrived. While I wait for her to be examined and for someone to come out and tell me what's going on, I scroll through her phone, which I also grabbed, to see if I can find someone to call. Spotting a group text pulled up, I can see she typed something just the night before, so I quickly input my information and wait for a phone call, unsurprised when my own phone rings within seconds.

"Who are you and why do you have my sister's phone?" a female asks, sounding angry.

"Like my text explained, I'm Manny Alvarez, and I found your sister sleeping in my shed this morning. She's sick or something, so I called 911 and an ambulance brought her to the hospital. Who is this?" I question. "Ivy or Lacie?"

"Ivy. What do you mean, she's sick? What hospital?" she inquires, still sounding slightly angry, but more worried than anything after what I've just said.

"I don't know what's going on with her," I admit. "She was clammy, feverish, and unconscious, but she moaned when I palpated her belly. The only reason I did that was because she was curled in on herself and holding her stomach, so I thought maybe it was her appendix or something."

"The baby," Ivy whispers. "Fuck, I bet that son-of-a-bitch hurt her again," she seethes. "Again, what hospital is she at?"

"Possum Run General," I reply, rage starting to course through me as I finally process the words she spit out. "What do you mean, *again?*" I ask.

I hear a lot of noise on the other end and pull the phone back to make sure we weren't disconnected, then hear, "Okay, sorry, I was getting into my car. Give me a second to pull it up on my GPS then I'll try to explain what I know."

"That's fine," I say. "They won't let me back there with her right now since they're doing an exam."

"She found out about a week or so ago, maybe even two now, give or take, that she was pregnant again."

"She's got kids?" I ask, interrupting her. "I didn't see any kids, though."

"No, and if you'd give me a second to finish without interrupting, I'll try to explain it all."

"Sorry, sorry. I was just worried that maybe there were kids in the car behind my shed," I admit. "I'll wait to ask any questions until you're done, will that work?"

A snort comes through the line, making me chuckle in response. "Yeah, that'll be fine. Sorry, I'm not usually a bitch, I promise. But here's the deal. She's not my sister by blood, but she's still my sister, if that makes sense, and I'm very protective of her. Lacie is too. Our parents were her foster parents and some old biddy who she was related to wouldn't sign off on our folks adopting her. However, she was always treated like one of us kids. Right after Mom and Dad died, when my brother decided to be a dick about the garage apartment Ricci was living in, she said she would move in with her boyfriend, Erik. He's a douche, by the way, and anyone who knows him, knows this for a fact. Anyhow, he hurts her, and so far, he's caused her to have four miscarriages. I bet he wasn't happy to hear she was pregnant again, he beat her, and she ended up having another one."

My blood is beyond boiling right now and my breath is coming out in short gasps as I stand and walk out of the waiting area. "I'm sorry, Ivy, give me a second," I rasp out.

Images of Luci swarm in my mind as tears start leaking down my face. Knowing that the tiny slip of a woman I found this morning has endured what my sister did? Has me wanting to track the asshole down and end him. This time, it would be on purpose, unlike what ended up happening to Turo.

"Take your time. Trust me, my sister and I have been sick with worry since she told us she was expecting again. He's not a nice guy and while I know why Ricci has stayed, she deserves the world."

I clear my throat a few times then say, "When I was a teenager, my sister's boyfriend killed her and my unborn niece."

She gasps then asks, "What did you do?"

"Beat the shit out of him," I reply. "Unfortunately for me, the asshole died from complications, so I spent some time in prison. He wasn't a good guy either, to be honest."

"Well, as much as I want Erik to pay for what he's done to Ricci over the years, I think you need to stay put," Ivy replies. "Because if she was staying on your property, she felt safe."

"I wasn't home at the time she started staying in my workshop," I admit. "In fact, when I got home, I thought things looked neater than how I left them, but I'm so busy, I didn't have time to investigate. Until this morning."

"I should be there in about forty or so minutes depending on how fast I drive. If she... if she wakes up, let her know I'm on my way. I'll call Lacie. Don't let her be alone, Manny," Ivy says, her voice sounding wobbly as if she's trying not to cry.

"I won't," I promise. "Be safe, I'll stay with her until you get here."

CHAPTER
TWENTY-ONE

Ricci

Beep.

"... appears to be suffering from an incomplete miscarriage."

Beep.

"... sign here for surgery, please."

Beep.

"... know why she wasn't seen at a hospital?"

Beep.

"... surgery went well. We're giving her broad-spectrum antibiotics to combat the sepsis."

Beep.

"... in God's hands now."

"Ricci, sweetie, it's time for you to wake up. You're scaring Ivy and Lacie."

"Mama B? What are you doing here? Where am I?" I ask.

"You're in a coma, Button," Papa B replies, coming to stand next to Mama B.

"Why am I here though?" I question. The last thing I remember is taking some Tylenol before crawling into my sleeping bag. "This is a dream, isn't it?"

"Yes and no, sweetie," Mama B says. "You were really sick, but a nice young man found you and got you help. They did surgery and have been giving you strong medicine, so now it's time for you to wake up."

"Surgery? Why did I have surgery?" I can feel my heart pounding and from far away, hear machines going nuts.

Mama B looks at me with tears in her eyes. "Because when you lost the baby, it was what they call an incomplete miscarriage. Some of the tissue was left behind which caused an infection that went septic."

"I'm sorry, I know I've disappointed y'all," I murmur as tears start to fall from my eyes.

"You've never done that, Button," Papa B replies, pulling me in for a hug. "We'll take care of your babies until it's your time, which isn't now. It's time to wake up, Button."

"I don't want to," I whisper. "It's warm and safe here."

"She's crashing!" a voice yells.

"Clear!" another voice yells.

Searing pain courses through me and I feel my body jump.

"Got a rhythm," a third voice states.

As hard as I try, I can't open my eyes, so I slip back into sleep, hoping that the next time I try, I succeed.

A steady, almost soothing noise slowly awakens me to a room that is somewhat dark, with only a light glowing behind me. Glancing to my left, I can see an IV pole and follow the hose down to where the needle is taped to the inside of my arm near my elbow. It's the machine beeping that roused me, apparently, but I don't know when or how I got to the hospital. The last thing I remember is answering a text from Ivy in the group chat.

"H-h-hello?" I rasp out. My throat feels like it's on fire, and my voice sounds as though I gargled with crushed glass.

A warm hand grips mine and I see brown eyes peering down at me. "You're awake," the man says. His voice is husky, as though I woke him up and my immediate response is to apologize. "No, no, it's okay, we've been waiting for you to decide to wake up for several days now."

"We?" I ask.

"Your sisters and me," he replies. "Here, let me get you some water then I'm going to get your nurse."

Scant seconds later, he's holding a straw to my lips, and I sigh in relief as the cool water soothes my parched, aching throat. "Thank you," I tell him once he pulls it away.

"You're welcome. I'll be right back."

Several minutes later, a nurse comes bustling into my room, a big smile on her face. "Well, Sleeping Beauty is apparently all caught up on her rest, isn't she?" she asks, coming to my side. She efficiently takes my vitals then checks the machine that's been steadily beeping. "Looks like you're due for another bag of meds, which I'll grab in a few seconds. How are you feeling? You sure gave your sisters and fiancé quite the scare."

Fiancé? What the hell? Before I can tell her she's mistaken, I see the man shake his head, so I keep my mouth quiet instead. "Am I okay?" I question.

"You were a very sick young lady, that's for sure," the nurse advises, not actually answering my question. "I'll put a call in to your doctor who'll be happy to hear you're awake. I'm sure your sisters will be thrilled as well."

"Thank you."

I'm not sure who the man that's standing next to me is, but I feel safe for some reason, as though he'd fight the devil himself to protect me. Once the nurse leaves with a promise that she'll return shortly with my meds as well as some crackers since I'm starving, I realize I don't know who he is to me.

"What's your name?" I ask after he's sitting in the chair that's pulled right next to my bed.

"Manny. Manny Alvarez. You were sleeping in my workshop," he replies. "Found you almost a week ago now, I think, although the days are kind of hazy."

"I'm sorry. I didn't mean to break in or anything, I was just looking for someplace to sleep," I admit, yawning. "There's no way if I've been out of it for nearly a week that I can be tired," I grouse, making him chuckle.

"Your body went through a lot, Ricci," he softly says. "Did you know you had a miscarriage?"

Tears well up in my eyes at the thought of losing yet another baby. Nodding, I sniffle, unable to control the emotion that wells up. "I figured I did."

"Can you tell me what happened?"

Briefly, I explain the series of events that led to me arriving in Possum Run. "He wouldn't take me to the hospital, said they didn't do anything anyhow, so I

figured I was just coming down with the flu or something because of the stress of the situation."

His own eyes are shiny as he clasps my hand
between his. "No, sweet girl, you didn't have the flu. The
reason doctors want women to be seen if they're having
a miscarriage is so they can examine you to make sure
that all the tissue passes. In your case, you had what
they term an incomplete miscarriage, meaning some of
the tissue was left behind. An infection set in then you
went septic. You nearly died, Ricci."

Closing my eyes, I think of the strange dream I had
about my foster parents. "I dreamt of Mama and Papa
B," I murmur. "They told me I had surgery, and it was
time to wake up, but I didn't know it was real. I just
thought I was imagining things."

"Not sure about your dream, but the rest of it was
real. The doctor did surgery, but yeah, it got scary for a
little bit. Your heart even stopped."

"Did... did they shock me?" I ask, causing his brows
to raise. "I remember while I was sleeping feeling as
though I was electrocuted or something. I can't explain it
right because everything's so blurry."

"Yeah, babe, they had to shock your heart. Never
been so fucking scared in my entire life."

"Ivy, Lacie, y'all need to go back home. I'll be fine," I argue, sitting up in my hospital bed.

"Yeah, no, not happening until they release you," Ivy retorts. "You gave us a damn heart attack, Ricci."

"I'm sorry, but y'all heard the doctor. He said I'm going to be just fine."

"Thanks to Manny finding you," Lacie replies, before tearing up. "If he had been out of town again, or God, not gone into his workshop, you'd have died, Ricci. So, no. We'll be here until they let you go. Speaking of, we've been looking for places around here for you to rent since you said you want to stay in Possum Run."

"I do. I still can't believe that Betty is going to let me come back to work once I'm released by the doctor," I murmur. When I didn't show up for the morning rush, she called my phone and Manny told her I was in the hospital. Her response? Tell her she's got a job when she's better.

"She can stay with me," Manny says. When all three of us look at him, he shrugs. "It's a huge house, plenty of room."

"But we don't even know each other," I hiss, causing him to chuckle.

"So? I'm busy all the time, Ricci, between my wood-working and the tattoo shop. Trust me when I say, there's plenty of room for you in the house. Or, if you'd rather, there's an apartment above the tattoo parlor that you're welcome to rent. You'd be within walking distance of the diner on nice days, and can drive when the weather sucks."

"I... I think I'd like to look at the apartment if that's okay? I mean, I've never lived on my own. I'd like to see if I can make it on my own," I reply.

"Then that's what we'll do once you're released," he says. I think I've disappointed him with my response, but if so, he doesn't show it in his mannerisms, which is a far cry from how Erik would react.

CHAPTER
TWENTY-TWO

MANNY

I won't lie and say I wasn't disappointed when she said she wanted to check out the apartment, because I was. Maybe because all those days spent sitting by her side, I had spun a fanciful story involving the two of us as the stars. But I understand where she's coming from, because I felt the same way after I was released from prison.

Granted the scenarios are totally different in several ways, but she's never been on her own, and I was never left alone during the years I spent in prison. As I take Ivy over to my house so she can gather some more clean clothes for Ricci from her SUV, which I've moved to my driveway, I mentally think about the condition of the apartment.

"Can we swing by where Ricci wants to live before we go back to the hospital?" she asks, breaking through my reverie.

"Sure. I was just thinking of how it looks after the last tenant moved out and what she might need, furniture-wise." And whether or not it needs a good cleaning. I make a mental note to let the woman who cleans the shop know I have an add-on job for her if she wants it.

"We've got stuff we can get here from our parents' house," Ivy suddenly says. "We've kept the house all these years, but the rest of us have our own places, so it's just sitting there. Maybe a new bedroom suite and that kind of stuff, but there's also a really nice set at the house, it just needs new mattresses because they're older than dirt."

I chuckle at her thought process while deciding I like her brashness. "Your sister is lucky she has y'all."

"We're lucky you found her," she replies. "You like her, don't you?" she suddenly asks, switching the subject.

I think about her words then nod. "Yeah, I do. But she doesn't need to get tied to the likes of me, Ivy. I'm an ex-con. Hell, half the town still thinks I deserved what I got, as if what happened to Luci didn't matter."

"Our parents taught us not to judge a book by its

cover, Manny. From what you've told us, you didn't mean for him to die. Now, that being said, it sounds like he was a piece of shit for how he treated not only your sister, but other girls he was involved with before her."

"He was, but Ricci deserves better," I state.

When I first met her sisters, who descended on the hospital as though the hounds of Hell were nipping at their heels, I wasn't sure what to expect. We've spent this past week getting to know each other and because I'm nothing if not above board about my past, I shared what led to me being arrested and imprisoned. It's good to know they aren't concerned about it, because I don't think I can let Ricci slip out of my life. We haven't really talked much, but she's someone I can see building a future with, provided she's willing.

"She deserves someone who's going to let her grieve her lost babies, help her understand she's worth being treated as though she's a queen, and who will protect her with everything they have. I think that someone is you," she says. "She just may need some time, because Erik was her only boyfriend and I can tell you from what she's shared over the years, he was not kind."

"How about we see what happens?"

"This is really nice," Ivy says as she walks around the apartment.

To access it, there's a door in the back of the shop with a flight of stairs that leads to the apartment, which takes up the whole upper portion of the building itself. Once you walk inside, the apartment is one huge room, more of a loft or studio set-up than a traditional one with various rooms. There's a kitchen straight ahead, with a counter that has a ledge for stools to sit beneath it. The cabinets are open-faced, with frosted glass inserts on several of them, something I put in when I converted the space into living quarters. Floor to ceiling windows give the whole area a light, airy feeling. Built-in bookshelves are just inside the door, and I can visualize a small, cozy living room once Ricci has furniture in place. A television mount on the wall immediately inside the door already has the hook up for cable, something that is covered with the rent since I have it for the shop and it's all on one account.

The far corner has a door which opens into an ensuite bathroom, with plenty of shelves, as well as a small closet, for linens and clothes. A small half-wall is the only thing that breaks up the room and I put that in to create the appearance of a bedroom area.

All in all, it's perfect for a single person, plus the added fact that it would be *Ricci* doesn't escape me.

"Thanks. My uncle owns the building and when I got

out, I saw the potential for this space since it was already wired and plumbed. So, between learning how to tattoo and getting assimilated back into society, I worked on converting it into what you see right now," I reply.

"It looks like it's pretty much move-in ready," she murmurs. "Just needs a good cleaning."

"Already going to take care of that," I say. "I have a cleaning lady who takes care of the shop. I'll have her do it."

"Let's go back to the hospital so I can tell Ricci and Lacie, then see what she might want from the house," Ivy suddenly says. "I took some pictures of the space so she can see it."

―――――

"Okay, and what about Mama's pots and pans?" Lacie asks, her pen poised over the pad of paper she whipped out of her purse once the three women began talking about what Ricci was going to need.

"Really?" Ricci questions. "None of y'all want them?"

"Honey, they're literally all just sitting in the cabinets," Ivy replies. "All her baking stuff is there too, and I remember how much you liked cooking with her. Hell, the two of you would bake up a storm whenever it was the holidays. We've got her recipe books too. Whatever you want, Ricci."

I hide my grin because she looks slightly over-whelmed, but she's trying to keep her game face on. While they continue to talk, I work on the finishing touches of the design for one of my newest clients, Sunday Blake. I had to push her appointment back when Ricci went into the hospital, which ended up working out for the both of us, because she had a few changes.

She's a decorated military veteran with some horrific scars she wants covered. After meeting her and seeing the sheer size of the tattoo she needed, I took her ideas and input and have been working on the design ever since, tweaking it after each contact with her and her husband.

Hearing my phone, I stand up and smile at the three women. "I'll step out to grab this," I tell them. "Carry on."

Their snickers follow me out as I hit the accept button. "Hey, man, how's it going?" I ask Jett, Sunday's husband.

"Manny, what you just sent is wicked as hell," he replies, referring to the picture I just snapped then texted to the two of them. "When do you think you can start? We know it's going to take a few sessions."

Looking up at the ceiling, I mentally review my upcoming schedule, then add in the fact that Ricci will likely be discharged in a few days. While she says she's 'ready to get out', the doctor wanted her to build up some strength since she was so sick.

"My calendar's pretty light right now, so you tell me when y'all want to come out and I'll make it happen," I state.

"How's this weekend?" he questions. "No games since we got a bye week, and I wanted to be there."

"Saturday? Maybe around ten? We can take a break for lunch, but I should be able to get the outline done at least."

"Sounds like a plan. See you then," Jett replies before hanging up.

Sliding the phone back into my pocket, I head back into the hospital room only to see all three women clam up. Realizing I likely interrupted a conversation they don't want me to know about, especially seeing as Ricci's face is blood red, I walk over to her and lean down before tucking a stray piece of hair behind her ear.

"Since you're in good hands right now, I'll run out and take care of a few errands I have," I tell her. "Mama is making a pan of enchiladas for y'all and will bring them up in a couple of hours, but I should be back by then. Try to stay out of trouble," I tease.

"Your whole family has gone through too much trouble for me," she says.

When Mama and Aunt Juanita heard about Ricci, they went and picked up a dressing gown along with 'girly' things they insisted she would need. Ricci couldn't believe that they'd do it for a complete stranger, but after I explained that my mother and aunt were forces to be reckoned with and slightly scary to me, she relented a bit.

"Too late to get away now," I reply, grinning at her. "I'll be back, ladies. If there's anything y'all need, just text me."

With that, I walk out of the room, knowing I'm probably the chief topic of conversation. At least, I hope I am.

Because while I know beyond a shadow of a doubt she's got some healing to do, I want to be there when she's ready to take a chance again.

CHAPTER
TWENTY-THREE

Ricci

I look at my sisters after Manny leaves and groan as the two of them burst out laughing. "Shut it," I grumble, picking at the blanket on my lap.

While he and Ivy were gone earlier, Lacie had helped me with a shower, so I am feeling a bit tired, but determined to stay awake as long as possible. But being clean for the first time since waking up, wearing the pretty gown that Manny's mom and aunt bought me, combined with fresh, crisp sheets, has my eyes drooping.

"I think he really likes you," Ivy softly says.

My eyes dart to hers as I slowly shake my head. "I'm broken, Ivy, remember?"

"You're not broken, just slightly bent from the storms

you've weathered," she counters. "I'm not saying you have to jump into something with him this second anyway! Take your time, get to know him and see where it takes you."

I'm about to protest again when Lacie pops in with her two cents. "We've only known him for a few days but already, he's head and shoulders above Erik, Sissy."

I grin at her use of the nickname they bestowed on me all those years ago. My name doesn't really have any derivatives, yet the Billingsleys found pet names to call me; Button and Sissy being two of them.

"Maybe you're right, I don't know," I confess. "But I like it here, like this town, and think it'd be a good idea to take some time to heal before I jump into anything with him or any other guy."

"Can't ask for more than that," Ivy concedes. "Okay, so as far as furniture from the house, this is what I was thinking."

I doze off only to wake up when I smell something absolutely delicious. Opening my eyes, I see a woman I presume is Manny's mother, sitting with my sisters and talking quietly. "Hey," I say while reaching for my water cup.

"Oh, I'm so glad you're awake," the woman says,

coming over to me. "I know you gave my Manny a big scare," she continues as she gently smooths the hair from my face.

"Hello, Mrs. Alvarez," I reply, holding out my hand. "Thank you again for what you and your sister bought for me. Manny brought it up to the hospital and I can definitely say, the gown is very soft and comfortable."

"None of that, sweetheart. Mrs. Alvarez is my mother-in-law, God rest her soul. You can call me Mama or Evangeline."

"Then you'd have a Mama A in your life," Ivy teases.

Evangeline turns to her with a puzzled look on her face. "What do you mean?"

"She called our mom 'Mama B'," Lacie replies. "You could be Mama A."

I can't help giggling as I retort, "As long as I don't have twenty-four more 'Mamas' in my life, that should be just fine."

His mother starts laughing before she walks over to the rolling table. "Let's get some food in you, you're too skinny, Ricci. I brought my enchiladas because Manny said you had no restrictions as far as what you could eat."

Raising my bed so I'm sitting up, I nod. "I don't. The doctor's just keeping me now to make sure I regain some of my strength or something."

She turns and her face is solemn when she says, "I

don't think you truly understand just how sick you were, Ricci. But when my Manny told me about you, I prayed to the Virgin Mother you'd get well."

Not sure how to respond, I simply shrug. "I just thought I was coming down with the flu or something. I mean, I knew I had miscarried, of course, but I honestly didn't know things could go so bad."

I watch her bring me a plate piled high with food and know I'll likely only eat a portion of it. She sets it down on the rolling tray next to my bed then adjusts everything so it's right in front of me. Lightly touching my cheek, she smiles. "Well, I thank God he found you. I believe life is going to be different for you."

Taking my fork, I put a bite of the enchilada in my mouth and moan as the flavors burst across my tongue. "This is delicious," I mumble.

Ivy grins at me while chewing her own food and says, "Don't talk with your mouth full."

"Says the pot to the kettle," Lacie retorts.

"Girls let's eat and then we'll figure out how to get the apartment set up for Ricci," Mama A decrees, grinning at my sisters.

I gaze around the 'apartment' in awe at what my sisters, Manny, and even his family, managed to accomplish in just a few short days. While I was lazing around the hospital, eating their food that was supplemented by what Evangeline brought up every day, Ivy and Lacie went with Manny's uncle, Jorge, and his brothers, Diego and Matias, and they brought back the furnishings from the house I grew up in. Not only that, but my sisters bought a new mattress and box spring for the bed, so even though the items are older, the bed itself is 'brand new', as are the linens and bedding, since Ivy *did* let me borrow her iPad and I ordered what I wanted, and had it delivered to the tattoo shop per Manny's instructions.

My new home positively gleams; the windows sparkle and the hardwood floor looks so shiny, I briefly worry about slipping and sliding. As I wander around looking at all the little touches my sisters added, I can hear Mama A and Ivy in the kitchen area as they pull out the trays of food Mama A and Manny's Aunt Juanita brought over as a housewarming.

"Do you like it?" Manny asks, coming up to stand beside me.

"It's beautiful," I whisper, staring up at the man who literally saved my life. "If I haven't said it already, thank you for everything, Manny."

"You're more than welcome. I have to run downstairs since I have a client in my chair who's taking a break. I just wanted to be sure y'all got settled okay," he replies, grinning down at me.

"Maybe one day I can see what you do?" I question.

"Absolutely."

With that, he turns, and I find myself momentarily alone, so I walk into my new bathroom to check it out.

Hours later, the food is gone, everyone has left, and I'm getting ready for bed. When I let Betty know I was finally home, she told me to take the next week or so before I came back to work. So, I'll use my time exploring my new town.

And maybe getting to know the man responsible for all the good in my life a little bit better.

CHAPTER
TWENTY-FOUR

MANNY

"Oh, Manny, I love it!" Sunday exclaims as she turns from the mirror.

It's been six weeks since the weekend that Ricci came home from the hospital and I started Sunday's tattoo. Today's session was to start the shading and color work, which came out well.

"Should just be one more session once that heals," I tell her, cleaning up my workstation. "We'll go over any areas that need it, maybe darken a few of the lines."

"Looks good, man," Jett says, handing me his credit card. When I shake my head he asks, "Why?"

"Because she's a veteran. She served our country

honorably and got those scars fighting to help others be free," I reply. When he attempts to protest, I raise my brow and say, "I do it for anyone who has scars, Jett. It's my way of giving back since I couldn't go into the military."

Left unsaid is why I couldn't go in; they both are aware of my history.

"Then we'll make a donation to the charity of your choice," Sunday announces.

I nod; this is more than okay with me. "There's a shelter called Helping Hands that works with women trying to get out of domestic abuse situations. I'm sure they can use the help."

My family and I donate our time and money there as a tribute to Luci. If there had been something available like Helping Hands when she found herself being physically abused by Turo, maybe she'd still be alive.

"That's what we'll do. Didn't know there was anything like that around here," Jett muses.

"It opened about six years ago, I think," I reply, now spraying off my chair since all my supplies are put up and my gun has been cleaned while we've been talking. "Let's go schedule the next appointment."

I felt my phone buzzing while I was getting Sunday squared away but I waited until they walked out the door to check, only to see a text from Ricci.

> Ricci: Betty wanted to know if you would like me to bring you today's special? It's meatloaf, mashed potatoes, and green beans.

> Me: That would be great.

> Ricci: See you soon.

She's settled in Possum Run like she has always been part of the community. While I don't want to examine why that makes me happy too closely, I'm glad.

Hearing the door chime, I look up since I'm not expecting anyone else today, only to see my former girlfriend walk in. "Hey, Manny," she says, smiling at me.

"Leanna. Is there something I can help you with?" I question.

While I was initially bitter that she hadn't stayed by my side while I was in prison, I let that go during a visit with Uncle Jorge. He told me that she wasn't the kind of woman who had staying power. When I asked him what he meant, he told me how when he and my aunt first got together, she had a cancer scare and ended up having a complete hysterectomy, which meant the children they wanted were impossible. She tried to divorce him, but he buckled down and told her he married her for *her*, not for the children they could've possibly had. Said that it took a few counseling sessions, lots of tears, and finally she accepted that he wasn't leaving her until he drew his last breath. Then, they adopted a set of twins, my cousins, Petrina and Gabriella.

"I'm home, Manny," she replies. "I wanted to see if maybe we could start over?"

I snort. "Start over? What's changed, Leanna? I'm an ex-con now, found guilty of manslaughter, remember?" I sneer. "You didn't want any part of that, if I'm not mistaken."

A flash of guilt crosses her face before her lips tremble slightly. "I was wrong," she murmurs, reaching out to place her hand on my arm. I barely resist the urge to shrug her off which is when Ricci walks into the shop.

Her face falls slightly before she shakes her head and pastes a fake as hell smile on and says, "Got your lunch, Manny." Handing me the bag, she starts to walk toward the back to head up to her apartment.

"Who's this?" Leanna asks, her voice sounding snotty as fuck.

"My tenant," I reply, keeping my voice even. "Thanks," I say, nodding at Ricci.

I remember how jealous Leanna was when we were growing up, and seeing the sneer on her face lets me know she hasn't grown out of that at all. I refuse to give her any ammunition to hurt Ricci, who is already showing how much she's healed from her past in the little things she says and does.

"You're welcome," Ricci replies. "Y'all have a good day."

After she leaves, with me unconsciously giving away my feelings since I stare at her the whole way, I turn to Leanna. Now, she's got a calculating look on her face as she smirks at me. "Looks like she's more than your *tenant*, Manny."

"Not your business," I bite out. "Now, unless you're here to book an appointment for a tattoo, there's nothing else we have to talk about."

"I want to try again," she insists. "We were good together, don't you remember?"

Sighing, I look at the ceiling before my gaze returns to her. "We were kids, Leanna. What I remember is a girl who didn't want to stand by her boyfriend when he got arrested. I also recall how said girl got jealous every single time I so much as talked to another female. Not only that, but you didn't like the fact that my family and I are close and resented the time I spent with them, or playing sports."

"I've changed," she retorts.

"How so? Rumor has it that you caused your ex-husband to be reprimanded and nearly lose his job because of your actions," I state. At her shocked expression, I nod. "Yeah, the whole town knows what you did.

And while you might not have matured, I had no choice in the matter. I've got a good life now and there's no room for you, so please leave."

She glares at me then says, "You'll regret that, Manny."

"I sincerely doubt it. Now get out of my shop."

Once the shop is locked up for the night, I grab my bag of food and head upstairs before knocking on Ricci's door. When she opens it, I don't miss the surprise on her face. Holding my food up, I say, "Thought maybe we could eat together then walk down for some ice cream or something."

I've been slowly getting to know her. I say slowly because I know what my end game is, but want her to realize she's got options of her own. I don't want her turning to me simply because she thinks it's what she needs to do. So, several times a week, I'll pop up with food and we'll watch a movie.

"I'd like that," she shyly says, opening the door wider and letting me in. "I just pulled my food out and put it on a plate. Here, give me yours and I'll get you set up."

I grin because when it's just me, I eat out of the styrofoam container, but when I come upstairs, Ricci insists on using real plates and silverware. "I'll grab us some drinks."

"Sounds good to me. How was work today?"

While she plates my food and carries it over to the counter, I tell her about Sunday's tattoo, as well as Helping Hands. She sits down across from me and starts peppering me with questions.

"Do you know what kind of things they accept for donations?" she questions, while seasoning her mashed potatoes. I grin, then take the salt and pepper from her to do the same.

"Pretty much any kind of household item, since they assist the women in finding new places to live again and they're starting over from scratch. Money, of course. Gently used clothing, furniture, old cars."

"Old cars? Why?" she asks.

"If the vehicle is still in running condition, they go over it carefully then sell it to the woman for a few hundred dollars. If it's inoperable, they sell it to a junk-yard that gives them book value for the car, then they use those funds for the residents who are there at the time."

"I wonder if Ivy, Lacie, and Stanley would be willing to donate what's left at the house," she muses. "Or maybe, we could do an estate sale and just give Helping Hands the money instead."

"Something to ask them about, that's for sure. I'm

working at the house tomorrow, would you like to come out and see what I'm working on now?"

She smiles and nods. "Yes! Did you ever sell that dresser with the tile on top?"

I start laughing at her excitement. "Yeah, I did. It seems as soon as I post a finished item on my website, I find a buyer."

"I can see why. You're very talented. Just look at the things you created for this place."

"Even though he was gone by the time I got out, I used the cabinets me and my granddad made in here. They were sitting in the workshop collecting dust, so I figured why not?" I tell her.

"They're a great addition, that's for sure. Do you want more water?"

I look down at my glass and realize I've finished the whole thing while we've been eating and talking. "Yeah, but I'll grab it," I insist, standing and heading to the refrigerator with my glass in hand.

***

"You like living here?" I ask as we walk back from the ice cream shop.

Watching her try to choose from all the flavors was definitely a treat; she was like a kid in a candy shop. Or, in our case, an ice cream parlor. She finally got Dutch chocolate in a waffle cone, complete with sprinkles. Watching her eat it is an exercise in control for me, however, since the sprinkles keep clinging to her lips.

Lips I'd love nothing more than to kiss.

She takes another lick of her cone before glancing up at me. "I really do. I mean, I never thought I'd enjoy living 'in town' so to speak, but literally everything is within walking distance. So, great exercise, plus I've met so many people. I really lucked up the day I stopped here for something to eat."

"What made you stop?" I ask, curiosity over-whelming me.

"Believe it or not, I liked the name of the town," she says, shrugging. "Did you grab any napkins?"

I hand her several then watch as she wraps one around the cone that's starting to drip down onto her hand. "May need to eat that a bit faster, Ricci," I tease.

"I just want to savor it, Manny," she replies, licking around the edge where the ice cream seems to be melting the fastest.

"It's not like we can't get ice cream again."

"This is true," she muses before quickly finishing off the rest of her cone. "Great, now my hands are all sticky."

I can't help the laughter that bursts out at her disgruntled face. "Come on, Princess, let's get you home so you can wash your hands."

"Thank you, kind sir," she retorts, grinning.

I leave her with the admonishment to be sure and lock up, as well as the promise that I'll pick her up around nine. When she tries to protest that she can drive herself, I decide to give her that out.

For now.

CHAPTER
TWENTY-FIVE

RICCI

After Manny leaves, I take a shower, once again luxuriating in my bathroom. Freshly clean, I grab my phone and call Ivy.

"Hey, girl, I was just thinking about you," she says as I prop myself up against my headboard. "How was your day?"

"It wasn't all that bad, but I saw something today and don't know what to make of it," I admit.

"What did you see?" she asks.

"Okay, so I'll go back to it, but first of all, I think I finally saw Manny's ex. She was in the tattoo shop when I stopped in to drop off some food for him. But earlier today, during the breakfast rush, she was in the diner with a teenage girl."

"And?" Ivy prods, her voice sounding impatient now.

"Ive, she looks just like Manny," I whisper. "As well as several of his nieces."

The day I came home to my apartment, it was overrun with Manny's family, including several nieces and nephews. While I was slightly overwhelmed, once his mom realized there were too many people, she slowly but surely got them to leave until it was just her, Manny, and my sisters toward the end.

"Do you think it's his?" Ivy questions. "Wasn't she married to someone else?"

"She was, yes, and they're divorced now, but the girl would be the right age if it was Manny's," I insist, quickly doing the math in my head. "She's a dead ringer for his one cousin, Maribelle."

"Shit, what are you going to do?"

I stop and consider what she's asking me. On one hand, if the girl I saw *is* his, he deserves to know. On the other, if it's his daughter, would I be pushing him back to his ex? I express my concerns to Ivy who starts laughing.

"Why are you laughing like a damn hyena?" I grouse. "There's nothing funny about this at all! His family has been through enough with losing his sister and unborn niece. I mean, his mom is one of the strongest people I've ever met in my life because if I had lost a child the way she did, I'd be curled in a corner unable to function."

"You did, sweetie," she softly says, bringing me up short. "Your babies were killed due to domestic violence, just like his sister and niece were. The only difference is you hadn't met your babies yet."

A lone tear trickles down my face as I think about what she's just said. Not a day goes by that I don't wonder about my babies; what they would've looked like, if they would've been boys or girls, how I would've been as a mom.

Before I can reply, she continues. "You'd have been the best mom, Ricci. You had our mom as a guide, remember? I suspect you'd be one of those 'Earth moms', getting your hands dirty as you taught them how to cook and bake, or craft."

"You give me a lot of credit, Ivy," I reply.

"I just give you the credit you deserve. Now, as to what you saw this morning, I think you should tell Manny what you saw. Let him make his own decisions as to how he wants to handle it. I know you really like him."

"I do, but you don't think it's too soon?"

She snorts which makes me giggle. "Not at all, sweetie. It's been a few months now since you left that asshole. You deserve someone who'll treat you the way Papa treated Mama."

"He already does," I murmur, thinking of all the little things Manny has done for me these past few weeks since I came home. When he goes to the store, he picks up things he thinks I'll like. He helped me change the oil in my SUV two weeks ago; we went out to his property and since he saw I knew what I was doing, he let me do it. Then, took my vehicle in and got it detailed before he filled up the gas tank.

All things that Papa B used to do for Mama B. Small things that on the outside looking in, probably wouldn't seem to be all that much. But for me, they show he cares. Even if it's only as a friend, I can live with that right now.

"Good. Now, tell me something funny that happened at work," she demands.

I immediately launch into yet another 'Betty's Diner' story, which soon has both of us laughing our asses off. It seems that Possum Run has its fair share of characters, and with football season in full swing, some of the locals get a bit hot under the collar about what the coach 'should be doing' which usually ends up with shouting matches across the diner. Betty says it's all in good fun, but I'm not too sure sometimes.

"I need to run, Ivy. I'll tell him this weekend about the teenager," I promise. "Love you."

"Love you too, Ricci."

"Manny, I have something to tell you, but I'm not sure how you're going to take it," I say.

We're in the workshop, the two barn doors open wide to allow the fresh air inside, while he sands several pieces he claims will eventually be a huge farmhouse table. I've already put all the tools where they belong, which had him grinning, then washed the coffee pot and mug before putting on a fresh pot for him.

"Just tell me, Ricci. You never have to worry about telling me anything. I might get upset or angry, but it won't be at you, understand?" he replies, glancing over at me.

Taking a deep breath, I begin talking and by the time I've finished, he's got his head in his hands and he's shaking. Whether it's in anger or distress, I can't say for sure, until he bolts off of his feet and says, "It would be just like that crazy bitch to do something like that!"

Pulling out my phone, I open up my pictures and swipe over to the ones I took of Leanna and the girl. "Here, I managed to sneak these," I tell him, handing my phone to him.

His indrawn breath has me glancing worriedly at his face only to see it's nearly ashen while his eyes appear glassy. "She looks just like Luci," he whispers, his finger caressing my phone screen. "Dead ringer."

"Are you okay?" I ask after several minutes of silence. "Should I go home?" Not that I can on my own since he picked me up, but maybe he needs to be by himself right now.

"No," he replies. "But I will be. Can you hold down the fort here for a little bit? I want to see what I can figure out and the only way I know how to do that is to find Leanna."

"Sure. Do you need me to do anything in the house?" I question.

He scoffs then grins. "And take away Gabriella's way to make money?"

"You're a good uncle, Manny," I reply. He gives his nieces and nephews who are old enough 'jobs' either at the tattoo shop or out at his house. For the boys, it's restocking shelves, cutting grass, and all the manual labor stuff. For the girls, it's cleaning his house and the shop, and grocery shopping, which he says he hates to do. Although he *does* pick things up for me, so there's that to consider.

"I want them to have what we didn't have growing up. Not that Mama and Papa didn't provide, but there were a lot of mouths to feed, so we all had something we did to help out. Luci babysat, I ran errands. Easy shit, but with all of us in better positions than we were growing up, it makes all of us feel good that we can do it for the kids, you know what I mean?"

"I understand. I earned an allowance when I was growing up too, but they also let me take on part-time jobs. I babysat, walked dogs, cleaned houses, and mowed lawns before I went to work at the little corner store."

He stops his pacing and stares at me. "You worked in a convenience store?" His tone is full of horror, and I understand where he's coming from.

"No, it was more of a mom-and-pop kind of catch-all store. There was a section with local produce from the farmers, and canned jellies, even venison jerky. They had basic stuff, of course, like eggs, bread, and milk, that sort of thing, but you couldn't do a full grocery shop. They didn't sell beer either. Just sodas and juices."

"I understand now," he replies. "I was picturing a gas station or something along those lines, and that's definitely not the kind of job a teenage girl should have."

I giggle at his words because he sounds a bit... sexist right now if I'm being truthful. Only, that's not his personality by any means.

"No, there's no way Papa B would've allowed me to do that," I tell him. "Now, since I don't need to do anything in the house, can I see about creating something out here?"

He's got a pile of scrap wood, along with bits of tile, and I've been toying with making some of those cutesy signs I've seen online for my bathroom, as well as the laundry room area.

"Help yourself, Ricci. I'll be back as soon as possible. You've got your phone, right?" he asks.

"Right here," I reply, patting my pocket.

"Good. Just be aware of your surroundings."

"Always am."

Humming to myself, I sit back and look at what I just made. I traced the word 'Laundry' on a decent-sized board and then glued pieces of tile into the word. Now I just need to paint around it, then figure out what Manny used to fill in the cracks. Hearing a noise, I turn and nearly pass out, seeing Erik standing in the doorway.

"W-what are you doing here?" I ask, backing up slightly as he moves forward, anger marring his face.

"Took me some time to find out where you went," he seethes, his hands clenched in fists. "If the pretty little bank teller hadn't asked me if I was joining my girlfriend in Possum Run, I would still be looking."

"Why do you care?" I question. "You were cheating on me, you hurt me constantly. Hell, your treatment of me killed my babies, Erik! I'd think you'd be happy I left."

"Look at how brave you are," he sneers. "You've turned into a mouthy little bitch, haven't you?"

"No, I just finally realized my worth," I taunt. I might be scared to death right now, but I refuse to allow him to see my fear.

He lashes out and I feel his fist connect with my cheek. While I was busy talking, I failed to realize he had moved closer. It's a mistake I won't make again.

Provided I survive.

Despite my best efforts, I'm flat on my back as Erik's fists rain down on my aching body. Regardless, I continue to scratch and bite at him, determined to hurt him if possible. But I'm running out of steam since I'm smaller and weaker than him and I feel sadness wash over me at the thought that Manny might very well find my dead body in a place he enjoys so much.

And then... I hear sirens which gives me a burst of adrenaline. Grunting, I thrust my hips upward, catching him off balance which allows me to roll away.

"Help!" I scream as I hear doors open and feet pounding on the ground. "Please, help me!"

"Police! Put your hands up!" a male officer yells as he breaches the doors. Another officer runs toward me as tears steadily pour down my face. I watch as Erik is handcuffed then see the first officer touch the mic on his shoulder to notify EMS the scene is secured.

As the paramedics run through the grass toward the workshop, the gurney between them, I see Manny overtaking them. He reaches my side and hits his knees. "Thank God I put cameras in here," he murmurs, his eyes taking in my bloody and bruised face and body.

"Y-y-you did?" I stammer as the paramedics get me moved to the gurney and start checking me over.

"Yeah, wanted to make sure I had nobody trying to break in again," he teases as his hand grips mine.

Once they have an IV started, we start the process across the yard, Manny never letting my hand go. As I'm loaded into the ambulance, I see Erik being put into the back of a squad car and smile.

"What's that smile for, Ricci?" Manny asks as the doors of the ambulance are closed and we start pulling away.

"I fought back. For the first time in my life, I fought back," I murmur, my eyes never leaving his. "Thanks to you, I found something worth fighting for again."

CHAPTER
TWENTY-SIX

MANNY

Once again, I'm reaching out to Ivy and Lacie. Once again, it's because Ricci is hurt. Only this time, her injuries are far less serious than when I had to contact them the first time. As I wait for the doctor to finish his exam, I think about what I found out earlier in the day.

When Leanna came back to town, she moved into her parents' house, which is in the ritzier section of town, if there is such a thing in Possum Run, that is. I rang the doorbell and when it opened, I came face-to-face with a young girl who so closely resembles Luci I nearly passed out. The look on Leanna's face was priceless, however, when she came to see who was at the door.

*"Marisol, who's... what are you doing here, Manny?"
Leanna asked, arching her brow at me.*

*"Looks like someone's got some explaining to do," I
answered, my voice taut with anger.*

*"I'm not sure what you're talking about," Leanna
sneered. "Marisol, why don't you go check to see if the
water is boiling."*

*As the teenage girl walked away, I glared at Leanna
before I said, "She looks just like Luci. Do you mean to tell
me you hid the fact you were pregnant from me all these
years?"*

She scoffed. "As if, she's my ex's daughter."

*"Unless your ex is related to my family in some way,
fashion, or form, I highly doubt it," I rebutted.*

*Finally, her bravado crumbled. "Look, Manny, isn't it
better for her not to know her father is an ex-con?"*

*"It's better if she knows the truth, Leanna. You know
damn well secrets never stay hidden. What are you going
to do then when she figures out the truth? My nieces are
dead ringers for her. I can't believe what you've done!"*

*"Mom? Is... is he my father?" the girl, Marisol, asked,
having come back unnoticed. While she waits for her
mother's response, she stares at me. "Mom?"*

"We'll discuss this later, Marisol," Leanna snapped.

*"No, Mom, we need to talk about it now. I've met two
girls at school, and we look alike."*

I raised my brow at Leanna. "See? Secrets, Leanna.

They always come to light." Then, looking at Marisol, I said, "I suspect they're your cousins, my brother's daughters."

"What are you going to do?" Leanna questioned, a look of fear briefly crossing her face.

"First of all, I'm going to confirm what I can actually see. Then, I'm getting my lawyer involved," I retorted. Looking at the teenager, I simply said, "I never knew you existed before today, but believe me, if I had known, I'd have been in your life."

Then, I walked down the steps so I could pick up some food for Ricci and me.

While I waited on the food, I got a notification from the camera system I installed in the workshop. Opening it up, I bellowed in rage seeing someone attacking Ricci. As Betty hurriedly bagged up our food, I called the police and broke every speed limit law getting back to my house.

"How is she?" Lacie asks, coming over to me with Ivy.

"Waiting on the doctor," I reply, standing to pull both women into a hug. "She fought back, y'all," I tell them once we sit back down.

Pulling up my phone, I start the video from the beginning, keeping the volume low so we don't disturb anyone else in the waiting room. I can see tears flowing down the cheeks of both women as they watch Ricci fend off her attacker, then growl out in anger when Ivy says, "How did he find her again?"

"Stupid fucking bank teller," Lacie retorts, once the audio plays. "Well, hope she's got someone to pay her bills because by the time I'm done, she's going to be looking for another fucking job."

I grin at Lacie's ferocity. "Need me to send you the video?"

"Absolutely."

Once they decide to admit Ricci for observation, we're allowed to see her. Several of the lacerations required stitches, and she's got a slight concussion, but considering it could've been so much worse, I find myself saying a silent prayer in thanks.

"Manny?" Ricci asks, reaching her hand out for me.

Walking to her side, I take her smaller hand in mine and lean in to kiss her forehead. "You okay, sweetheart?" I question.

"They gave me some good stuff," she teases, slightly slurring her words.

"Sounds like it," I reply, grinning down at her. I note her pupils are dilated which is due more to the medication than the concussion. "Do you want me to get you anything from your place?"

WHISPERS OF LOVE

"Did the cops talk to you?" Ivy asks.

"Yeah, they just left before y'all came in," she replies. "I told them I wanted to press charges this time." Then she looks at me and softly says, "Not just for me, but for Luci. All women should be safe."

"Men too," Lacie adds. "Although, typically, it's women who are abused, I know men are as well."

"Hopefully, he'll see some actual jail time," Ivy murmurs. "He tends to get away with stuff all the time."

"The cops said he probably would," Ricci says, now sounding sleepy. "Said you had it all on video and they were going to ask you to send them a copy or something like that."

"We'll run to your place and get some stuff together, then come back tomorrow," Ivy states. "Manny, are you staying with her?"

"Absolutely."

By now, she's drifted off to sleep, so once Ivy and Lacie leave, I send a text to my mom and ask her if someone can bring us some decent food before I settle into the reclining chair next to her bed and doze off.

Hours later, after my mom has descended with enough food to feed an army, despite it being just the two of us, we're awake talking. I decide to take the bull by the

277

horns and tell her how I feel, what I want, and who I want it with—her.

"Ricci?"

"Hmm?" She turns her head to look at me and smiles. "What has you thinking so hard over there, Manny? I know you heard your mom tell you that your brothers went and cleaned all the blood out of the workshop then locked it up for you."

"It's not that, sweetheart," I reply, clearing my throat. "I know things are up in the air where Marisol is concerned, but I want you to know I'd like a chance with you."

"Me? But... but I'm still broken, Manny," she murmurs.

Reaching out, I take her hand in mine and lace our fingers together, never letting my gaze drop from hers. "We've discussed this before. You're just a little bent, never broken, and today proved that better than anything anyone could tell you."

"How so?"

"Because you fought back, Ricci. For whatever reason, you didn't give up. I overheard nurses in the hallway talking about the man they treated who had deep scratch marks as well as bites all over his upper torso. *You* did that, honey. No one else. Not Ivy, Lacie, or hell, even me. You."

She shrugs so I decide to continue. She needs to start

seeing herself the way I do, the way her sisters do. "I've met truly broken people, Ricci, during my time volunteering at Helping Hands. Oh, they go through the motions of physically healing, but they have no fire, no life behind their expression any longer. Hopefully, they'll continue with therapy so they learn differently, otherwise they'll find themselves in the same position they were in before they arrived. In the time since our first meeting, you've recovered from nearly dying, moved into your own place, found a job you enjoy, started online therapy sessions, and have started making friends, including me."

I watch her face, her beautiful, expressive face, as she ponders everything I've just said, and my smile grows bigger as I watch her entire body change. She's now sitting up straighter, there's a clarity to her eyes that wasn't there moments before, and she's smiling as she turns to me.

"I think... I think you're right," she finally says. "My therapist and I have been working on my past, which is where I think I started believing the shit I heard in so many different foster homes."

"What did you hear?" I ask, growing angry that a mere child would believe what some assholes would say about her.

"That I was a troubled kid, I was defective. Hell, you name it, and I probably heard it about myself," she murmurs, lost in thought again. "But when I went to live with Mama and Papa B, everything changed. No matter how badly I behaved, they never gave up on me. So, what I thought I knew about myself changed and I stuffed those things away. Then after they died and I went to live with Erik, he changed in how he treated me so slowly, I didn't realize it was happening."

"Like a frog in boiling water," I state.

"What do you mean?" she asks.

"If a frog is put into a boiling pot of water, it'll do whatever it can to flee, right?" At her nod, I continue. "But if they're put in a pot of regular water and the heat is slowly increased, by the time they realize there's any danger, it's too late. Erik was probably nice in the beginning, wasn't he?"

God, it galls me to even say his name, but I want her to grasp my meaning, so I suck it back and wait for her to respond.

"He was, actually. Took me out on the town, brought me flowers when he came home from work, treated me like I was important. Then, it slowly changed," she muses, "The compliments stopped, and the accusations started. I felt like I was getting whiplash because one day, the way I folded towels was the 'right' way, and the next time I did them, they were wrong and needed to be done again."

I squeeze her hand to keep her with me, instead of

lost in a past that no longer bears weight on anything she does, except maybe in her mind. "Sweetheart, however you can fold the fucking things so I don't have to? I'm good, I promise."

Her giggle has me grinning at her, happy to see the sparkle in her eye. Despite the bruising and swelling, she's the most beautiful woman I've ever seen. But it's more than her outward appearance; she's genuinely kind to everyone she meets. Betty told me earlier in the day how the customers almost fight to sit in Ricci's section now because she'll listen to their jokes and even come back with her own.

"So, laundry isn't your thing," she teases. "Duly noted."

"Growing up, the boys had certain chores while the girls did others," I reply. "My sisters were responsible for the laundry and ironing. Us boys handled the outside stuff for the most part."

"Mama and Papa B let me learn and do whatever crossed my mind," she says. "It's why I know so much about fixing cars. I helped Papa B get mine 'road worthy' as he called it. But I also played softball, learned how to play the piano and dance, and also how to cook and bake."

"Well rounded, I like it," I drawl out. "You're the perfect woman for me."

She rolls her eyes at me, and I burst into laughter.

"Whatever. So, you think you want to take a chance with me? I mean, I don't even know if I can have children and from the look of things, your family is rather prolific."

"Ivy and Lacie both told me that every doctor who you saw after your other miscarriages advised you that there should be no problem at all with you carrying to term. But saying that, if we can't have kids, we'll do what my uncle and aunt did, we'll adopt."

"Your cousins are adopted?" she asks.

"Yep."

"I would've never known."

"They're family, sweetheart. Now, saying that, we should probably get more sleep because I'm sure your sisters will be descending on us as soon as they're allowed to do so tomorrow morning."

"Good night, Manny," she says, trying to pull her hand away from mine.

I hold on tighter, even though I know my arm will probably go numb at the position and reply, "Good night, Ricci."

CHAPTER
TWENTY-SEVEN

RICCI

"Stop laughing, Ivy, and help me figure out what to wear!" I grumble, glaring at her through our FaceTime call. "He's going to be here soon."

She sticks her tongue out at me then replies, "In about three hours, you goose."

Sighing, I flop down onto the bed and groan. "I *know* but gah, I'm so darned nervous!"

It's been a week and a half since I got out of the hospital for a second time since coming to live in Possum Run and tonight is our first 'real' date. The only reason I'm defining it like that is because as Ivy so astutely reminded me a few minutes earlier when I was in a full-blown panic about what to wear, he's seen me at my worst already. Plus, since the first hospital stay, we've actually spent a lot of time hanging out. But, like I reminded her, that's different than a date, although... Ivy's voice breaks into my thoughts and I focus once again on her.

"You're thinking too hard, Ricci," she says. "Really, you are. The man has been taken with you since the first time I met him. He barely left your side, remember? Not only that, but you yourself have told me and Lacie both how often y'all do stuff together. This isn't really any different, sweetie. The only difference is that this time, you've labeled it as a date."

I consider what she's just said. He has seen me in everything from a hospital gown to my work uniform to jeans and a T-shirt. I've been beaten to hell and back, worn no makeup, had my makeup virtually melted off because of the heat, and been fresh from the shower. My hair's been a tangled, bloody mess, a sweaty, fevered mess, and clean. Yet regardless of the countless ways I've been in his presence, he always treats me the same.

As though he *wants* me there.

"Keep talking, you're getting through," I whisper before sticking my tongue out at her.

"It's about time, you're under three hours now," she teases. "Did he say where y'all were going?"

"Yes. Possum Run has an annual festival and it's in

town. They've got rides, food, and even animals! Oh, and games of course."

"Alright. Wear your new jeans, the cute ones that have the fabric behind the holes, plus the red shirt with those rhinestones. You'll be easy to spot in a crowd because the lights will make you all sparkly. You should probably either wear your hair in a high ponytail or maybe even braid it, although your braids are usually uneven. Dammit. Okay, I'm on my way so I can French braid your hair for you," she declares. "Be there shortly."

"Fine, Miss Bossy McBosserson," I retort, grinning at her. "I'll go and take my shower and get dressed. Just use your key."

I've got my license and debit card tucked into my back pocket, some money shoved into the front, and am playing with my phone while I wait for Manny to arrive. Even though Manny sold the dresser that was in the workshop when I came to town shortly after finishing it, he hadn't had a chance to deliver it until now. Between finishing Sunday's tattoo, taking care of me after my first hospital stay and now this assault, then getting me moved into my new apartment, he has been a busy man, so today, he went to deliver it to the new owner. Ivy just left with instructions 'not to do anything she wouldn't do' and to call her in the morning, so now I'm sitting patiently.

Or maybe not.

Because even though I wasn't sure initially I wanted to ever get involved with a man again, Manny's had my attention from the beginning. He's hardworking, committed to his family, and despite the way so many in town still treat him, he doesn't lash back at them. When I asked him why he didn't put them in their place, he told me they only knew the rumors of what happened, so what they thought didn't matter.

A knock on my door has me smiling as I glance around my apartment while heading in that direction. Because he's fussed at me before for just opening the door, once I get there, I call out, "Who is it?"

"Some tattooed stranger who wants to take you for a ride," his voice teases through the wood. "It's me, sweetheart. You ready to go?"

Opening the door, I smile up at him and say, "Yeah, just need to grab my keys." With that, I snag my keychain that hangs on the rack just inside the door, handing them to him so he can lock up the apartment. Then, he takes my hand in his and we walk back down together then out through the back to his truck.

Which, I might add, he's had detailed since earlier in the day when I saw him after dropping off some food for him, Sunday, and Jett. He opens my door for me, something he always does, reminding me of how Papa B was with Mama B, then once I'm safely inside, he closes my door and rounds the front of the truck. Once he's inside and we're both buckled up, he grins at me.

"Ready, Ricci?"

"I'm ready."

I can't stop laughing as we exit the haunted house. Why, you ask? Because while going around one of the last few corners, a masked man with a chainsaw jumped out and Manny screeched like a teenage girl.

"Stop, you're giving me a complex," he grumbles, grabbing my hand and lacing our fingers together.

"You have to admit, it was funny," I tease.

"I wasn't expecting anything else," he points out, leading me to the countless food trucks.

"Expect the unexpected," I reply. "It's what Papa B always told me."

"He sounds like a wise man. Do you want food or junk?" he asks, as we stop in front of several trucks.

One has Italian sausage, which I love, but the other has funnel cakes. "I like them both," I admit.

"Then we'll get both. Whatever you can't eat, I'll finish." Leading me over to a table, he grins then leans down and lightly pecks my lips. "Be right back, hold my spot."

While I wait, I people watch, seeing a lot of folks who are regulars in the diner. I briefly wonder if I should think about looking for another job, but I genuinely enjoy what I do, plus I only work about four or five hours first thing in the morning, then I have the rest of the day to do what I want.

"What has you thinking so deeply?" he asks, arriving at the table with his arms laden down with food. I quickly grab the drinks and set his across from me, then watch as he divvies the rest up, placing a stack of napkins in the middle.

"I was wondering if I should get a different job," I admit.

"Do you like what you do?" he asks, opening up a mustard pack and handing it to me.

I'm not sure if he realizes it, but him doing those simple, almost unconscious things, makes me feel special. And it's all just a part of who he is as a person, it's not an act to try and get into my pants.

"Yes, but I'm not using my degree. Shouldn't I?" I question, taking the second packet he's opened and slathering it across the bun before I roll the sausage, so it's thoroughly coated.

"I mean, I guess if you want to, you should. I've

always been big on doing what made me happy since I was released."

"I know you enjoy tattooing and building things," I say. "You're good at both. Probably better than good, but I can't think of the word right now."

"It's a delayed reaction from the haunted house," he teases, smirking at me. "What's your degree in?"

"I have my Bachelor's Degree in Business with a minor in Accounting," I reply, once I've chewed and swallowed what I had just bitten off of my sausage before he asked his question. "Only, I'm not sure I'm cut out for corporate America."

The thought has me shuddering, to be honest. Both Ivy and Lacie work in offices and some of the stories they've shared about how catty some of their coworkers are has me debating on whether or not I want to put myself through that or not.

"Did you say accounting?" he questions. "Because I've got a CPA for all the tax bullshit, but I absolutely *hate* paperwork. I'd be willing to offer you a job just to get that taken care of for me so when I go see her, she doesn't want to strangle me."

I giggle and ask, "Do you show up with a box full of receipts?"

"Something like that," he replies, grinning at me. His expression changes when he glimpses someone coming up from behind me. Turning, I see his ex stomping her way over, her face livid.

"I can't believe you're going to go through with it," she seethes.

Since I'm kind of in the dark about what she's referring to, I continue to eat but don't say a word. I know Manny had a DNA test done on Marisol to prove she was his, but with everything else that was happening, I haven't asked him what his plans were. Although, having been around his family, I feel pretty sure he's going for custody of some sort, and I don't blame him one single bit.

"Why don't you believe it? She's my *daughter*, Leanna," he retorts. "A daughter I had absolutely no fucking clue even existed. Hell, I have what, maybe two or three years at most with her before she goes off to college, which is barely any time at all. I can't believe you're so foolish as to think your secret would stay that way when you came back to a town full of my family."

"Well, you're not going to get away with this at all, *Manny*," she taunts.

"Seems as though I already have," he replies. "The hearing is on the docket for next month, and until then, I plan to get to know her, which you cannot stop me from doing."

Seeing she isn't getting the reaction she thought she'd

get, she grunts out a screech of some sort that has me thinking of a dying hippopotamus, then spins on her ridiculous high heels and stomps off. Her screech is heard again when she manages to walk through a puddle from the earlier rain.

"I'm glad you're going to try for custody," I tell him once we're alone again. I'm pulling apart my funnel cake, which has the perfect ratio of gooey goodness and powdered sugar.

"I have to, Ricci. She's my flesh and blood."

"Have you talked to her at all?" I ask, curiosity winning out.

"Briefly. She came into the tattoo shop the other day and we talked for about an hour or so. She figured out pretty quickly that I had no idea she existed, but she also knows I want a relationship with her. I know it won't be the same as if she were a little girl, but she needs to understand if me or my family had known about her, we'd have been in her life. The fact Leanna hid her not just from me, but from all of us, pisses me off so much."

I realize the conversation is taking him to a place he doesn't need to be in since we're on a date, so I ask, "So, tell me more about this job?"

"You're a woman after my own heart," he says a few hours later. We're standing in line for another funnel cake after having walked through the livestock barn.

"How so?"

"You like your sweets," he teases, looking down at me.

I pat my stomach and grin before saying, "Maybe so, but you don't look like you indulge all that often."

And he doesn't. Even in a T-shirt, it's obvious he's got muscles. Meanwhile, I have a small pooch that doesn't go anywhere despite how hard I try. Thankfully, all the walking I do around town has helped tone up other areas, but I'm nowhere near as physically fit as I was when I lived with Erik. Mainly because I realized his obsessiveness about my weight and size was another means of controlling me. Once I figured that out, I decided I didn't have to spend hours in the gym; as long as I was frequently active, I would be just fine.

"I run and work out so I can eat what I want," he admits. "And trust me, you're perfect just the way you are, Ricci. No complaints from me at all."

Since I'm unsure how to respond, I simply smile then wait as he tells the clerk what we want. As we walk away with another plate full of greasy, doughy goodness, I sigh in contentment. "I've had a good time tonight, Manny."

"So have I, sweetheart. Let's sit here," he motions,

letting me sit down at a small table. He then sits right next to me and I almost swoon when he pulls a piece of the funnel cake off and places it at my lips. "Open up," he teases, which I oblige, moaning at the sweet taste.

When I open my eyes it's to see him with an odd expression in his. "You okay?"

"Yeah. You've got a bit of powdered sugar," he says, leaning in and lightly caressing my lips with his own, "right there. Got it!"

Erik wasn't much into kissing; in fact, he didn't really care for body fluids of any type, which is weird considering he refused to use a condom when we had sex. One of the things I have done since leaving him is get myself tested to make sure he didn't leave me with anything that would screw up the rest of my life. Because I know he cheated on me. He doesn't know I was aware, but his side chicks always made themselves known to me. It really frustrates me that I thought so little of myself that I stayed.

"What has you thinking so hard, baby?" he asks, before feeding me another piece of the cake.

I shake my head, unsure if I want to put a damper on the good time we've been having. "Not sure I want to bring it up right now," I confess once I realize he's not going to let it go. "Because we're having a good time, you know?"

"Ricci, good or bad, I always want to know what's on your mind," he replies. "Hell, we had Leanna interrupt us earlier. Not only that, but if things go where I think they're going, you'll have a stepdaughter."

My eyes widen in shock at his words. I mean, I know he said he wanted a chance with me, one I'm willing to give, but that's a far cry from what he just stated was eventually going to happen.

"I was just wondering why I thought so little of myself that I allowed a man to treat me like I was a piece of shit," I slowly state. "I mean, he had *multiple* affairs over the years, so why he wanted me around is beyond me. You would think he'd be happy not to be 'saddled' with me any longer, right?"

"We talked about this, sweetheart. You know now that you're worth everything. Especially to me," he whispers, leaning in and placing a soft kiss on my lips. I can taste the confectioner's sugar and briefly wonder how it would feel if he deepened the kiss, but he pulls back. "You ready to go or was there something else you wanted to do while we were here?"

"Can we check out the vendors? I'm impressed that so many in town are involved in this, it's a really big thing," I reply.

"Absolutely. Normally, I'd have a booth for some smaller pieces, but didn't have the time to do much."

"That's my fault," I murmur, taking his hand so he can guide me toward where all the booths are set up.

"No, it's mine, sweetheart. I've been focusing on bigger pieces, trying to finish up things my grandfather started but didn't get done before he passed away. Plus, I'm a tattoo artist down right now as the other guy who was working at the shop decided to move across the country. So, I've been a bit busy trying to keep all the balls in the air. By the way, I like the sign thing you made. I think there's a market for those, so if you want, you're welcome to come out and 'do your thing' whether I'm there or not. Totally up to you."

"I think I'd like that," I admit.

We spend another hour or so walking through the various booths set up and I can't hold my giggle when I see he's got every bag I've managed to fill running up the arm that's not occupied holding my hand.

"You know you're killing me, right?" he teases as we head toward where he parked his truck. "It's a man's job to carry everything in one trip. I just had no clue my woman would want so much stuff."

I can't help the laughter that bursts free because he sounds aggrieved, but I know he's only teasing me based on his smirk. "When will I find stuffed llamas again?" I question, standing next to the truck to wait for him to put all my bags in the back seat. Once he has that done, he crowds me a little until my back is against the door and I'm looking up at him.

"No clue, but knowing how you women have the ability to find things, I wouldn't be surprised if you did," he replies, placing a stray curl behind my ear. "I've had something on my mind for a few hours now, but I'm still going to ask. Is it okay if I kiss you?"

"Yes."

CHAPTER
TWENTY-EIGHT

MANNY

"Yes."

One simple word. Yet, it has my heart rate accelerating as if I just ran the last quarter mile in a race.

Reaching out, I tuck a stray tendril of hair that's managed to escape from her French braid before cupping her face in my hand. Stroking my thumb across the apple of her cheek, I move closer and lean in, running my nose along hers and making her giggle. I can see her pulse racing in her throat and realize she's as affected as I am right now. Only, hers is probably increased because of the situation she came out of with that piece of shit.

I realize that slow will be the name of the game

when it comes to Ricci and am glad that I'm no longer that teenage boy who had no patience. While neither of us are innocents, I know she's likely far less experienced than me simply because when I got released from prison, I had my share of fun. Now, I want to settle down in the farmhouse where my grandparents raised their family and do the same with her.

Leaning in, I brush my lips against her and can still taste the powdered sugar from our shared funnel cake. When she makes a little noise in the back of her throat, I deepen the kiss and soon, our tongues are tangling as I stake my claim. When I feel as though there's no oxygen left in my body, I pull back slightly and lean my forehead on hers.

"Wow."

I grin then tell her, "We're doing that again. As often as possible, just so you know."

"You won't hear me complaining, Manny," she whispers, reaching up to run her hand along my jaw.

Who knew such a simple touch would feel so charged with emotion? Because right now, I feel poleaxed. Starting over again after I left prison, I pushed so many of the dreams and desires I had to the back of my mind. Sure, I got my dick wet from time to time, but those encounters were always out of town and casual at best. One-offs, my brother calls them. But with Ricci, I see forever.

"Good."

I take her lips again in a kiss that promises everything without saying a word. Which isn't a bad thing, since we both seem to be at a loss for them.

Eventually, I get her into the truck, and we head back to her apartment. She's nervous now, likely thinking I'll push this issue since there's no way she didn't feel my erection pressing against her stomach when we kissed. Reaching over, I take her hand in mine, lacing our fingers.

"Ricci?" I ask, pulling her away from staring out the side window.

"Yeah?" Even her voice sounds unsure now, and it's killing me inside.

"You know this, all of this, is at your pace, right? You dictate when things go further because I'll never pressure you for more."

"Really?" Her gaze is now fully on my profile, and I squeeze her hand in affirmation.

"Really and truly," I reply, turning to grin at her. "I'm a grown ass man who can take care of things until the woman I want is ready for more. Trust me on this."

"I got tested," she whispers. "When I was in the hospital the first time, after I woke up, I told a nurse I thought I should, so she sent a bunch of blood off. Thankfully, everything came back okay. I mean, it wasn't because of you or anything, I just had to know."

Squeezing her hand again, I run my thumb over hers before I say, "That was probably a good idea based on what you've shared, sweetheart."

She laughs, sounding carefree, then states, "Yeah, I thought so too seeing as I was one of many. Which is definitely cringeworthy to me. I'll get tested again in a few months just to be sure nothing shows up that wasn't there for my own peace of mind."

Having reached the back of the shop, I park the truck then turn to her. "That's more important to me than anything, Ricci. So again, we're going to take things at your pace."

"Okay, Manny." Then, in a quieter voice, she says, "Thank you for that. I was overthinking, which is something I tend to do when I get nervous."

"You never have to worry around me, honey. Now, let's get your million bags upstairs so I can kiss you good night, then you can call Ivy back."

She starts sputtering which has me laughing as I get out of the truck then head to her side, help her out, then start pulling the bags from the back. "How, what, how did you know that's what I was going to do?"

"Sisters, babe. I know a little about how women think when it comes to going out on a date," I reply.

Once we're inside and headed upstairs, with me watching the sway of her hips as she walks in front of me, I silently groan.

Yes, I'll be patient.

Yes, I'll probably jack off every single day in the shower.

But it'll be worth it in the end when she's completely mine.

After several long minutes of kissing her good night, I head back out toward home. My phone rings and I push the button so the call comes into the cab. Hands-free might be a pain in the ass sometimes, but if there's anything worse than people who decide to drink and drive, it's those who are distracted by their phones.

"Hello?"

"Hey, boy, got some news I thought you'd wanna hear," my uncle says.

"What's going on, Tio?" I ask.

"Well, it seems that asshole who hurt your girl is dead."

"Wait, what? He was still locked up waiting for trial, wasn't he?"

As if I didn't know. I've kept a close eye on him because if he was bonded out, I planned to have a discussion with him about staying away from my woman.

"He was, but there are other charges that came to light, and he apparently found out he was a suspect in the rape of a teenage girl," Uncle Jorge states. "So, some-time between one check and the next, he hung himself. They got him down, but it was too late."

"I can't say I'm sorry," I murmur. "At least now Ricci doesn't have to face that prick in a trial or anything."

"You got that right. Also, your mama told me about your daughter. You need to see if she wants to meet the rest of us because the girls are already friends with her."

Chuckling, I reply, "I'll get right on that the next time we see one another."

"You do that, mijo," he instructs before hanging up.

Once at home, I lock up before taking a shower and heading to bed. As I drift into sleep, I think about the future. My future with Ricci.

CHAPTER
TWENTY-NINE

RICCI

"You weren't kidding about your books," I grumble at Manny, who's standing in the doorway of his office.

For the past week, ever since our first date, I've been coming to the shop after I'm done at the diner. While he has a computer program that will track receipts and also do print outs of his sales, splitting them between cash and card transactions, he seldom uses it.

"I told you, babe, that paperwork and I are not friends," he teases. "Do you want to take a break and go eat at the diner? I've got about two hours before the next client comes in."

"That sounds wonderful," I reply, just as my stomach rumbles, causing me to blush.

He's laughing as we leave the shop once he has everything locked up. Taking my hand in his, we start walking to the diner, only to stop when we see Marisol heading in our direction. She looks a bit distraught, which I can tell has Manny gearing up for mayhem.

Just like Papa B would've done for his girls. That thought has me smiling slightly as she reaches us, wringing her hands together. "Um, can we... can we talk?" she asks.

I can see she's unsure what to call him, which is totally understandable given the circumstances.

"Absolutely. We're going to the diner, would you like to join us?" he questions. "Oh, and this is Ricci, my girlfriend."

The spark of hope and happiness that's been steadily building since our first date flares to life. True to his word, he's been letting me set the pace of our relationship, which I appreciate more than I can express.

"Hello, Marisol," I reply, holding out my hand. "It's nice to finally meet you."

"Um, hi," she says, running her hands through her hair. It's something I've seen Manny do countless times and I find it endearing that she has some of his habits despite just finding out he was her father. "That, yeah, that's fine."

"Then lead the way," he says. She turns and we fall in line, silence surrounding us.

I wonder what's going on to cause her distress, then realize if things go the way I hope they do, I will be her stepmother someday. That means, I need to foster a relationship of some sort with her.

Once we're in the diner and settled in a booth with her setting across from us, Manny reaches out and takes her hand in his. "What's going on, Marisol? Why are you so upset?"

"My mom hasn't been home for a few days," she murmurs, looking around to make sure no one is listening.

"What do you mean? Have you been by yourself all this time?" Manny questions. I can feel his anger boiling beneath the surface, but he's holding it back so he doesn't scare his daughter.

"She came home from the fair the other night really angry. Said she was going to fight you in court or something. Then the next morning, she went to work and hasn't been home since."

"A week? It's been a week, baby?" he asks, his voice now soothing since Marisol looks freaked out. "Why didn't you call me?"

"Because... because she does that sometimes. She takes off and leaves me by myself for a few days. So, I didn't worry or anything because it's happened before. But today, when I got home from school, there was a message on the answering machine from her boss."

"What did it say?" I ask, instinctively knowing that Manny's trying to keep his cool at the fact such a young girl has been left to her own devices for a week.

"That because she hadn't shown up for work and hadn't called, she was fired," she whispers, looking at her hands. "I think... I think something must have happened, but if it did, why didn't anyone call me? She only ever took off and left me on the weekends unless she had to go in to work a Sunday shift."

"We'll find out what's going on, Marisol. In the meantime, I think you should come stay at the farm," Manny decrees. "I don't want you by yourself. It's not safe. Now, let's get something to eat, then we'll go back to the shop, and I'll make some calls, okay?"

"Okay."

———

Manny ended up canceling his appointment so he could take the route he thought Leanna would take to work. Meanwhile, I have her with me and we're shopping for things for what's going to be her room out at the farmhouse.

As we meander through the bedding department, I softly say, "I was in foster care from the time I was a little girl until I aged out of the system."

Her shocked eyes stare at me and it's like looking at

the man I'm slowly falling in love with, one I can't imagine *not* being in my life. "Really? What happened that made you go into foster care?"

"My parents died in a car accident. I was in a lot of different homes before I was moved to the Billingsleys' house."

"Were they nice?" she asks, having stopped in the middle of the aisle to listen to me.

I smile in remembrance. "Yeah. At first, I was a little shit, not gonna lie, because so many of the homes I'd been placed at weren't very nice and I was picked on a lot. But they were patient with me, and I grew to love them as if they were my parents."

"Why didn't they just adopt you?"

"There was an aunt, I don't remember whose side of the family she was on, but while she wasn't physically capable of taking me in, she was unwilling to let me be adopted," I reply. "But Mama and Papa B treated me as if I was their little girl."

"They sound nice," she replies. Her wistful tone has me glancing at her, so many questions on the tip of my tongue.

I want to know what her life was like growing up. Was Leanna a hands-on mom or was she neglectful? Based on the little Marisol shared when we were at lunch, I feel as though it was the latter, which is a crying shame in my opinion.

"They really were. I have two sisters and a brother because of them." At her shocked expression, I giggle. "Well, I don't think Stanley really claims me as his sister, but Ivy and Lacie do, that's for sure. As far as they're concerned, I'm theirs even though there's no official paperwork."

"What does that have to do with me?" she inquires, now looking at a really pretty comforter set.

Despite her nonchalance, I can tell she's worried about what's happening with her mother. Plus, she really doesn't know Manny all that well. Taking a deep breath, I reply, "I don't have a good feeling about things, Marisol. I know you said your mom would leave you for a few days from time to time, which I'm not crazy about by the way, but with it being a week? I think maybe something happened. I hope I'm wrong because girls need their moms."

"If something bad did happen to her, what happens to me?" she whispers, a lone tear tracking down her face.

"Well, I know you know that Manny is your father already. So I suspect you'd go to live with him."

"My dad didn't like me." At my look, she clarifies what she means. "My mom's husband, that is. I've known for a long time that he wasn't my real father. He's got blond hair and blue eyes, and so does my mother. I look nothing like him, or even her for that matter. Not sure what she was thinking."

Since I don't want her to have bad thoughts where her mom is concerned, despite my own feelings about her, I shake my head. "I think she was thinking she was a seventeen-year-old girl who just found out she was pregnant and her boyfriend, the father, was going to prison. Being that young, she likely didn't think she had any other options. The important thing is, you know who your dad is now, and you've got a huge, loving family waiting to welcome you into the fold."

I might not like Leanna because of how she did Manny, but I know beyond a shadow of a doubt, he'd have been there for his little girl who isn't so little anymore. She's on the cusp of womanhood; a beautiful girl with a somewhat troubling childhood from the sound of things. I'm sure once Manny's family 'officially' meets her, she's going to be surrounded by the love she's gone without, and I find myself wanting that for her.

"So, what do you think of this one?" she asks, changing the subject.

Looking at the pattern she found, I grin. "I like it. Do you think he'll let us paint the room you're going to use? Maybe some complimentary colors to make the comforter set pop?"

"I hope so," she says, grinning at me as she grabs the set and puts it in the cart. "What else?"

"Well, I think the room has its own bathroom, so

how about some new linens, maybe a shower curtain and all the matching accessories?" I ask.

"Sounds like a plan to me."

We're on the way out to the farmhouse, the back of my SUV loaded down with bags. Because once we outfitted the bathroom, we looked at paint colors and picked up a few samples just in case. Plus, we grabbed the snack things and drinks she likes since I know it's highly unlikely Manny keeps that kind of thing around. He tends to eat healthy most of the time, but teenage girls need their junk food, especially during that time of the month.

When my phone rings, I see it's Manny and I answer saying, "You're on speaker."

"Where are y'all at?" he asks, not giving anything away in his tone.

"Headed out to your house," I reply. "We probably went a little bit overboard." However, when he pulled out his card along with a wad of cash, he told me to spend whatever I wanted as long as she got what she needed.

Now sounding distracted, he says, "That's okay. I need y'all to come back into town to the police department."

I hear Marisol gasp beside me and reach out to grip her hand in mine. "We'll be there shortly."

Disconnecting the call, I look for a driveway to turn around in, only to hear a slight sniffle. Once I get us headed back to town, I grab her hand again and say, "We're not going to borrow trouble. It may be something, it may be nothing, but your dad and I are by your side."

Tears stream down my face as I watch Manny console his daughter. He was waiting outside for us when we pulled in and once I parked and shut the SUV down, he was at the passenger side pulling Marisol into his arms. I followed behind them as he led us into the police department then toward a little room off to the side.

There, we found out why Leanna hadn't been home for a week. It seems that she lost control of her car and went off the road. Because of the heavy foliage, her vehicle wasn't seen by anyone until Manny went driving around looking to see if he could find anything. She was found dead in her car, but right now, it's unknown if she died due to the injuries she sustained or if she lingered for a few days.

Personally, as awful as it sounds, I hope like hell she died on impact. Nobody should have to suffer what I know my own parents suffered. Both sets of them. I'm lost in my thoughts of everything that needs to be done when I hear him say, "Come on, let me get my girl home."

As we walk out, I head to my SUV while they go to his truck. Since he doesn't say anything, I figure he wants to be alone with her, so I get in and head home, refusing to cry because he never once really glanced in my direction.

"It's not about you, Ricci," I mutter to myself as I pull behind the shop and park. Once I gather the items I purchased, I lock up my SUV then head inside. "I'll just send him a text later."

CHAPTER
THIRTY

MANNY

Never in my wildest dreams did I expect the outcome from my earlier ride. When I saw the black skid marks, I pulled over and parked my truck, then looked around until I saw tire tracks that went off the road. Following them, I came across a car against several trees, and could see a body in the driver's seat. I called 911 and relayed what I found then got closer to see if maybe I could help.

Only to see Leanna's lifeless eyes staring straight ahead. The car was beyond fucked up; the airbags were all deployed, and the front end was crushed in and pushed into the passenger compartment. I couldn't even see Leanna's legs as they were covered by the dashboard.

Still, I opened the door since the windows were busted and reached in to see if there was a pulse, but there was none to be found.

Hours later, as I hold my daughter in my arms while she cries, my thoughts are spinning everywhere. I sent her and Ricci off to do some shopping for her room at my house, but that was so we could start having overnight visits. I never anticipated or expected that I'd have her living with me, but there's no one else and quite frankly, I *want* her there. Too many years have been wasted and I refuse to waste another minute.

Leaving the police department, I just presume that Ricci will follow us since she was heading out to my place when I called and had her turn around. So, when we arrive and she's not behind me, I'm confused as hell.

"Did Ricci say anything?" I ask Marisol once we get inside the house.

"N-n-no," she replies, still sniffling from her crying jag. "I thought she was following us. She has all the stuff for my room."

"Hmm. Okay, let me show you around, including your room. It used to be my aunts' bedroom, so it has an attached bathroom because my grandfather refused to fight for a toilet when he had to go."

My comment does what it was intended to do; she starts giggling as I give her the grand tour of her new home before taking her upstairs to her room. There's not much inside; a matching bedroom set, complete with a vanity, a walk-in closet, and of course, the bathroom.

"Can... can we paint it?" she quietly asks after checking everything out.

"Absolutely. Did you have any particular color in mind? I'll get my brothers out here and they can get it done in no time flat."

"Ricci and I picked out some of those paint chip thingies," she says as we walk back downstairs into the kitchen. "We also got snacks and stuff I like to drink because she said you probably didn't have that kind of thing."

I chuckle because she's right. If I feel like I want something sweet, I usually eat it when I'm getting lunch. If it's not around the house, I'm less tempted. "Let me give her a call then, because I don't want my girl to be without her snacks. Feel free to help yourself to whatever's in the fridge."

As I wait for Ricci to arrive, I try to push down my frustration. I sure as hell didn't anticipate the reception I got when she answered, especially since we started dating and I thought we were on the same damn page as far as where things are going. According to her, Marisol and I need 'time' to get to know each other so while she's bringing out the stuff they bought, she doesn't plan to stay.

Something I desperately want her to do. I *need* her. Not because I find myself with a teenager living under my roof, but because she makes everything better. There's a calmness to her spirit, one that helps me stay focused. So her saying that she's backing off doesn't sit well with me.

I can hear the television through the screen door as I sit on the front porch drinking a beer. Today has definitely been one for the record books, with me having to put my mother and the rest of the family off while I get Marisol settled. Still, that doesn't mean I don't want Ricci by my side, which I plan to tell her when she gets here.

Seeing her SUV pull into the driveway, my heart accelerates. Her eyes look puffy, and she won't hold my gaze as she opens the rear hatch then gets out of the car. "Hey," she says, looking over my shoulder instead of directly at me.

"We thought you would be behind us, sweetheart," I reply, moving to where she's now standing at the back of her vehicle.

"I just figured you'd need some time alone together," she states, pulling the bags closer.

I start adding bags to my arms, determined to get the fifty-five thousand they bought inside in one trip. She smiles seeing what I'm doing, then grabs the final two before pushing the button to close the back. She follows behind me to the porch then waits as I navigate opening the door with two fingers.

"Oh! Hey, Ricci," Marisol says, jumping up from the couch to try and take a few bags from me.

"I got them, baby," I tell her as I head to the kitchen. "Let's get your snacks and stuff out first, shall we?"

We leave Marisol in her room so she can start getting things put away and I walk outside with Ricci. "Sweetheart, talk to me," I state, pulling her into my arms. "What's going on in that head of yours?"

"I just think... well, maybe we should take a step back until you get her settled in, Manny," she replies. "I'll still come in and work on the books, of course, but she needs to be your priority right now, not me."

I growl out in frustration. "I need you by my side. What do I really know about teenage girls?"

"They just want to be loved and feel noticed," she whispers.

Her comment breaks my heart because I know that

until she was placed with the Billingsleys, she really didn't have that once her parents passed away.

"This isn't over," I tell her as she moves to get into the driver's seat. "Not by a long shot."

"Take care, Manny. We'll see how you feel once things settle, okay?"

CHAPTER
THIRTY-ONE

RICCI

"You're an idiot," Lacie says.

"Honestly, I have to agree with her this time," Ivy adds.

It's been a month since Marisol moved in with Manny. A long, lonely month. While I see him when I go into the shop to do the books, now that I've got everything caught up, I only have to go in once a week as opposed to daily like I initially had to do.

I know from the chatter at the diner that Marisol is struggling a bit, and it breaks my heart for her. From what I understand, Manny has her in counseling, and his family has been helping get everything at Leanna's house sorted out. I did attend the funeral, but sat in the back and left before he could reach me.

"Maybe I am, but it's not like he's reached out to me," I retort, suddenly angry at my two sisters. "The phone works both ways, you know."

"Yeah, it does, and if memory serves, he told you he was waiting on you to make the first move, remember?" Ivy asks, pointing her finger at me.

We're at our weekly lunch, thankfully *not* at the diner, and I've spent thirty minutes listening to the two of them gang up on me regarding my choice to back off from Manny. Don't they know what he's come to mean to me? I cry myself to sleep every single night, then I feel guilty because his daughter's mother died. She needs him more than me right now. I'm a grown adult while she's still a child.

"So what do I do?" I question. "How do I tell him I screwed up?"

"Just like that, sweetie. The next time you go to the shop and he's not busy with a customer, flat out tell him, 'Manny, I fucked up. I miss you. Can you forgive me?'" Lacie retorts.

"What if it doesn't work?" I whisper.

"Then he's not the man we thought he was," Ivy says, patting my arm. "Now, what are we having for dessert?"

The ringing phone rouses me from a deep sleep. Grabbing it, I hear, "Ricci?"

"Marisol? What's wrong, honey?" I ask, already throwing my covers aside. I can hear her crying and without thinking, I slip my feet into my slippers, grab my keys and purse then head out to my SUV.

"I... I had a bad dream," she whispers.

"I'm on my way. Do you want to stay on the phone until I get there?" I ask, switching over to hands-free.

"Yes, please," she says, sniffling.

For the next fifteen minutes, I listen to her ramble about school, the therapist she's seeing, how hard it's been going through stuff at her old house. When I pull into the driveway and park, she practically flies down the steps and into my arms.

"It's okay, I've got you, sweetie. Where's your dad?" I ask. I don't see his truck in the driveway which is odd.

"He had to deliver some furniture and is on his way back. I was with my grandma today, but I told her I'd be alright since he was going to be home tonight. I'm not a little kid, you know."

"No, you're not. You're a responsible young lady. Come on, let's get inside and see what we can find to snack on, okay?"

Several hours later, after finally getting her settled back down, I head to the couch where I curl up underneath the throw that was on the back and fall back to sleep. I haven't slept well since I told Manny we needed to step back and the adrenaline rush from Marisol's phone call, then subsequent crash has me snoozing quite soundly.

So soundly I don't hear Manny arrive, or even stir as he carries me upstairs to his room and settles me in his bed. What wakes me up is my full bladder, only when I rouse enough to get up, I realize I'm no longer on the couch but on a bed and there's a firm, muscular arm holding me down.

What the hell? My heart rate slows slightly when I realize it's Manny, but still, it's a bit discombobulating to fall asleep in one place and wake up in another. I manage to wiggle my way out from underneath his arm then head into his bathroom, where I quickly take care of business.

Since I'm up, I decide to check in on Marisol and find her peacefully sleeping. Her face is still puffy from the tears she cried earlier, but hopefully, her dreams are sweet. Turning, I run into Manny's hard chest with an oomph.

Instead of saying anything, he takes me by the hand and after closing Marisol's door, we head back to his bedroom, where he closes and locks the door before turning to me. "What happened tonight?" he quietly asks, his gaze never leaving mine.

He looks tired. Stressed even. Somehow, I know some of it is because of me and I feel bad.

"I'm sorry, Manny," I reply. When he goes to say something, I hold up my hand. "Please, let me just say this first, then I'll tell you what happened to cause me to be here, okay?" At his nod, I continue. "First of all, I fucked up when I said we should take a step back. I understand you might not feel the same way any longer, but not a day has passed that I don't regret what I said to you. We should be together since Marisol is now living with you, and if you needed time, you would've said something. That's on me and trust me, I've spent hours talking it over with my therapist, as well as my sisters."

"What did they say?"

"My sisters said I'm a dumbass, of course. My therapist kind of said the same thing, but she didn't use those exact words," I mutter. He bursts into laughter and pulls me into his arms.

"You're not a dumbass, sweetheart. And while I appreciate your apology, I promise, I'm not angry or upset. I actually understood why you did what you did, and respect the hell out of you for your compassion. It's definitely not been easy, she cries a lot of course, and because of me being in prison, I missed some of the normal teenage girl angst and drama that my mom says is perfectly normal. Now, what happened tonight?"

"She called me crying, saying she had a nightmare. I didn't think, just ran out of the apartment and headed here. Then I found out she was alone since you were coming home, so I decided to stay with her. We probably ate our weight in junk food, by the way, so I'm sure you're going to need to restock the ice cream."

He chuckles again at my words. "I've been considering getting a second freezer for the ice cream and what-not," he advises. "Because it's one of her favorite go-to foods."

"Mine too, although I typically add chocolate syrup, sprinkles and even sometimes chopped nuts," I admit. "None of which you have, by the way."

"I'll add it to the list," he promises. "Now, why don't you get comfortable in my bed again, where I've wanted you for so long. I'm going to grab a quick shower to wash the road off of me then we can get some sleep." It's then I realize that he fell asleep on top of the covers while I was tucked underneath them.

He then proceeds to kiss me until I'm breathless before turning me and giving me a slight push toward his bed. "I missed that," he says, stalking into his bathroom. He doesn't fully close the door, so I can hear him going about his nightly routine before the water turns on in the shower.

I'm curled on my side waiting for him to rejoin me as I think about where we're currently at in our relationship versus where I want to be.

I want him.

I don't care if he served time and is a felon.

I don't care if he's got a teenage daughter.

The fact of the matter is he treats me like I'm something precious to him. That's something I watched growing up with Mama and Papa B. I thought I had it with Erik when we first got together, but that was obviously not the case.

As he slips into the bed, he looks at me and asks, "What has you thinking so hard over there?"

Taking a deep breath, I reach out so my hand is covering his and reply, "Make love to me, Manny. Make me yours."

CHAPTER
THIRTY-TWO

MANNY

Getting home after a long, frustrating day of driving, I didn't expect to see the woman who's occupied every waking thought curled up asleep on my couch. Immediately, I wonder if Marisol is okay, but a quick check shows she's also sleeping, although her face is puffy as if she had been crying.

As I head back downstairs, I notice Ricci's face looks the same and wonder what happened tonight to have my two girls crying. Shaking my head, I make my rounds, checking all the doors and locks, before I approach Ricci once again. She hasn't moved at all and seeing the dark circles under her eyes, it dawns on me that she probably hasn't slept well this past month.

Well, neither have I if I'm completely honest with myself. Between helping Marisol plan her mother's funeral, wading through her house so my girl can take what she wants, then overseeing the estate sale so there's money for Marisol's college, I feel like I've been run over by a truck multiple times.

Because in addition to all of that, I hired a new artist to help take some of the load off me at the shop, but have also had people reaching out for some custom pieces they want made. I feel like I run from sunup to sundown these days, plus a few hours afterward.

But seeing Ricci in my house settles the noise in my head. It feels right that she's here, regardless of the reason, so I gently pick her up then head up the stairs to put her in bed. My plan is to lay her down then grab a shower, but fatigue hits me hard and fast so I figure I'll just rest for a little bit then do it.

I wake up when I feel her slip out of the bed but when she leaves the room, I decide to follow her to see what she's doing. As she goes into Marisol's room, I watch her care for my daughter and my feelings for her grow even stronger than they already were. After our brief discussion about the reason she was at my house tonight, I push her toward the bed and head in to take the shower I meant to take earlier.

I never expect her to say what she does; immediately, my dick, which has been at half-mast since she fell asleep, fills with every drop of blood in my body and I'm convinced I can nail steel spikes into railroad ties.

Reaching out, I smooth her sleep-tousled hair back and ask, "Are you sure, sweetheart? There's no rush."

Her little growl of frustration makes me grin, even though my heart is beating so fast right now, I'm sure she can hear it. "Manny, I'm serious right now. I've been miserable since we've been apart. I've done a lot of soul-searching this past month. I know I'm probably still a bit of a hot mess, but when I'm with you, I feel like I can do anything."

"You can, Ricci," I reply. "You're one of the strongest women I've ever met, sweetheart. Most of the things you've endured would have broken a lesser person. Yet you've persevered and come through the fire stronger. But just so you know, if we do this, there's no going back for us. You'll wear my ring and my name, and eventually, we'll fill this house with babies. Do you understand?"

"Kind of like this bossy side of you," she teases. Her smile is radiant, and I know, even though we haven't said the words yet, that we're on the same page with regard to our feelings. "Although I hope that the actual proposal is better."

Leaning in, I nip her lip then say, "It'll happen when you least expect it, baby."

"Then I'm sure about what I want. You."

Since I'm almost positive that Erik never really worried about whether or not Ricci enjoyed herself during sex, I know I need to make sure she's ready for me. Pulling her closer so we're touching from chest to toes, I focus on kissing her and soon, I'm lost in her taste once again. Her soft moans as my hands lightly stroke along her sides has my dick throbbing, wanting to be inside her inviting heat, which I can feel through her pajamas and my sleep pants.

As my hand slips underneath her top, I pull back slightly and ask, "Is this okay?"

"Mmhm," she murmurs, before she sits up and pulls her top over her head.

I've never had a particular part of a woman's body I was obsessed over like some guys, but right now, seeing her full breasts, the nipples already distended? I may be a boob man after all. Reaching up, I cup them in my hands, feeling how plump they are as I bring my mouth to one. Licking, nipping, and sucking, I shower attention on one side before switching to the other until Ricci is writhing beneath me, her soft sounds making my dick even harder.

"God, you're luscious," I say as I pull back to see the expression on her face. Her lids are at half-mast, her skin is lightly flushed, and the nipples I've been laving with attention are turgid peaks.

"Never felt like this before," she admits, her hands running down my arms.

"We're not discussing before," I growl out, causing her to giggle. "Suffice it to say, I figured as much, sweetheart." When she starts to look distressed, I lean in and lightly nip her chin. "I'm not upset by that fact, Ricci. You deserve the world, so if I can show you what it should be like, I'll feel like a million bucks."

"Less talking, more showing," she teases, her thumbs stroking my nipples, which have never been particularly sensitive. Only now, each touch has my dick jumping and I realize I need to move away from her, or I'll come in my sleep pants before I ever get inside her.

"If you insist," I reply, before dropping back onto my calves so I can look at her body. "Seems I need to get rid of these," I muse, staring down at her pajama bottoms, which have little coffee cups on them. "These are cute."

She snorts. "Ivy got them for me. I'll drink coffee if it's the only thing really available, but I prefer hot chocolate."

"I'll keep that in mind," I say, my fingers dipping below her waistband to feel the soft silky skin beneath her pajamas. When she giggles, I ask, "Are you ticklish?"

"Just a little bit," she advises, her breathing now choppy and labored. As I tug at them to pull them off her so I can feast on her body, it stalls completely, and I glance up to see her eyes almost impossibly wide.

"Sweetheart? We can stop," I tell her. It would kill me, but I mean what I say. If she's having doubts, we'll wait.

"Don't you dare," she hisses, making me smirk. She then lifts her hips which allows me to easily remove the bottoms as well as her panties, leaving her bare to my gaze.

"You undo me," I murmur, my eyes roaming from the top of her head to the apex of her thighs where I can see her desire glistening on her slightly spread thighs. Reaching one finger between her legs, I swirl it in her essence and ask, "Is all this for me?"

"Yeah," she shyly says, her face flushing once again.

Not wasting another second, I lower myself so my shoulders are between her legs, forcing her to open them further. As I breathe in her scent, I groan before running my tongue through her folds, causing her to gasp out loud. "You good?" I ask, focusing on the feast before me.

"I-I think so," she whispers.

Suddenly, I realize it's likely that fucktard never went

down on her, and I am determined to show her how good it can be. "Relax and just feel," I instruct, before I focus on bringing my woman to ecstasy.

As her flavor bursts across my tongue, I moan then begin licking from her pussy to her clit, giving that sensitive bundle of nerves a slight suck each time, until she's clutching my hair in her hands and writhing back and forth. When I introduce a finger into her tight, hot sheath, I hear her shakily calling my name and feel her pussy fluttering. Thrusting in time with the motion of my tongue, I add a second digit and know she's about to come if the pressure from her thighs is any indication.

"Manny!" she keens out, her back arching off the bed, as I continue my ministrations while she rides out her release. When she flops back, a soft, contented sigh coming from her parted lips, I slowly make my way back up her body, kissing her exposed skin until I take her lips in a demanding kiss.

I'm just about to notch my weeping dick at her entrance when I hear, "Condom?" Reaching blindly toward my nightstand, I quickly grab a foil packet and within seconds, have my straining member sheathed and poised at the gates of heaven.

"You ready, sweetheart?" I ask, looking down at her.

She raises her hand and smooths back my sweaty hair while smiling up at me. "I feel like we're poised at the top of a cliff about to jump or something," she teases.

"We are, it's called making you mine," I reply, slowly entering her pussy, which is still slightly pulsing from her orgasm. My eyes cross when I'm fully seated; she's so fucking tight, I'm afraid I might end up being a two-pump chump.

As I pull back then quickly thrust back inside, she circles my hips with her legs, her feet pressing into my ass. Setting a steady rhythm, I watch her face so I know what she enjoys, which is obvious by her moans and soft sighs.

"I feel so full," she murmurs, her hands now clutching my biceps, her nails lightly scoring my skin.

"You feel like heaven," I grunt out, adding a swivel when I bottom out which causes her to gasp.

Soon, the only sound in the room is our labored breathing and the slapping of our sweaty skin as we both climb higher and higher. I feel my balls draw up and tingles at the base of my spin so slide my hand between us to circle her clit.

As her pussy clamps down on my dick, my release shoots into the condom, making me briefly wish it was filling her instead. Finally sated, I roll with her still attached and smooth my hands down her back before kissing her.

"That was... that was phenomenal," she whispers, her eyes somewhat glassy. I suspect her emotions are out of control right now, so I simply nod.

"Better than that, but I'm not sure what word to use," I admit, grinning at her.

"I... it's never... it's never been like that," she replies.

"And it's only going to get better, sweetheart."

"How so?"

"The longer we know each other, the more we'll figure out what we like," I state. "Now, as much as I would love to go a second round, I think we need to clean up and get some sleep because Marisol is going to be up before we know it."

She might be a teenager, but her previous life with her mother didn't allow for her to 'linger' in bed all day, so she tends to get up very early. Since she had a bad night earlier, I want to be there for her when she does wake up.

CHAPTER
THIRTY-THREE

RICCI

Having never showered with anyone before, I wasn't prepared for my shower with Manny. A second round of lovemaking commenced by the time we were done washing, so after we completely wiped out all the hot water, we finally got some sleep.

Waking up, I smile because last night was everything I ever dreamed it could be. I can tell he's already up, so after stretching, I roll out of the bed and head into the bathroom to take care of my screaming bladder. Thankfully, after multiple UTIs early on in my relationship with he-who-shall-no-longer-be-named, Ivy told me the trick about peeing after sex, so this is just the normal morning, so to speak. After I wash my hands, I go ahead and brush my hair, then my teeth before it dawns on me that I wore my pajamas over here.

"Son of a biscuit eater," I mutter.

"What has you cursing so early today?" Manny asks. When I shriek, he chuckles, causing me to turn and glare at where he's leaning up against the door jamb. "What's the matter, sweetheart?"

He looks extremely relaxed, almost like a contented cat this morning and I preen a little inside when it dawns on me that I'm behind his mood.

"I uh, I realized I wore my pajamas over here last night. I don't have anything I can wear back home."

He bursts into laughter at my confession then pulls me into his arms. "Well, your pajamas aren't too revealing, sweetheart, so you should be just fine driving home to get dressed. Which you need to do as soon as possible."

"What? Why?" Maybe last night didn't mean as much to him as I thought it did, which has my heart sinking.

"Not for any other reason than I want to take my two best girls to breakfast before we check out a local estate sale. My granddad used to take me when I was a kid and he often found items that he was able to repurpose. Thought y'all would like to go with me."

"It sounds like fun. Okay, I'll head out so I'm ready when y'all come to get me."

"Not before kissing me good morning," he growls out, before tugging me into his arms and thoroughly kissing me.

By the time he pulls back, I'm breathless and wondering if we can just spend the day in bed instead, which he must pick up on because he laughs. "If we could, we would, babe. Unfortunately, unless my other best girl is with family, that's unlikely to happen. The good news is, she'll be off to college in a few years."

"If she goes. She might decide to go to a technical school or something. Do you know what she wants to do?" I question, moving away and putting my slippers back on.

Yes, my slippers. Why I didn't put on my flip-flops or hell, even a pair of sneakers, is beyond me. Nope, I have my fuzzy chicken heads on which has him doubled over now, laughing his ass off.

"What, they're cute!" I defend my footwear choice.

"They are, sweetheart. We won't be far behind you, Marisol is showering now. We'll get some breakfast at the diner, then head over to the sale."

"What will you do with that?" Marisol asks Manny, looking at a huge hutch he just bought.

"Not quite sure yet, but I'm positive I'll come up with something," he replies.

I love watching the two of them interact; they don't realize just how many of their mannerisms are similar. Today has been an absolute blast. Despite my concern, Marisol didn't bat an eye when she saw me coming out of her dad's bedroom. Instead, she linked her arm with mine and thanked me for being willing to come over the night before.

"Maybe I can help," she shyly says.

"You like creating things?" he questions.

"Yeah."

"Then when we get this beast home and I have your uncles come over and help me unload, I'll show you the workshop, see what you think. Your great-grandfather taught me everything I know, plus I've taken a ton of classes in different techniques. If you want to learn, I'll be happy to show you all I know," he says.

"I'd like that a lot."

Once he pays the man overseeing the sale, he maneuvers his truck over to where several items he bought are waiting. Several men come over and help him get them loaded, then he attaches a gazillion bungee cords to secure everything before he gets in the driver's side.

"Y'all ready?" he asks.

"Yes!" Marisol exclaims.

"I think you should build us a she-shed," Marisol decrees as we watch Manny's brothers help him unload his purchases. "That way, we can create things without getting in your way."

"You think there's enough room out here for one of those?" he teases. "Because I suspect you two will want one of those cutesy things I've seen online, one that has a porch and an overhang. Chairs, that kind of shit."

"Of course," I state, joining in on the conversation. "And tables inside with good lighting so we're able to see what we're doing."

"There's plenty of room in here," he muses, a grin on his handsome face. "I could put some tables over there in the back. Yep, plenty of room."

"Dad," Marisol drawls out. "Your workshop is cool and all, but it won't be as cool as the one Ricci and I will have if you make us one."

I see him fighting not to roll his eyes or start laughing because she's being serious. He finally shrugs when one of his brothers says, "They've got pre-built ones for sale at the big hardware place in town, Man. I think they're even pre-wired. At least then, you'd still have your own cave of sorts."

"I like him," I whisper to Manny. "He's on our side."

"He's got a house full of girls," Manny retorts.

"Well, seems to me, you're trying to catch up," his brother teases.

"Fine. Let's go into town and check this thing out, then we'll head out to my mom's house. We've put it off long enough."

Apparently, while Marisol has met some of the family, she hasn't met everyone yet and today's the day.

"I still can't believe it'll be delivered next weekend," Marisol says as we head home after a fun afternoon out at her grandmother's house. Many of her cousins are either the same age or close to it, so now she's got a built-in support system that I think will go a long way to helping her heal.

"They could've done it during the week, but I've got clients, Ricci works, and you're in school. Although, they have to have an adult on the premises before they'll deliver so even if you were home, it wouldn't matter," Manny says. "Are we dropping you off at the apartment or do you want to come home with us?" he asks, squeezing my hand.

"You should totally come back to the house with us, Ricci. We have to plan how we want to decorate our craft shed," Marisol advises, causing me to giggle.

I'm pretty sure that's not why Manny extended the

invitation, but since it'll be a few more hours before bedtime, talking about our plans for the building Manny cheerfully paid for so we'd have our 'own place' is fine with me.

"Then that's what I'll do," I reply.

CHAPTER
THIRTY-FOUR

MANNY

Since Ricci and I worked things out, the past two months have been busy as hell. Once the 'she-shed' was delivered and fully set up on the cement pad Diego and I poured, Ricci, Marisol, Ivy *and* Lacie, as well as my nieces, Gabriella and Maribelle, spent hours in there crafting. When I asked why the rush to make things, I found out that the high school was planning to do a winter festival complete with booths and Marisol wanted to sell some things so she'd have the money for Christmas shopping.

"She's come a long way in such a short time," Uncle Jorge says, watching as she and her cousins do some crazy TikTok dance challenge.

"Yeah, she has."

Initially, she was angry at her mother for keeping her from me, which warred with her grief over Leanna's death. Thankfully, I found a therapist for her to talk to and after a few false starts with regard to school, as well as some behaviors that had to be corrected, she's a fairly well-adjusted teenage girl.

She talks to her girl cousins about every little thing, making me glad I have an unlimited data plan through my cellular carrier. At least she now puts her phone on silent when she goes to bed. The constant chiming had my ears ringing, which made Ricci laugh.

She also talks to her aunts, as well as Ricci. It's as if she's so starved for female attention and affection, she can't get enough, which makes me sad on her behalf. I don't think she realized just how little she was getting from Leanna as a mother figure until my family fully descended. Even Ivy and Lacie have taken her under their wings, much like I suspected they did to Ricci when she first came to live with their parents all those years ago.

"You planning to make her a permanent part of your life?" he questions, nodding toward Ricci. "Because she fits in as though she's always been around, mijo."

"Yes." I've known for a while now that I love her beyond measure. Have I told her? No, not yet, but that's mostly because during the week, she stays at her apartment since she enjoys walking to work at the diner, then on the weekends, when she stays at the house with us, we're busy doing family things together. By the time we fall into bed at night, I have other things on my mind.

"Better make it soon. She's definitely a catch," he teases. "Don't want someone stealing her away from you."

"Steal who away?" Ricci questions, walking over to where I'm standing. She faceplants against my chest, slightly wheezing.

"You okay?" I ask, tipping her chin up so I can examine her face.

"I think I'm too old to hang with the younger crowd," she replies.

I've noticed she's been more fatigued lately but chalked it up to how busy she's been between work, our nighttime activities, and crafting with Marisol and the rest of the girls. At her words, I take a closer look and realize her face is slightly fuller, and she has a more pronounced pooch. Not that I give that first fuck, because I definitely don't, but I know there's something else going on that has her feeling the way she is right now.

Nodding at my uncle, I take her by the hand and walk by her side until we're up on the back deck before I sit down and pull her into my lap. "Is there anything you want to tell me?" I quietly ask.

Ivy and Lacie clued me in two days ago about their suspicions, but today was the first day I was able to look closely at her. I feel relatively confident that she's worried about how I'll react, but the truth is, I'm ecstatic.

Her face flushes slightly at my perusal then I see tears well up in her eyes as she begins to shake.

"Ricci? Sweetheart, not sure where your head's at right now, but you *never* have to be afraid of me. Tell me what's going on, please?"

"I... I think I'm pregnant, Manny," she whispers. "I don't know when it could've happened because we've always used a condom." By now, she's wringing her hands together and she won't hold my gaze.

"Look at me," I command. When she finally lets me see her beautiful eyes, I lean in and kiss her. "Do you know how fucking over the moon I am? The thought of you carrying a child we made together? One who will be raised and surrounded by love? The words don't exist yet to express how I'm feeling. Have you taken a test?"

"I've been too scared to," she admits. "I bought one and have been carrying it around with me."

"Let's go take it," I say, standing with her now in my arms.

"Manny! I think you have to do them first thing in the morning and it's afternoon now," she protests.

"Baby, if you're as far along as I suspect, I don't think

it's going to matter if you piss on a stick in the middle of the night or when you first wake up."

She walks out of my bathroom, her cheeks flushed pink. I heard the water turn on then off and know she washed her hands once she was done. With my arms now wrapped around her, I ask, "How long did the directions say we had to wait?"

"I don't know."

Shaking my head, I lead her back into the bathroom and bite back a chuckle when I see she tore off a sheet of paper towel from the linen closet and has the test sitting on it instead of the counter itself. While I'm sure there's a minimum timeframe, as I peer over her shoulder since she's got her face turned into my chest, I can see two lines that are getting darker the longer the seconds tick by.

I crouch down and cup her stomach, then lift her shirt and kiss it. "Looks like you wanted to be here, little one," I murmur. When I stand, both lines are dark blue and as if that wasn't enough of an indicator, the words 'pregnant' are displayed as well. "Congrats, sweetheart, we're going to have a baby," I whisper.

"Now you'll be stuck with me for the next eighteen years," she replies, tears slowly trickling down her face.

Before I answer, I get down on one knee and slip the ring that's been burning a hole in my pocket for months now. Gazing up at her, I take her hands in one of mine and say, "After the way Leanna broke up with me and crushed my teenage heart, I swore then and there I would never love anyone ever again. And until you came along, I kept that promise to myself. While I haven't told you how I feel, I've tried to show you every single day just how much you mean to me. Ricci Adams, I love you and want to spend the rest of our days together. Will you marry me?"

"Yes, yes, I'll marry you, Manny. I would be proud and honored to be your wife."

I slip the ring on her finger then stand and draw her into my arms. Kissing her thoroughly, I don't stop until we're both breathless and I can hear the pounding of feet in the hallway. "Let's go tell our family."

Later that night, after I spent quite some time showing her just how ecstatic I was that not only was she carrying my baby, but she was going to be my wife, she quietly says, "I was afraid to tell you before that I loved you because everyone I've ever loved has gone away. But I do love you, more than my next breath. More than I ever imagined possible. Thank you for being willing to take a chance on me. On us."

"There was never any doubt in my mind about where we were going when I asked if you wanted to try with me," I reply. "Now, I suspect a certain teenage girl will be up early as she always is, especially since she's so excited about helping to plan a wedding."

Her giggles have me kissing her and soon, sleep is forgotten as she takes charge and shows me how she feels.

CHAPTER
THIRTY-FIVE

RICCI

Marisol and I are at my apartment, packing my stuff so I can move out to the farmhouse. Since Manny and I are getting married next month, it made no sense to keep going back and forth. Well, that was his logic anyway. He's downstairs finishing up a tattoo, and plans to let his employee close it down tonight.

I'm about four months along, further than either of us suspected, but after the infection I got when I had the incomplete miscarriage, my period was somewhat sporadic, and since we always used protection, pregnancy was never on my radar.

As I wrap up the glassware, I find myself crying. It seems that everything lately has the waterworks going, and since I've never made it this far in a pregnancy, I wasn't prepared. My emotions have been all over the place with each week that has passed, and I'm pretty sure that I'm driving everyone in my life crazy. At least, that's how it feels to me. Manny, however, takes everything I say and do in stride, while Mama A and Aunt Juanita have been absolute godsends, allaying each and every fear that pops into my head. I've worried about everything from how big the baby is going to grow inside of me, to whether or not the infection from my last miscarriage will cause problems when I deliver. Right now, feeling the fluttering of my baby move inside me, something I've never felt before, has me nearly sobbing in gratitude and I can't wait for Manny to be able to feel it.

"Why are you crying?" Marisol asks, having come out of the bathroom with a box full of towels.

"What if I'm not a good mom?" I reply, crying harder, both of my hands now caressing my growing belly. "I mean, I had Mama B who taught me a lot when I was a kid, and she was the best kind of mom, but I also saw a lot in the homes I was placed in before I moved in with them."

She wraps her arms around me in a hug and states, "You're going to be the best mom, Ricci. I miss mine every day, but she was probably one of those people who should've never had kids. Yet since you and my dad came into my life, you've loved me like I was your own kid. Plus, with all the family my little brother or sister is going to have, how can you even think that? Grandma is so excited and will probably have to be beaten off with a stick so you can do things for the baby on your own. I wish you were mine, actually." She almost sounds wistful as she rubs my back while I try to control my tears.

I can't help the giggle that escapes despite my distress because even though she has a boatload of grandkids already, Mama A is beside herself about our baby. She's been crocheting and sewing since we shared the news. At the rate she's going, the baby won't need a darned thing. Plus, Ivy and Lacie have been shopping up a storm in preparation for the baby shower they're planning, even though it's at least four months from now.

"Sweetie, I just tried to be to you what my sisters were to me when I first went to live with their parents. What's not to love about you? You resemble your daddy, your Aunt Luci, and of course, Maribelle and Annabeth. If I denied loving you, I'd have to do the same for your dad and that's simply not going to happen."

"Good to know, sweetheart," he says, having snuck into the apartment during mine and Marisol's little heart-to-heart talk.

"How long have you been here?" I ask as he gently takes the two of us and tucks us under his arms.

"Long enough to hear what Marisol said," he admits. Looking down at her, he asks, "Did you mean that?"

"Yeah, Dad, I did. I love and miss my mom, but after being with you, I can see how far off the mark she really was as a parent."

"I think that probably had more to do with her age than anything," I state. "She was a kid raising a kid herself."

Manny glances down at me and winks. "Baby, that there is one of the reasons my girl loves you so damn much. You could bash her for the things she did to me, or didn't do for Marisol, but instead, you show compassion for her circumstances."

I shrug. "It's how Mama B raised me, Manny. I don't know any other way to be."

When I feel the fluttering again, I grab both of their hands and ask, "Can y'all feel the baby moving?"

Smiling now, even though a few tears still trickle down my face, I watch the wonder cross both of theirs when they feel the new life my body's growing move.

"I can't wait to meet you, little one," Manny murmurs, kissing my temple.

Later that night, after a dinner of pizza at the local pizzeria, then a movie complete with popcorn, we're in bed after a thoroughly satisfactory shower when he turns to me and asks, "Would you be willing to adopt Marisol?"

"Do you think she'd want me to?" I counter. "I don't want her to think I'm trying to replace her mother."

"Sweetheart, I heard everything she said to you. I think she'd be thrilled if you legally considered her your daughter."

"Ask her and if she's okay with it, then yes. I'll be glad to adopt her."

"How much more do you have to get done for the festival?"

I stop and think about all we've made so far. "I think we're pretty much done. I know she's excited about earning her own money."

He chuckles then says, "Yeah, I may see if she can pick up something part-time at the diner after school, because she's determined to save her money like you told her you did when you were a teenager."

I blush a bit because Marisol and I have had a lot of great talks. I haven't hidden my past from her, wanting her to know she should always know her value and worth. That particular nugget came about when she shared there was a boy in her class who was picking on her a lot. Some of the other girls had told her it meant he liked her, and I reminded her that if a boy truly did like her and want to date her, he wouldn't call her names or be mean like he'd been doing. She took that back to her cousins and all of a sudden, the boys had a 'talk' with the teen and he's no longer messing with Marisol.

"She's got a good head on her shoulders, Manny."

"Mostly because she practically raised herself. Maybe with a little bit of help from Leanna's parents while they were alive."

"But now she's got you and the rest of the family," I protest.

He leans in and kisses my nose. "And you. She's got you in her corner, Ricci."

CHAPTER
THIRTY-SIX

MANNY

"Do we need to have 'the talk', mijo?" Uncle Jorge asks as we wait in the back of the church.

"The talk? What do you mean?"

"About the birds and the bees. I'm sure my sister tried her best, but she's a woman, you know," he teases, causing me to burst into laughter.

"I think, considering that I've fathered one child and have another on the way, I have it down," I finally reply once I've gotten myself under control again.

"Just saying, if you need any tips, I can..."

"No, Uncle Jorge. I do *not* want to know about you and my aunt and your sex life."

He snickers just as my brothers walk into the room.

"You ready? The priest wants us to go stand at the altar because it's almost time."

My heart starts beating a little faster knowing that in less than thirty minutes, I'll have a wife. Even the fact that she's now almost seven months pregnant doesn't faze me. When she realized how long it would take to plan the wedding she wanted, she asked if we could wait until after the baby was born, but I nixed that rather quickly.

I pat my jacket, feeling the paperwork my lawyer dropped off to the tattoo shop earlier in the week. It's the official adoption paperwork, already signed, proclaiming that Ricci Adams Alvarez is now the mother of Marisol Alvarez, and as such, will be treated as though she is Ricci's natural-born child. Once Ricci signs it, my lawyer will file it so we can get a new birth certificate and social security card for our girl.

"Let's do this," I reply, taking the jibes from my brothers in stride. I know my whole family is beyond happy about the turn my life has taken.

I'm the last one out the door and hearing a noise, I look over to the window to see a red cardinal on the sill. "Hey, Luci. Thanks for keeping her safe and bringing her to me. You're so missed and will always be loved."

"I now pronounce you man and wife. You may kiss your bride," the priest intones.

I raise Ricci's veil, which Mama B wore when she got married, and cup my wife's face in my hands. "I love you," I whisper before kissing her.

"I love you too, Manny," she softly replies.

"I'd like to introduce you to Mr. and Mrs. Manuel Alvarez."

As the music starts, I hold out my arm for her to take, then we walk back down the aisle and out into the foyer of the church. Thankfully, the photographer got all the poised photos earlier, and since we asked for no formal ones, just candids, we won't have to wait forever to eat since I know my wife is currently eating every two hours.

According to her, that's what the baby needs. Since I try to give my girls what they need, I indulge her as often as possible. When the rest of the bridal party arrives, the photographer takes one 'posed' picture of all of us before we head over to my mother's, where the reception is being held.

Once I have her in my truck, which required some assistance because of her dress, I move to the driver's side, ignoring the jeers from the males in my family. "Just y'all wait, your turn will come," I retort before sliding into my seat.

I crank up the truck to get the heat going since it's

surprisingly cool. Granted, it's October so it's technically Fall, but we had a cold front come in overnight and the temperature drastically dropped.

Pulling off, I hear the cans banging behind me and know my nieces and nephews had a part in decorating the truck. As Ricci giggles, I just shake my head before grabbing her hand and lacing our fingers together.

"You looked so beautiful walking toward me," I say.

"You look mighty handsome yourself," she replies.

"Now that the toasts have been made and the cake has been cut, we're going to get changed," I tell Mama. "Ricci is shivering in her dress, and I don't want her to catch a cold."

"Go, Manny. Take care of your wife. We'll do dinner in about an hour, will that give you enough time?"

I smirk then nod. "Yeah, Mama, that should be more than enough time."

Taking Ricci's hand, I usher her up the stairs and to my old room where our clothes are waiting. As I unbutton the back of her dress, I kiss the exposed skin, causing her to shiver for an entirely different reason. When I slide it off her shoulders and down her arms, she turns to me, wearing nothing but a lacy corset complete with a garter belt and hose.

"Fuck me," I mutter staring at her. Reaching out, I touch a curl that Ivy managed to tame somewhat and watch it bounce back.

"That was the plan, wasn't it?" she sasses, grinning at me. "At least I hope it was because the further along I get, the hornier I get."

"Well, let's take care of that, shall we?" I ask, quickly stripping off my own clothes until I'm standing there naked in front of her, my dick bobbing against my abdomen.

"Can I go for a ride?" I watch her bite her lower lip and nod, climbing onto the bed and laying back.

"Show me what you've got, woman," I instruct, my voice husky.

Even though she's seven months along now, she's all belly and boobs. She crawls up the bed, undoing the lacing on her corset so her breasts pop free and I feel myself begin to salivate. Her nipples have gotten so sensitive that I know playing with them will have her ready to take me in no time flat, something my dick is totally on board with, if the pre-cum steadily leaking from the tip is any indication.

"What about your panties?" I question once she's straddling my thighs.

"Oh, these?" she teases, reaching down and popping two snaps, exposing the lower part of her swollen belly, along with her pussy that is already

ready, if the slickness on her inner thighs is any indication.

"I think I like that thing," I murmur once she's hovering over my dick. When she grasps me in her hand, I hiss out a breath, eager to fill her up. Once we realized she was pregnant, condoms went by the wayside and every time I'm inside her tight, wet sheath, I have to focus on not coming too fast.

"Me too. It's why I bought it," she admits, slowly sliding down my length until she's balanced in the saddle of my hips.

Raising my legs so she has something to lean against, I thrust upward as she begins to move, my hands cupping her breasts. When I stroke my thumbs over her distended nipples, she whimpers, and I feel her pussy flutter.

"Don't think this is going to last too long," I warn, already feeling my own telltale signs of my imminent release.

"Don't think I care," she pants out, moving faster. She swivels on the downstrokes, her clit coming into contact with my pubic bone and hisses. "Manny," she moans. "Every time gets better and better."

"You gonna come for me, beautiful?" I ask, doing my best to 'do all the work' so she doesn't exhaust herself.

"Yes, if you keep doing that," she teases. "God,

more," she demands, before reaching between us to rub at her clit.

Mere seconds later, we both detonate together, with me filling her full of my release as she throws back her head and tries not to scream. I curl up, using my abs, and take her lips in a kiss, which has her yelling out her orgasm down my throat. Finally spent, we slump back, laying there until our breathing returns to normal.

"I love you, Ricci Alvarez."

"I love you more, Manny Alvarez."

CHAPTER
THIRTY-SEVEN

RICCI

I'm now a hundred years pregnant, wondering if I'll give birth to a toddler, as I make my way into the school gymnasium. Today is the Winter Festival and Manny, as well as his brothers, got Marisol's booth all set up. Since I haven't been sleeping well the past few weeks, I waited until Mama A came and picked me up.

"Mija, wait for me," she calls out, coming to my side. "You should let us help you, you're not as stable as you once were now that the little one has grown so big."

"I didn't think I'd have a big baby," I admit, looking at how my abdomen announces my presence these days. I had to stop working at the diner because I couldn't balance a tray anymore.

"All of my babies were what my George called whoppers," she states. "Even Luci was ten pounds."

"Ten pounds?" I ask, feeling nauseous.

"Mama, are you scaring my wife again?" Manny asks, walking over to us. I smile when his hands wrap around me to cup where our child is currently dancing around in my stomach. "I think your child just kicked me," he whispers.

"So, this baby is mine when they do something to you?" I tease.

Most nights when we're relaxing before bed, we watch the acrobatics display in my belly and try to guess what body part is 'revealing' itself. I'm pretty sure we're wrong most of the time, but the intimacy it's given us is something I absolutely love. I'm so wobbly now that Manny showers with me so I don't fall, and he's even taken over shaving my legs for me. When I had mentioned it needed to be done, he told me he didn't care if I was as hairy as Bigfoot, then my hormones struck because I heard it differently in my head, so what did my husband do? He got a fancy electric razor and has taken great pleasure in 'grooming' me.

"No fear, just facts," Mama A retorts, grinning at him. "I just wish you had wanted to know what you were having."

"Mama, those gender reveal things are over the top most of the time anyhow," Manny says. "We know the baby is healthy, and it's not as if we can't get gender specific clothes once he or she arrives."

"But that means the room is so generic."

"It's really not, Mama A," I interject. "We went with a baby jungle animal theme which is perfect for a boy or a girl." It's freaking adorable is what it is, and my sisters have been heavily involved in getting the nursery ready. Well, them and Marisol. I swear, the three of them are constantly coming home with things 'for the baby' which is almost to the point of ridiculousness.

"Si, si, I know. I just want to know if I'm buying overalls or tutus," she grumbles, making me laugh.

"Let's go see how your other granddaughter is doing at her booth," Manny suggests, guiding me through the crowd of people to the far corner where I see a massive line waiting.

"It looks like she's doing good," I exclaim, seeing Ivy and Lacie both taking money while Marisol bags up purchases.

Manny made me sit down when he saw my legs were starting to swell but I wasn't willing to go. Not when my girl was slowly selling out of all the things we made. While we had some of the usual things you see at a Christmas bazaar, like wreaths, and small, painted trees, we also had the tile signs, birdhouses painted with the school's mascot, decorative holiday towels, and wooden toys that Manny and his brothers had made. Marisol's booth was definitely a family affair as even Mama A donated several quilts, as well as a few crocheted lapghans.

"Do you want something to drink?" Ivy asks, startling me out of the lists I was making in my head of everything I still need to do before Christmas. Most of the presents have been bought and wrapped, but I have a few more small things I want to get for Marisol, as well as stocking stuffers for all the adults' stockings. Of course, as overprotective as Manny is these days, I'll probably have to go online to shop.

"No, I think I need to use the bathroom. I'll be right back," I tell her, awkwardly standing to my feet.

I'm nearly to the ladies' room when I feel a gush of fluid flow down my legs. Looking down, I see a puddle forming at my feet and realize the small pains I've been having are labor pains. "Manny!" I call out, drawing not only his attention, but everyone else's as well.

Within seconds, he's by my side. When he sees the problem, he scoops me up in his arms bridal style and shoulders his way through the crowd. "Marisol, we're headed to the hospital," he calls out as we pass her booth.

"Go, go," Gabriella, Manny's niece, says. "All of you,

go. The prices are marked, I've got this. Just someone come and get me when this is over."

Since there's maybe an hour left and so little remaining of Marisol's items, I put my hand on Manny's arm and ask, "Can Diego or Matias stay until she's done then bring her up to the hospital? That way, they can take all of this down and you won't have to worry about coming back."

"Good idea." He stops and asks Diego who agrees to stay with Gabriella while the rest of the family falls in step behind us.

I don't know what to expect when we arrive at the hospital, but nurses practically running around as the doctor barks orders isn't it at all.

"Manny?" I whisper, pulling on his shirt sleeve. I've been changed into a hospital gown, had an IV inserted, and been checked by the doctor, which is what preceded all the chaos currently going on around me. "What's wrong?" I ask when he leans in to hear me over the medical staff.

"I think you're further along in the labor process than they thought you'd be with a first-time birth, sweetheart. Are you in any real pain?"

I think about it and shake my head. "No, not really. More like twinges if anything."

"Well, young lady, that's a good thing because there's no time for an epidural," the doctor announces, while washing his hands. I watch him dry them then slip on a pair of gloves. "Because we're about to have a baby. Are you ready?"

"Kind of too late if I'm not, isn't it?" I tease.

He looks at Manny and smiles. "This might be the most enjoyable delivery I've ever had. Usually, the woman is threatening to geld the man. It's difficult to be between her legs when she's got violence on the mind, you know?"

Manny chuckles while taking my hand in his. As always, he laces our fingers together, which I'm grateful for when I feel a wave of pain roll through me. "Doctor? I'm feeling some pain," I advise.

"Totally understandable considering I'm watching a baby's head come out of your vagina," he replies. "Now, push, Ricci. Push hard."

Manny helps me, using his back to prop me up as I push until the doctor tells me to stop. He watches the monitor that's next to me that's showing my contractions and when another starts to indicate its arrival, he says, "Push, push, push, push. Good girl."

Over and over again, I push when I'm told to,

breathing like the Lamaze instructor taught us in class, yet the baby seems determined to park itself in my vajayjay.

"I'm probably so stretched out a Mack truck could drive up there," I whisper, sweat and tears intermingling on my face.

"Sweetheart, I promise, it'll go back to what it was before," Manny says. "And even if it doesn't, I'll still love you."

"How do you know? I mean, you've never given birth, have you?" I sass. "Sorry, sorry. Just worried that our baby isn't wanting to meet us after all this drama."

"You mean having your water break in the school gymnasium?" he questions.

"Yeah, that. Shit, I hope someone cleaned up the mess."

"I'm sure by now they did, honey, since the whole family is in the waiting room for this one's arrival," he says.

I'm about to say something snarky when the doctor says, "Now, Ricci. Push, push, push, push, push."

I grunt and groan, the pressure almost unbearable until suddenly, there's blessed relief, and I hear the unmistakable cry of a baby. Glancing down, I know my expression must be puzzled because Manny looks at me and asks, "What's that look for?"

"They said I was measuring to have at least an eight to nine pound baby," I reply. "But the baby looks no bigger than a peanut."

The doctor interrupts us when he looks between my legs then says, "Because the other one was hiding this whole time."

Manny's eyes grow wide, and he glances at me before he says, "Twins? We have twins?"

Hell, I don't even know what the first baby is other than Baby A as I just heard the nurse announce. Right now, the little one is being held on my abdomen against my skin while the second baby pretty much pops right out. No fuss, no muss, no drama.

"Let's see what we've got, shall we?" the doctor asks, almost rhetorically. "Ah, Baby A is a little boy, Baby B is a little girl. Congratulations, Mom and Dad! Dad, would you like to cut the cords?"

———

It takes a little while to get both babies weighed and cleaned up, but while Manny is overseeing the nurses as they take care of that, the doctor is sewing up my episiotomy after I delivered the afterbirth. Once he's finished and congratulates us again, two other nurses come in and help me get cleaned up. Although, truthfully, that will involve a full shower, none of that baby wipe crap. Granted, they did have one of those small basins, so it was better than wipes, but even still, I feel slightly disgusting.

When the babies are brought over to me, I carefully take each one, with the nurses helping to prop them up in my arms.

"We'll let your family know you'll be out shortly but won't say a word about it being twins," one of the nurses says. "And, like the doctor says, this was one of the best deliveries we've had in a very long time. Congratulations, Mom and Dad."

"What should we name them?" Manny asks once we're alone.

"What about Lucinda Noelle and Javier Luis?" I reply. "Lucinda for your sister, Javier for your grandpa?" I see the tears well in my husband's eyes and lean against his arm. "Thank you, Manny. If I hadn't started over with you, and you with me, we wouldn't have these two miracles from Heaven right now."

"Yes. Are you ready for our family yet?" he teases, grinning down at me.

"Definitely. Looks like the girls will need to go get another crib, hmm?"

"As if any of the women in either of our families has a problem shopping."

"I bet your mom has stuff for a little boy and a little

girl already," I tease, snickering. "But just in case, let her know she needs both overalls *and* a tutu." She so wanted us to do a reveal, but that just wasn't for me.

"Be right back, and you're probably right. Thank you, wife, for my babies."

———

Hours later, after our families have left with promises to return in the morning after they shop, I doze off while watching Manny talk to our children.

"They're beautiful, Button," Papa B says, hugging me.

"You know?" I ask, looking around. Once again, I'm in that strange place I was in before. On one hand, I know he's no longer alive, yet he's standing right in front of me.

"Yes we do, sweetie," Mama B replies. "We're so proud of you and couldn't have asked for a better daughter." When I go to protest, she shushes me. "You were ours, Ricci. We didn't need a piece of paper to tell us otherwise. Now, go enjoy your family. I foresee plenty of laughter and love in the following years."

"Will I see you again?" I ask.

"Someday, a long time from now, you'll be with us again. We'll check in on you from time to time, though."

"Okay. I love you both so much."

"Sleep now, Button. You've got some busy years ahead of you."

I wake up with Papa B's laughter in my head and smile over at Manny.

"What's going on, sweetheart?" he asks, having just settled Luci and Javier in the isolettes the nurses brought in for us.

"I just had the strangest dream. Mama and Papa B were there, and they congratulated me on the babies and marrying you," I reply, still kind of in a daze. "It happened before too, when I was so sick. Is that even possible?"

"I think, in times of great sadness and also joy, that those we love are able to reach through the veil and communicate with us. Mama has told us stories of how Papa talked to her."

"Well, I don't care whether it's true or not, I believe it happened and that's all that matters. Now, are you sleeping on that cot or climbing in with me?"

He chuckles while slipping off his shoes before he slides into my hospital bed and pulls me into his arms. "Third best day of my life so far."

"What were the first two?" I ask, my curiosity roused.

"The first was the day I found you in my workshop. The second was when you became my wife."

"What about Marisol?" I whisper, not wanting our oldest child to be left out.

"Any of our kids will be included in the third best day, sweetheart," he replies, kissing me. "Now, get some sleep. I suspect our babies will be awake and wanting to eat soon."

"Night, Manny," I murmur, already sliding back into sleep.

"Night, Ricci."

EPILOGUE

MANNY
(MANY, MANY, *MANY* YEARS IN THE FUTURE)

"Who would've thought all those years ago when I stopped in Possum Run on a whim because I liked the name that we'd have such a beautiful life?" she asks, gazing out at our family surrounding us.

It's our seventieth wedding anniversary and while the past few years have been hard health wise, our kids, grandkids, and even great grandkids have been by our side. Seeing how the whole family came together to do this for us has me holding back my tears. I've apparently become an emotional old man in my dotage, as our oldest daughter constantly reminds me any time she spies me tearing up.

"Who would've thought that a tiny, curly-headed sprite would unharden my heart enough that I could give her this life?" I reply, leaning over to kiss her.

"Ten kids, Manny. *Ten*," she whispers, giggling a little. She's had a few glasses of champagne, something I know she shouldn't be drinking due to her cardiac problems, but how many people live long enough to celebrate seventy years of marriage?

And they've been good years. Sure, there were some tough times, especially since we had two sets of twins rather close together, followed by five hard years of miscarriages, then five single births. But the farmhouse had plenty of room for all the laughter, yelling, tears, and teenage drama that ensued as we raised our brood.

"Closer to twenty if you count the ones who weren't born," I softly reply. We lost two sets of twins, then had two stillbirths, plus she had four miscarriages before we ever met.

"No wonder my poor hips never fully recovered," she teases.

"Sweetheart, you never changed a bit."

"Now I know the eye doctor screwed up when he did your cataract surgery." She giggles some more. "Because I've gone up two pant sizes since then."

"You could've gone up thirty sizes and I'd love you the same," I tell her. "Because you'll always fit into my arms."

"Grandpa, you can't say something like that!" Stella, our youngest granddaughter states. "There are little kids around."

I chuckle then say, "Stella, if that's the worst they've heard with our family here tonight, they can count themselves lucky."

"Yeah, you're right. Grammy, you shouldn't be drinking."

Stella is a doctor, although she's not ours. However, that being said, she watches the two of us like a hawk.

"I only had two, dear heart," Ricci replies.

Fibber. She's had four. But I've never denied my wife whatever her heart desires, and I refuse to start now. If she doesn't deserve to drink champagne after the two of us have accomplished this milestone, I don't know who does.

"Okay, but just saying, no more after you finish that glass," Stella retorts before winking at me. Yeah, our girl knows.

Our 'nanny' as Ricci calls her has just finished settling us into bed for the night. After my quadruple bypass surgery then Ricci's near-fatal heart attack, the only way the family would let us live on our own was if we allowed a live-in nurse, at least at night, since we both refused to go into an assisted living facility. We both have those ridiculous life alert buttons too, but if it gives our kids peace of mind, so be it.

"Do you want to watch that movie you enjoy?" I ask.

"Which one? There are so many, you know."

"The one that always makes you cry at the end. The kids who meet as teens, are separated, then she comes back? It was based on a book, remember?"

"You mean *The Notebook*?" she questions.

"Yes, that's the one," I reply. "Even though you always sob."

"It's a beautiful love story."

"Our love story is my favorite one of all," I tell her, flipping through the channels until I find the correct station. "Now, come closer and let me hold you."

As she curls into me, she whispers against my neck, "Ours is my favorite as well."

Looking around, I realize I'm somewhere I've never been before except one time, years ago during my open-heart surgery. A sense of peace washes over me then I hear, "Mijo!"

Turning, I see my mama, her smile just as radiant as it was so many years ago. I pull her into a hug while she murmurs about how much she's missed me.

"Mama? Why am I here again?" I ask as several people I don't recognize move toward me. I can see my grandad, as well as my Uncle Jorge and Aunt Juanita in the distance as well.

"You must be our button's young beau," the man says as he approaches, holding out his hand for me to shake.

The woman next to him, who bears a striking resemblance to Ivy, lightly taps his arm. "Honey, he doesn't know who you are." Turning toward me, she smiles and says, "We're Ricci's parents, Mama and Papa B."

If I had to choose one word to depict the way I feel right now it would be stunned. While I never doubted Ricci's experiences as she described them, never did I anticipate having her family show up in my own dream. Maybe there was something wrong with the enchiladas and this is just a bad reaction.

"It's not a reaction, Manny," Mama says. "We've been waiting for a very long time now."

I can't catch my breath when I process what she's saying. "No, Mama! I can't leave her alone. She's my everything. This will kill her if what you're implying is true. Please wake up, Manny, wake yourself up, dammit!"

Several small children appear next to Mama and Papa B, and they look so much like my beloved Ricci that I instinctively know they're the babies she lost long ago. But when I see four more sidle up to my mama, then spy Luci, my precious sister, walking over to our group, I fall to my knees in despair, wailing out my grief and anguish.

"Manny Alvarez, why are you kneeling on the ground?"

Her voice wafts over me, melodious yet gentle. Turning my head slightly, I see her, my Ricci, walking to my side.

"Because I thought I had gone without you, sweetheart," I admit.

"One of the reasons I always cried watching that movie was because I didn't want to live without you and knew you felt the same way. We started a second chapter together over seventy years ago, now it's time to spend eternity with our loved ones while we wait for the others. Are you ready?" she asks.

Even the children we lost wait to hear my answer as I regain my feet to truly look at everyone surrounding me. My mama? Doesn't look like she did when she passed from her earthly life. No, she's middle-aged again, healthy and whole. It's the same with Luci, who appears just as she did the year before she started dating Turo. The child who clings to her is the niece I never got to meet on Earth. None of the children now surrounding us are infants; they're all around five years old or so, almost as if God Himself allowed them to be the perfect age.

And when I look at the most precious one of all, my Ricci? I see she's not white headed with small wrinkles around her eyes and mouth from all the years of laughing *and loving, she's just as she looked when we first met. Gazing at my own weathered body, I see that the muscles that had begun to atrophy due to lack of use are no more; instead, I'm as muscular and virile as I was in my own middle age.*

Taking her hand in mine and lacing our fingers together, I draw her closer then kiss her. "What do you say we meet our children?"

"I thought you'd never ask," she teases. "Thank you for a beautiful life, Manny Alvarez. I'm so glad I started over with you."

THE END

Sunday & Jett's story can be found in "What I Like About Sunday" and you can read about Loki and Kaya in the Poseidon's Warriors MC series (starting with Poseidon's Lady). All are available on Amazon and in KU.

ABOUT THE AUTHOR

I am a transplanted Yankee, moving from upstate New York when I was a teenager. I'm a mom of four and grandma of nine who has found a love of traveling that I never knew existed! I live with the brat-cat pack (all rescues) as well as my dog, Bosco, 'deep in the heart of Texas', as I plot and plan who will get to "talk" next!

Find me on Facebook!
https://www.facebook.com/darlenetallmanauthor
Darlene's Dolls (my reader's group):
https://www.facebook.com/groups/1024089434417791/
permalink/1063976267095774/?comment_id=
1063979757095425&notif_id=1539553456785632&
notif_t=group_comment

DARLENE'S BOOKS

The Black Tuxedos MC

1. Reese - The Black Tuxedos MC
2. Nick - The Black Tuxedos MC
3. Matt - The Black Tuxedos MC

Poseidon's Warriors MC

1. Poseidon's Lady
2. Trident's Queen
3. Loki's Angel
4. Brooks' Bride
5. Atlas' World
6. The Warriors' Hearts (novella)
7. Kaya's King

8. Chelsea's Knight

9. Orion's Universe

10. Glacier's Thaw - releasing 10/23

Zephyr Hills Phantoms MC (Mayhem Makers)

The Enforcer

The SAA (2023 release TBD)

Writing in the Rogue Enforcers World

Paxton: A Rogue Enforcers Novel

Esmerelda: A Rogue Enforcers Novel

Charisma: A Rogue Enforcers Novella (with Liberty Parker)

Writing in the Royal Bastards MC world (Roanoke, VA chapter)

Brick's House

A Very Merry Brick-mas

Banshee's Lament

Jingles' Belle - releasing 12/23

Standalones

Bountiful Harvest

His Firefly

His Christmas Pixie

Her Kinsman-Redeemer

Operation Valentine

His Forever

Forgiveness

Christmas With Dixie

Our Last First Kiss

Draegon: The Falder Clan - Book One

Scars of the Soul

Hale's Song

Mountain Ink: Mountain Mermaids Sapphire Lake

Knox's Jewel: A Dark Leopards MC Novella

Desire: A Savage Wilde Novel

Contraryed: A Heels, Rhymes & Nursery Crimes short

story

Sashy's Salvation

Search & Find

Little Red's

What I Like About Sunday

Starting Over With You

Rebel Guardians MC (with Liberty Parker)

1. Braxton

2. Hatchet

3. Chief

4. Smokey & Bandit

5. Law

6. Capone

7. A Twisted Kind of Love

Rebel Guardians Next Generation (with Liberty Parker)

1. Talon & Claree

2. Jaxson & Ralynn

3. Maxum & Lily

New Beginnings (with Liberty Parker)

1. Reclaiming Maysen

2. Reviving Luca

3. Restoring Tig

Where Are They Now? RGMC updates on original 7 couples (with Liberty Parker)

Braxton

Hatchet

Chief

Nelson Brothers (with Liberty Parker)

1. Seeking Our Revenge

2. Seeking Our Forever

3. Seeking Our Destiny
Rebellious Christmas (A Christmas Novella) (with
Liberty Parker)

Nelson Brothers Ghost Team Series (with Liberty Parker)

1. Alpha
2. Bravo

Old Ladies Club (with Kayce Kyle, Erin Osborne and
Liberty Parker)

1. Old Ladies Club - Wild Kings MC
2. The Old Ladies Club - Soul Shifterz MC
3. Old Ladies Club - Rebel Guardians MC
4. Old Ladies Club - Rage Ryders MC

The Mischief Kitties (with Cherry Shephard)

The Mischief Kitties in Bampires & Ghosts & New
Friends, Oh My!
The Mischief Kitties in the Great Glitter Caper
The Mischief Kitties in You Can't Takes Our Chicken

Raven Hills Coven (with Liberty Parker)

1. Rise of the Raven

2. Whimsical

3. Enchantment

4. Prophecy Revealed

Tattered and Torn MC (with Erin Osborne)

1. Letters from Home/War (novella)

2. Letters Between Us (novella)

3. Letters of Healing (novella)

4. Letters from Mom (novella)

5. Letters to Heaven (novella)

6. Letters with Love (novella)

7. Letters from Nanny (novella)

8. Letters of Wisdom (novella)

9. Band of Letters - all 8 novellas in one volume

10. Her Keeper

11. Her One

12. Her Absolution

Made in the USA
Columbia, SC
19 May 2024

35488522R00217